Second Chance Highway is the exciting sequel to the highly acclaimed *Always Think of Me.*

Praise for *Always Think of Me*

"A brief encounter has a profound impact on two quite different people in the moving spiritual novel *Always Think of Me.*"

Foreword

"The story delivers a poignant message about embracing your ordained purpose and finding beauty in starting over… Many will find this an inspiring tale, one that highlights the impact of our interactions and the preciousness of life."

—BlueInk Review

"*Always Think of Me* tells it like it is… love, friendship, and the debilitating effects of trauma on a person's life. Lori Keesey has created completely relatable characters in this beautifully written, compelling story."

—Debbie Terry, author of *When Love Wasn't Enough… Because I Loved Him*

"I love *Always Think of Me* largely because of its accurate depiction of why people become susceptible to abusive relationships. This is an unusual love story that also delves deeply into what really matters in life. A must-read for everyone."

—Marcia Messer, Board-Certified Counselor I

"This is my first time reading Lori Keesey but it definitely won't be the last. I love books that make me think, have great characters and great world building… *Always Think of Me* checked all of those boxes. Can't wait to read more by Lori Keesey!"

—Kimmie Coleman

"*Always Think of Me* is a heartfelt, four-star read that stands out for its emotional depth and unexpected twists… It's thoughtful, hopeful, and quietly powerful, leaving you with that lingering, reflective feeling long after the last page."

—Katie Burgess

"I could not help myself but to fall in love with the main characters. This book made me cry happy and sad tears. I could not help but to finish the book in one sitting. I can't wait to see what she writes next."

—Heather Bass

"*Always Think of Me* is a second-chance contemporary romance that once I started reading, I had a hard time putting it down… This is my first book by this author and I look forward to following her as she brings us more stories."

—Dawn Daughenbaugh

"*Always Think of Me* by Lori Keesey sucks you in big time. It's the story of TC and Ginny, but more than that, reading their story makes you sit back and think about your own life and the wish for second chances for yourself… This is a tragic story, but there are times when it was funny as well. Keesey did a wonderful job balancing both. Great quick read."

—T. Turner

"A beautifully heartbreaking story about one's journey to discovering their true purpose in life and how forgiveness can set us free from the demons of the past… Keep the tissues close!"

—Chloe McRae

SECOND CHANCE HIGHWAY

A SEQUEL

LORI KEESEY

CLAY BRIDGES
PRESS

Second Chance Highway: A Sequel

Published by Clay Bridges in Houston, TX
www.claybridgespress.com

ISBN: 978-1-68488-160-4
eISBN: 978-1-68488-161-1

Special Sales: Most Clay Bridges titles are available in special quantity discounts. Custom imprinting or excerpting can also be done to fit special needs. For standard bulk orders, go to www.claybridgesbulk.com. For specialty press or large orders, contact Clay Bridges at info@claybridgespress.com.

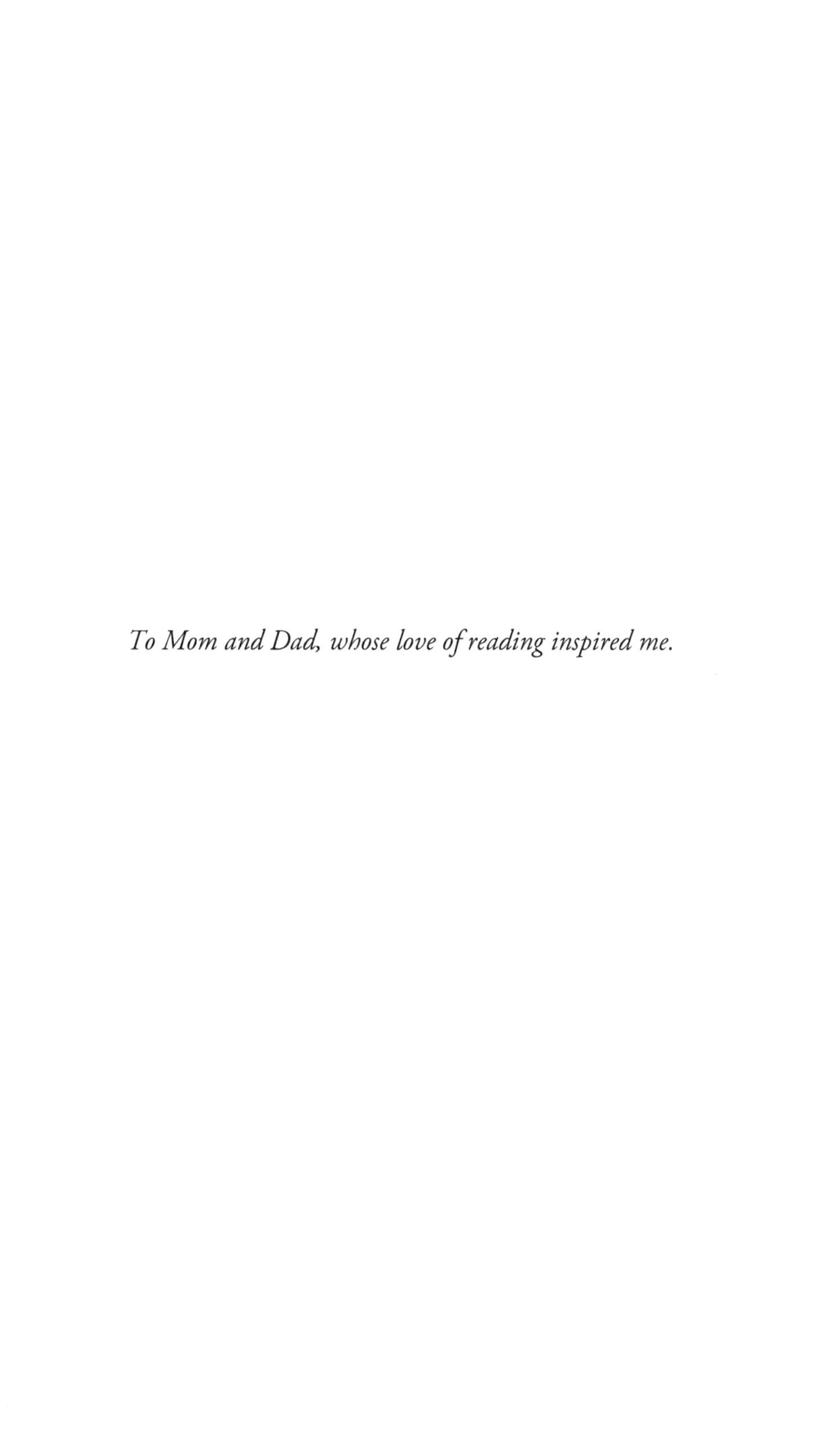

To Mom and Dad, whose love of reading inspired me.

CHAPTER ONE

Ginny

Call me. Now!!!!

My heart races—no, it pounds—as soon as I notice that message. My stomach tightens, and a wave of nausea rises, forming a thick lump in my throat. Despite wiping my clammy palms on my jeans, they still feel damp, a sign of my spiraling anxiety. I try to take a long, deep breath, but the nausea only worsens, aggravated by the smell of grease and coffee that fills this diner west of Oklahoma City.

Under normal circumstances, the signature aroma would have had the opposite effect on me. It would have wrapped me in a warm blanket of tender memories. My grandmother and I visited a place like this every Saturday morning, a standing date. While devouring biscuits and gravy, I'd gab between bites about the silliness only a child would find important.

"Oh my. Now, that is a story, Ginny Carmichael," she would say, her blue eyes shining, the color of a robin's egg. "You are my sunshine."

If only I could go back in time to those sunlit mornings.

I clench my fist, willing myself to breathe deeply, to stay calm. But the positive self-talk feels like a lie. Jacob Hudson—my fiancé, who has money and powerful connections—is probably the reason for that unwanted text from Melinda Anderson, one of the few people I can trust. The image of him combing every street, interrogating every passerby to find me won't go away. I glance over my shoulder, half expecting to see him lurking around the corner. How naïve I must seem, clinging to the hope that I can escape him.

I glance at my baby, Laurel. She's nestled against me, her tiny fingers curling around the bottle. Her rhythmic suckling soothes my frayed nerves, but the sensation doesn't last. Thoughts return to Jacob and how he might explain my sudden disappearance from the pristine illusion he's built—the one where he *plays* the devoted husband and father, who must protect me, his fragile and broken *wife,* from even myself.

Hard to say.

But count on a lie.

He lies about everything.

Laurel, my sweet innocent Laurel, may be his daughter, but I most certainly am *not* his wife.

Three days ago, I felt a flicker of optimism. I began to believe that I could create a new life for myself, far from the prison that my life had become in Atlanta—trapped, living with Jacob in his lavish house in the posh neighborhood, initially deluded by his empty promises of marriage. I shudder at my mistakes.

Then, that hope grew stronger, unshakable, when I stopped for a refill at a gas station on the outskirts of Tupelo, Mississippi.

Running on adrenaline, caffeine, and little else, I spotted a white-clapboard church across the street. It beckoned me inside. Only then, sitting in a pew polished smooth by decades of use, did the tension in my neck and shoulders begin to unravel. I laughed out loud, surprising myself.

Thank you, sweet Jesus. I can do this.

I strapped Laurel into her car seat, and I continued the journey, barreling past Memphis and Little Rock. Not even a tropical storm could diminish my resolve. I drove through the cloud-cloaked Ozarks, past wrecks and ambulances, until I reached Oklahoma and spotted the multistory Cherokee Casino and Hotel, which rose from the ground like a mythical phoenix.

Yes, the old me could die, and a new Ginny could rise from the ashes.

But that was then, and this is now. Sitting in this booth, numbed and in disbelief, I pick up my coffee, only to realize that I've already drained the cup, my eyes then falling on a turquoise-colored memory bracelet dangling from my wrist, a gift from TC Chaver, my dearest friend—a man I could've fallen for if I hadn't been so blind. His gift of gab was just one of the traits that drew me to him when we met by chance at an outdoor music festival one year ago.

I still haven't processed the extent of my loss.

The night before I packed my stuff and fled Georgia, he came to visit me in an otherworldly encounter that no one would believe. As the sun had begun to set, he caught me staggering around my bedroom drunk, planning ways to free myself of Jacob's torment. Of course, he'd been shocked at the state I was in. He was the fun-loving, free-spirited party boy known for over-imbibing.

I was not.

However, despite my impaired thinking three nights ago, TC's message resonated with me. Light began to penetrate the dark corners of my mind. TC was spot on; I would never find true peace until I recognized my value and buried the hurts and grudges that had led me to get involved with Jacob in the first place. The first step—TC insisted in his effusive and straightforward manner—was to leave Jacob. He understood my predicament and had experience with people like him.

In all fairness, my relationship with Jacob hadn't been *all* bad, and it didn't become toxic overnight. Always cautious of others, I initially approached him with care. He called me daily, asked me out on dates, and showered me with gifts and sweet words. He wouldn't take no for an answer. Over time, my resistance faded, and I became more confident in my exalted position at the center of his universe. Nothing seemed too good for me. I fell in love with him, believing his promise to marry me.

Now, I sit fearful and alone inside a roadside diner, wondering what he'll do next.

Everything feels impossible.

The diner's only visible waitress is an older, heavyset woman with a frizzy halo of steel-gray hair. Crow's feet appear at the corners of her eyes, and reading glasses dangle from a rhinestone lanyard hanging around her neck. An embroidered *Oralyn* over her right breast pocket tells me her name. She delivers my scrambled eggs, hash browns, and toast, and spots my empty coffee cup.

"Want a refill, honey?"

I nod.

"Okeydokey. Back in a jiffy."

I glance at Laurel, the only positive from my hellish relationship with Jacob. "What would I do without you, sweet pea?" My Southern accent doesn't turn heads here, just hours from Texas. And that's my hope. Keeping a low profile seems important, as that text might suggest.

Laurel smiles around her bottle, her blonde hair sticking up in all directions, as milk dribbles down her chin. I pull the bottle from her mouth and grab the paper napkin next to my untouched plate. Her happy kicks stop, and her dimpled hands twirl around her downturned mouth.

"Slow down, baby girl." I dab her face and reinsert the nipple before she can squawk, unaware that the waitress, Oralyn, has returned with a pot of coffee.

"Honey, what's wrong? You haven't touched your breakfast." She peers into my face, frowning, perhaps wondering why I'd let a perfectly fine breakfast congeal on the plate. Her weight shifts from one foot to the other, and she winces.

"Oh." My eyes swivel to the plate and then back to her. I offer a tiny smile as butterflies flutter about my empty stomach. "Nothing—"

"Well, you aren't fooling me. You look like you're fixin' to die, and then what would this little girl do?" She leans over and caresses Laurel's cheek. "My goodness, she's pretty. Favors you." She straightens, ready to say something else, but another customer interrupts, asking for a refill. She nods, then limps off toward the counter, the soles of her sneakers squeaking against the diner's checkered floor.

Am I that obvious?

Her observations are correct. I do feel like I'm fixin' to die. Furthermore, Laurel could be my clone, which means my angel baby resembles my mother. Blonde hair and blue eyes run in our blood, overriding the genetic contributions of the men who fathered our children.

Poor taste in men runs in our blood, too.

Before launching this half-baked journey across the South, before collecting our belongings and scrubbing away any evidence of my existence in Jacob's world, I made Mom the end point in my journey. As TC made clear, her absence in my life was the root of my issues. "Forgive her," he advised when he came to me. The cycles of dysfunction that had nearly shattered me needed to end—for my sake and Laurel's. This process would begin with an unannounced visit to my mother.

Mom lives in Las Vegas, but that's all I know. In my frenzy to disappear before losing my nerve, I'd forgotten to call Aunt Adele, my mother's estranged sister, to see if she had Mom's contact information.

Now I'm not sure about anything.

My phone is within reach next to the plate of untouched eggs. I should respond to the text, but I can't bear the truth. My happy bubble *had* kept me aloft over uncertain terrain for the past three days. Even with countless unknowns in front of us, I felt joy. Real joy. Freedom. And now, I'm afraid of proof that, despite my best efforts, Jacob won't let me go. He plays a game of cat and mouse, making sure he never loses.

* * *

With shaking hands, I lay Laurel next to me on the red-vinyl-covered booth, my breakfast still untouched, and try to distract myself by tickling her now-full belly. She kicks her feet and makes happy noises, oblivious to my strangled breathing and rapid heart rate. I'm delaying the inevitable.

Just respond to that text and make the call.

I hear chairs scraping across the black-and-white-tiled floor. Four construction workers are set to leave. If they catch sight of me, they'll see only the top of my head, my hair pulled up in a messy updo, tendrils hanging down my now-clammy neck. I don't want their attention. I don't want anyone's.

"See ya later, Oralyn, darlin'," one shouts as he and his companions lumber toward the door. I lift my head and see Oralyn standing next to the counter, waving her hand, as if shooing away pesky gnats.

"Maybe, maybe not. My days serving your breakfast are coming to an end." She laughs. "And if I felt any better, I'd drop my harp plumb through the cloud."

"Come on, Oralyn Strumpf," the man teases, lingering at the counter. I don't dare sneak another peek. Fingers drum on the counter. "You ain't leaving. No way, no how. What else would you do with your time, a widow and all?" He chuckles—another knuckle rap on the counter. "I'm off. See you tomorrow…as always."

The door opens, and the diner goes quiet. Except for Oralyn.

"What'll I do?" she mutters to herself as she rounds the counter and pours herself a cup of coffee. "Garden? Catch up on a good book? Travel? Jeez, I have plenty of ways to occupy my time. What do men know?"

Excellent question, and I wonder the same about Jacob.

I peer out the plate glass window, draped in red-and-white-checked curtains. The men pile into a Ford F-150, festooned with oversized tires and chrome trim, so different from the rusted pickup truck that my beloved Granny used to drive.

I breathe a sigh of relief. My mother might enjoy attracting attention from strange men, but not me. She's in a league of her own in that department. But then, she could have changed, found Jesus, and realized her troubles began and ended because of her own unforgiving spirit and poor choices in men.

Why can't I stop thinking the worst of her?

What will Aunt Adele say when I finally reach out to her? I should have contacted her before leaving Atlanta, but I didn't think about it at the time. Will Aunt Adele support me? Or will she come up with a laundry list of reasons to steer clear of Mom?

Ignorance is not bliss. Pull yourself together.

I reach for the phone to make the now long-overdue call, but a loud discussion from across the diner catches my attention. Oralyn is leaning against the doorjamb leading into a back room, hidden by the griddle, deep fryer, exhaust fans, and metal shelving stacked high with white plates and bowls. She smacks her thigh with her green-colored order pad.

"Monty, what do you mean I can't retire? I've been here since you came on the scene, you old fool. My legs can't take it anymore."

A deep baritone rumbles from behind the stainless-steel workstation, though I can't see who the voice belongs to or hear precisely what is being said.

"Why don't you come out and see for yourself, Monty?" Oralyn snaps, moving like a glacier to an empty counter stool. She pulls up her pant leg to make visible a network of swollen, purplish-colored, rope-like veins that twist beneath her thin skin. "Have you ever wondered why my wardrobe consists of long pants even when it's boiling outside?" Her voice amplifies. "People would take one gander at this gruesome mess and run from this little establishment of yours. Think it's catching."

A stranger's troubles supplant my own. I've never seen a worse case of varicose veins, and now I understand the source of her limp.

"Well, I can't afford to lose customers." The man called Monty chuckles as he appears from the back, wiping his hands on a white apron. He's a mountain of a man and wears his reading glasses not on the tip of his nose but on his broad forehead, which appears larger because of a receding hairline. Whatever hair that does remain is gray and carefully combed. He bends over and inspects her exposed leg, his face creasing in concern. "I've never seen so many ropes and lumps. How do ya walk on those pegs?"

Oralyn throws her hands up in the air. "That's what I'm trying to tell you. Standing all day makes them worse. I need to prop them up occasionally, which isn't possible around here."

"Okay. Okay. Okay." He lifts his head and makes eye contact with Oralyn. "But can you give me a few days to find a replacement?" Monty holds his breath, catching sight of one of the diner's other waitresses. She's mopping the floor. "Finding help is next to impossible these days. Except for you and her," he says, angling his head in the other waitress's direction, "no one wants to work hard." A pimple-faced teenager, who'd been scraping the griddle with a large spatula, ducks behind the shelving, ostensibly to avoid Monty's wrath.

And apparently for good reason.

"More elbow grease on that griddle, son. No shortcuts. I've shown you how to do it. Now do it."

Monty's gruffness and eye roll may be an act. Oralyn winks at the teenager, who gives her a sheepish grin—just another day in the life at a diner.

"Of course, I'll give you time," Oralyn says. "And I'll do one better. I've already talked with my niece, Shannon. She used to work here in high school. Remember?" Monty massages his temples and nods. "Her kids are old enough to take care of themselves, and she's interested in making some money. The breakfast and lunch shifts would work for her."

Monty's vigorous temple massage dislodges his readers. He repositions them on his forehead before asking, "When can she start?"

"Tomorrow. I'll come in and show her the ropes."

He gives her a long look. "Gonna miss you, Oralyn. We've shared lots of laughs over the years. How long has it been?" He scratches his shiny crown. "Thirty, forty years?"

"For crying out loud, I'm not dying. I'm retiring. Starting tomorrow afternoon, someone will finally be serving me."

He takes in a cleansing breath and returns to the back, and I wonder how old they are. Sixties? Seventies? Hard to say, and my mind turns to my mother. The only photo I have of her was taken just before I was born. Hard living and time take a toll on most faces. And my mother has lived hard. Will she be recognizable if I manage to find her?

Oralyn pockets the order pad before sliding off the stool. With slow, practiced movements, she wipes down the shellacked tables, their surfaces layered with old photos, each one a window into a distant time. Laurel and I are the only customers in the diner.

"Excuse me, ma'am. I want to pay my bill."

"Oh my gosh, I forgot you were there, honey." Oralyn hobbles to our booth and lays the bill next to my phone before looking past my lap to see Laurel fast asleep on the bench.

"Oh my, how I miss those days. So precious." She pats my hand and glances at my untouched plate. "How do you expect to take care of that little one if you're running on empty yourself? You need to take care of yourself."

"Yes, ma'am. I will." I pause. "Oralyn, right?"

She nods.

"My name is Ginny." I extend my hand. "I apologize for eavesdropping, but compression stockings or socks can ease the pain." I point to her legs. "They helped my grandmother and my patients… I'm a nurse," I say to clarify.

The corners of her mouth turn up. "Well, thank you." But she says nothing more as she gathers my plate and coffee cup and heads for the back, where Monty appears to spend most of his time, moving slower than before.

I leave a twenty and carry my sleeping baby and multicolored cloth satchel to my aging Honda, a source of contention between Jacob and me. Within weeks of my agreeing to move in with Jacob—another decision that disappointed Granny—he started insisting that I park my ratty old car in the garage. He would not allow it to tarnish his image as a mega-wealthy real estate developer—the only heir to his father's successful firm. But the snobbery was a godsend. I could pack my bags without anyone noticing, ensuring a clean getaway to address the mommy issues that had blinded me to Jacob's motives.

Once settled behind the wheel, I take in the sign affixed to the diner's roof, its lettering warm and welcoming. I feel drawn to this clean, well-lighted eatery, a close replica of the one Granny and I once frequented before I had deviated from the values she had instilled in me. Wrapped in shiny stainless steel, *Monty's Diner* feels like a beacon of hope. Here, I don't have to worry about my future. Here, I'm infused with Granny's wisdom.

I shake myself. I should be on the road, not dawdling outside. *Stop procrastinating.* I search my bag, looking for my phone. My lifeline to the world hides beneath the lavender-scented wet wipes, lipsticks, brushes, baby gear, and, of course, the treasured memento of my otherworldly visit with TC.

I take a deep breath and hit the call button under Melinda's name on my phone.

* * *

Melinda Anderson, a former nursing colleague, answers on the first ring. There's no hello or greeting, just an avalanche of words.

"Oh my gosh, Ginny. Did you read my message? I sent it more than an hour ago, just after Jacob left. I should've called..." Her voice cracks at the end, shaky with panic.

The scene from three days ago replays in my mind. Her eyes widened and her mouth dropped open as I confessed the reasons for leaving Atlanta. She had never cared for Jacob, she admitted as we sipped coffee in his kitchen. But she never suspected the extent of his cruelty, either—confidences I had never shared with her. Then she begged for my forgiveness. Some time ago, she had seen him holding hands with a tall, red-haired woman. The word "platonic" didn't describe their behavior. She kept his infidelity quiet because she thought I would hold it against her. Good grief. What a sad sack I had become. I had no idea he was cheating on me.

Pathetic.

Melinda stops talking, and I check my phone to ensure we haven't been disconnected. I then hear muffled sounds, as if she has covered the phone with her hand. I can't make out her words, but her husband's voice comes through clearly. Whatever happened this morning has shaken her. It may have affected Hank as well. For a moment, I think about her rock-solid husband, a former Navy SEAL, who wants nothing more than a quiet life focused on family and faith. "The things that matter," he had said one night when I stopped by, pregnant and feeling lonely—something that happened often during my time with Jacob.

"Jacob stopped by your house this morning, Melinda?"

"I'm trying to tell you."

As I listen to her story, a knot forms in my stomach. Jacob is many things, but showing up unannounced at someone's front door—especially a home occupied by people he's met only once or twice—shocks me. Although Jacob had discouraged me from connecting with my few childhood friends, he hadn't ended our relationship. If he suspects her involvement, he will make her life a living hell. Now, I regret her participation in my escape.

"This morning, after breakfast with the kids, Jacob knocked on the door." She takes a breath. "He was aggressive, like he was amped up on PCP. He kept looking past me to see if you were hiding in the house somewhere."

"What did you tell him?" My stomach twists again.

"I told him I had no idea where you might be, and that's the truth. You didn't tell me. You only told me that you had unfinished business with your mother in Nevada." Melinda's voice ratchets in intensity. "I pretended I didn't know you had left—that we had no contact since I drove you and Laurel home from the hospital after she was born."

My mind soars to that awful day about four months ago when Jacob stranded me at the hospital. The doctors had released me after my emergency cesarean, and I wanted to go home. I had called Jacob and left messages, asking him to please pick us up. But he had gone missing. So, I called Granny, who choked back bile whenever Jacob's name came up.

"I'm on my way. You're *not* going back to *that* man," she said. "You're comin' home with me, where I can keep you safe. He's no good."

But Granny never made it.

She crashed into a concrete barrier on Interstate 75 and died minutes later, an insurmountable emotional loss for me. Granny meant everything to me. Although my out-of-wedlock pregnancy went against the values she had taught me, she loved me unconditionally. Jacob didn't want the baby, and when I told Granny, she said that the good Lord had created my child, and it was my responsibility to see the pregnancy through. I was grateful for her kindness.

Disappointing her was never my intention, nor was falling into his web of deceit.

By then, I was so beaten down. The hospital no-show was just one of many hurts. It did not matter how much I loved or supported Jacob; I would never be anything more than a plaything to him, a person he could control and manipulate. Granny's death compounded my misery and poisoned my mind.

I felt trapped.

Alone.

With Granny gone, where would I go?

That's when I hatched my twisted plan. The night TC came, I had planned to take a fistful of painkillers on top of all the wine I had drunk. Melinda, unaware of my mental state, agreed earlier to stop by Jacob's house the following morning to check on me. I figured she would find me dead and then take Laurel home with her. Crazy. I know. But that's how desperate I'd become.

So caught up in the memory, I nearly miss what Melinda says next.

"Jacob called me a liar and accused me of withholding information. He kept clenching his fists. I thought his head would explode. Hank was having none of that."

Hank, from my interaction with him, doesn't suffer fools, and I can see him jabbing Jacob's chest with his finger and ordering him off his property. No one would speak to his wife in that manner.

"Jacob calmed down then," Melinda continues. "He apologized to the point of groveling. Said he was beside himself with worry and had no intention of causing trouble. He urged me to call him the moment I heard from you. But before climbing into that red BMW convertible of his, he laughed. As if he knew something that I didn't."

In my car, with the windows closed, sweat rolls down my face, mingling with tears brought on by memories of Granny and regret from my misguided thinking a few nights ago. *What if TC hadn't come?* I start the car and crank up the AC before glancing at Laurel, sound asleep in her baby seat behind me. Her hairline is beaded with perspiration.

"Ginny, he then pulled out his iPhone and tapped the screen. He told me to pass along a message."

My stomach lurches. "What's the message?"

"He said, 'Tell Ginny she can run, but she can't hide.' Where are you?"

"Oklahoma. Outside a diner."

"I don't know Jacob. He could be following you or just playing a game. But play it safe. Ditch the phone. Now."

Despite trying to put as many miles as possible between us and him in Atlanta—which is not easy traveling with a baby—a tsunami sweeps over me. Everything makes sense. No wonder he hadn't blown up my phone with calls and texts, demanding to know where I was. There was no need to. He *did* ask for my permission to track my phone.

I worry when you work late-night shifts, he had said, pulling me into a bear-like hug that used to make my skin tingle. He took my phone, adjusted the settings, then handed it back to me and told me to approve his access request. I did, even though I didn't fully understand what was happening. "Thanks, Ginny," he said, a smile spreading across his face. "I'll sleep better now."

It was an award-winning performance, like so many. I hadn't yet fully grasped his true motivation, his modus operandi. More like it, I was purposefully ignoring evidence of his controlling nature.

Earlier this morning, as I lay in my hotel bed, I felt sure of myself. Yes, I was a little anxious about finding my mom, afraid of how I'd react if she turned her back on me again. But at least I had freed myself of Jacob. He was seven hundred miles away and would never find me. I could contact him when I was good and ready, if ever.

Back in the car, I rest my head on the steering wheel, still holding the phone to my ear. "So sorry for this," I say in a whisper. "Your friendship—"

Melinda speaks over my apologies. "You could turn off location services, but if I were you, I'd go dark. Get rid of your phone and buy a burner...pronto. Whatever you do, make sure you loop me in. Promise me."

"Okay." I squeeze my eyes shut, unable to form a coherent sentence. "Gotta go."

The phone lands in the cup holder, and I begin to rock. My head bangs the steering wheel with each forward motion as I weep. *Why God? Why me?*

That's when someone taps on the window, and I jump.

CHAPTER TWO

Jacob

I settle into the front seat of my car, parked in the driveway of Melinda's cookie-cutter home—a modern eyesore in the Atlanta suburbs. I'm confident that I've instilled the fear of God in Melinda and shown her who's in control, which was my only reason for visiting her. There's no doubt in my mind. Melinda is sure to relay my warning.

Ginny might think she can run, but she can't hide because I know her hidey-hole.

I hit the push-button ignition and put the car into gear when her husband, whose name escapes me, shouts for me to wait. Curious, I comply even though it might be a mistake. His military bearing, much like my father's, intimidates me, as do his eyes. They're squinting and not from the glare of the sun, which is hiding behind a bank of clouds.

"You told me to leave, and that's what I'm doing." I hold myself upright, trying to give myself a more commanding presence, which is difficult sitting in a low-slung car. I touch my chest where he'd jabbed me earlier.

He bends over and invades my space. "I'll kick your pathetic carcass from here to Sunday if you ever darken my door again." His voice is controlled, but there's no mistaking the menace. He straightens and takes a few steps from my car. "I hope I've made myself clear."

"Oh, loud and clear. But why can't you, a family man, understand my perspective? My wife and child are gone, and I have every right to question those who know her best."

Before he can say another word, I back out, shaken, resisting the urge to peel out with tires squealing. As I drive down the street, a glance in the rearview mirror reveals the scene is still unchanged. He stands there, watching, his mouth pulled into a tight, hard line. I round the corner, and he disappears. I breathe a sigh of relief.

My fingers rap on the steering wheel as I debate next steps. At some point, I should call dear old Mom and Pops and share my little sob story about Ginny picking up and leaving, a discovery made late last night following my two-day romantic escape in Savannah with Rachel, the red-haired hottie who hangs onto my every word.

Much like Ginny used to do…before the kid came and her meddling old Granny died—all within a day or two.

I never saw this happening. Ginny had threatened to leave before, accusing me of cruelty and indifference, but my powers of persuasion worked their magic. She always unpacked her bags.

What lit a fire under her behind this time?

The last time I saw her, she was stumbling around, completely toasted. The bedroom was an absolute pigsty. Picture my surprise as I moved from room to room, shouting Ginny's name, only to find a *Dear John* note taped to the refrigerator. The bedroom confirmed her written kiss-off. It was clear she had cleaned the place out. Her clothes—at least the ones she came with—were gone. She left behind the things I had bought for her.

Whatever.

I pull into the driveway and stare at the garage doors that once concealed Ginny's ugly old Honda. She celebrated the day the title arrived in the mail, like the payoff of a used-car loan called for a standing ovation. How tiresome. Pedestrian. Do I want to continue this charade? The red-headed Rachel—my sexy *Red*—will do just fine...at least for now—no shortage of fine-looking women who seek a lifestyle that only wealth can afford.

No, finding women isn't a problem.

Getting played by Ginny is. I still can't believe her nerve. Her ingratitude. I gave her an enviable life. And this is how she repays me? Rage pulses through my veins. Only days ago, I wanted to wipe my hands of her, annoyed with her sniffling and slovenliness. Didn't I tell my father that Ginny might need a professional intervention? Her drinking had worsened, and it appeared she might be abusing painkillers.

But that was then.

My fingers drum the steering wheel as I think about what would be best for me. Red makes a splash and excites me with her come-ravish-me leers, but Ginny perfects my image. Everyone raves about her quiet, unassuming grace, brains, and beauty; therefore, they seem to think better of me. The kid doesn't hurt the image I project, either.

Why change anything?

Sweet little Ginny's out-of-the-blue departure has altered my view of her. I'm up for a chase, and it won't take much to reel her back in. This time, however, I will marry her. Isn't that what she always wanted? Ha! She will think twice before abandoning me again.

I press the garage-door opener and pull into my customary slot. The garage is bigger and cleaner now that Ginny has split. Melinda is probably on the phone now, relaying my message. Everything is going well and according to plan. Keeping Ginny guessing is what I do best.

* * *

I stand inside my home's grand foyer, struck by the silence. Ginny isn't a loudmouth like Red, but she annoys me with her pot banging and chitter-chatter with the kid, whom she perches in an infant seat that stays planted on the kitchen island—another annoyance. Clutter in communal spaces makes me cringe. I head for the kitchen and see the blasted seat still sitting there.

One sweep of my arm sends it clattering to the hardwood floor. I stand over it for a moment, looking at it in pieces on the floor, a mutilated reminder of the chaos she brings into my space. I sit on one of the stools, running my fingers through my auburn-colored hair, one of my vanities. First things first. I scroll through my contacts and tap a number.

"Hi, Adele. This is Jacob." I rest my head in my hand and roll my eyes, listening to her polite inquiries into my health, Ginny's health, and, of course, the baby's. She sounds uncertain, as if she's wondering why I might be calling.

We're not exactly best buds.

I met Ginny's aunt at Granny's funeral about four months ago, and two impressions registered. Though put together in her choice of hairstyle and clothing—selected to mask the flaws of a middle-aged face and body—Adele hit every branch on the ugly tree. No wonder she never married.

And two, she, like Melinda's meathead husband, didn't appear to suffer fools. Not that I'm a fool, of course. I'm just saying. She did not do small talk and seemed immune to flattery. In the end, though, I won her over. I blew a fair bit of bunkum up her backside, including the little white lie that Ginny and I were blissfully wedded, something I tell everyone despite Ginny's protests and pleas that we tie the knot.

Given the Hudson family's social position, Dad's political aspirations, and maybe even my own one day, I should care about loyalty and commitment—qualities that the institution of marriage and family stand for. But neither interests me much. As I always say, "Fake it until you make it." So, that's what I do. I fake it. It is amazing what people believe, including hard-nosed types like Adele.

"I'm fine," I say, "but I'm not sure about Ginny...or the baby. I got home from a business trip last night, and they were gone." I then launch into my practiced story, having already decided to omit specific details, such as the fact that I've tracked her down. The only reason for this tête-à-tête is to play on Adele's heartstrings and bring her over to my side. It might prove helpful if Ginny refuses to come to her senses.

Adele draws in a deep breath, which I can't interpret. I have never gotten a handle on their relationship because Ginny never talks about her family...except for that grandmother of hers. Adele, if mentioned at all, is mentioned only in passing.

"What do you mean she and the baby are gone?" By the sound coming through my phone, I know that she is shuffling papers, likely in her office, playing the titan of finance for that big-name Wall Street investment firm. But suddenly, the rearrangement of paper stops. I have her attention now.

"I was hoping you could tell me." Sincerity drips from my mouth. "Have you spoken with her recently?"

"No, we haven't talked in a while. Have you tried calling her?"

"Uh, no. I'm honoring her wishes. She left a note and told me not to call."

"Well, Jacob, she does need time to sort things out. My mother's death came as a big shock...and it didn't help that my sister refused to attend the funeral." Adele sounds like she's gagging on curdled milk with the mention of her sister.

"Yes, she did take the death hard," I agree, as the gears turn inside my head. Ginny's mother? I need to redirect the gabfest back to her. I continue with more details about *my wife's* state of mind. "Maybe I should have called sooner...before she left... and I apologize for that. Ginny's depression is scaring me. She's struggling."

"Jacob, be specific." Adele's no-nonsense, facts-only persona takes over.

"Because she started drinking...a lot."

I let that tidbit steep before telling Adele about Ginny's sack of pills—the very same painkillers I had encouraged her to take after the kid's birth. I spotted the bag on the nightstand, amid a jumble of papers and empty wine bottles. It was clear that the once-fastidious Ginny had become a genuine slob, with her dirty clothes, greasy hair, and mascara smudged beneath her eyes. This was all true, of course, because that was the way I left her before my tryst with Red.

"You love your niece. So do I." My words implore. "She and the baby are my world. I'm beating myself up. I thought she could muscle through the grief." My voice rises in volume. "Adele, she ran off with my child. She could be using. Her mother might have ideas on where Ginny might go. No one wants to see this end in tragedy."

That comment serves as a test of the waters. Until a few seconds ago, I had no idea about the status of Ginny's mom. Whenever I asked Ginny about her people, she would avoid the question, only mentioning that Granny became her legal guardian after her father passed away from a heart attack and her older sister died of cancer. According to Ginny, her mother could not support her only surviving offspring.

Oh, the fiction Ginny spun.

It did not take long for a private investigator to uncover the truth, discovering that Ginny's father, a reprobate named Jimmy, was very much alive. He was serving a life sentence in a South Carolina prison for the murder of Ginny's older sister, Laurel—the kid's namesake. As for Mommy Dearest, the investigator was still working on it.

"You'd be very much mistaken if you think Audrey Smith can help." Adele's voice drips with venom. "She doesn't lift a finger for anyone, including my mother, who had no choice but to raise Ginny when she walked out." Adele has worked herself into a lather. "My sister is dead to me and Ginny. We've both had a bellyful of her."

This is getting better and better. This is not the story Ginny told.

"Perhaps it's a waste of time, but shouldn't we try contacting your sister?" I feel myself smile. Uptight Adele is full of interesting factoids. I tamp down my excitement. "Did I hear you call her Audrey Smith? I thought she and Ginny shared the same last name."

After an interminable pause, Adele answers. "Didn't Ginny tell you? My sister didn't marry Ginny's deadbeat father. Certainly, she would've told you that."

"Of course. What's wrong with me?" I feign memory loss due to the stress of Ginny's unexpected departure. "But I don't know how to contact Ginny's mom. You've been in touch since Granny's death. I sure would appreciate a phone number or an address."

The tapping of a pen or pencil reverberates through the phone. She pauses as if weighing the pros and cons of revealing more. "Audrey lives in Las Vegas, the last I heard. Look, try not to worry. I'll call Ginny as soon as I hang up with you. I'll give you a call back."

I didn't get everything I wanted, but I received enough to get started. Indeed, my heart-to-heart with Adele went even better than expected.

CHAPTER THREE

Ginny

The air conditioning blasts through the vents, but it does little to cool the heat pulsing through me. My T-shirt clings to my back, damp with sweat, and my vision is blurry from the tears still streaming down my face after my conversation with Melinda. I lift my head off the steering wheel—the cold, hard plastic digging into my forehead—and squint through the fogged-up window to see who's knocking.

Oralyn stands next to the car. I roll down the window.

"Ginny?"

I nod.

"I saw you boo-hooing and thought I'd better find out what's going on. You're upset and shouldn't be driving anywhere." She furrows her brow, the lines carved as deep as the crow's feet at the corners of her eyes.

"Ma'am, thanks for your concern, but I'm okay."

Her head does a quick little shake. "I'm not so sure about that." She clamps her hands on her hips before telling me that the Lord speaks to her. And when He does, she listens. "Well, most of the time… But I *can* spot trouble from a mile off." She says this with the certainty of a prophet.

Her words transport me across space and time to the day Granny drove hundreds of miles over never-before-traveled roads to the ramshackle trailer in South Carolina where I'd lived with my older sister, mom, and so-called dad. She arrived within minutes of Jimmy kicking the life out of my sister and then beating Mom within an inch of her life, me hiding in the bedroom, my hands shaking, as I called nine-one-one.

Granny's arrival—long before the advent of navigation apps and devices—was a miracle and happened only because she was obedient to God's instructions, taking the roads He told her to take. She was adamant about this point. Because she listened, Granny believed my life had changed. Despite the hot mess I was born into, I *would* live an ordinary life, filled with love and security, if I never forgot the source of my blessings.

She was right, of course, but I chose a different path. Despite counseling, anger festered in unseen places. I was determined to prove that I was nothing like my mother. Jacob provided the means to achieve this goal. He adored me—or so he claimed before I popped up pregnant—and his success and social standing were icing on the cake. However, I paid a hefty price to uphold this illusion. I overlooked his lies and compromised my core values. I gave up everything to prove I had risen above my mother's poor choices.

"What's troubling you?" Oralyn asks. Her bluntness throws me.

She taps her foot—a gesture Granny would make when impatient with me. My eyes flit in all directions except at Oralyn. "You want to steer clear of my troubles." I wipe more moisture off my face, eyeballing the treacherous phone that hijacked my plans to leave without a trace. "I really must go."

"Well, honey, that's a decision I can make all by myself. Whether to butt into your mess. How about you go back inside and eat something—and coffee doesn't count. Haste makes waste on an empty stomach. I'll tell Monty it's on me."

I roll my neck to relieve the kinks from more stress. Why would this stranger concern herself with my predicament? Does Jacob know my location, as Melinda suggested? Is he on his way?

I stare at the rubber memory bracelet inscribed with Philippians 1:3: *"I thank my God every time I remember you."* TC had given it to me at the festival after I shared details about my traumatic childhood—secrets I could never reveal to Jacob for fear he would reject me. In that moment, it felt cosmic. We had transformed from strangers into close friends.

Oralyn is waiting for an answer, but I am unsure how to reply. I touch the bracelet, a sort of talisman, and think about the Bible verse and Granny's conviction that we should remember the special people who come into our lives—even if the connection lasts only a fleeting moment. They enter our lives for a reason, placed there by God, at the perfect time to encourage us as we journey through life. Without them, we might lose sight of our potential and miss the plan for our lives. TC was one such person; he was someone I was meant to meet.

Is Oralyn another?

Doubts flood my mind.

Too much trauma.

Too much loneliness.

And yes, too many losses.

Granny is gone, and so is TC, the two people I could have counted on during a time like this. The reason for these losses may elude me, but I am sure the phone must go. I cannot risk it. Credit cards are probably off-limits, too. Thankfully, I had started saving cash—lots of it—but I can't take credit for that. Despite my backsliding, God's still, small voice managed to get through. He told me to prepare, and this time I obeyed.

Beep. Beep. Beep.

I look past Oralyn, still standing next to my car, and see a garbage truck backing up to the diner's dumpster. In a burst of urgency, I swing open the car door, practically knocking her off her feet. "Sorry!" I call out, but I'm already sprinting toward the dumpster, phone in hand. I aim for the open lid but, of course, miss the mark. The device hits the pavement hard, and the glass shatters.

Oops.

"Whatcha doing, lady?" the driver yells from the window. "Move."

I raise my hand like I'm directing traffic and snatch the phone with the other. Despite the cracked screen, the phone appears otherwise functional. A new text has come through, this one from Aunt Adele—a bad omen, considering we barely talk. Why is she calling? It's too late to worry about that now. Jacob is a hunter, and I'm his prey. With a frustrated huff, I take another shot. My phone sails through the air and lands squarely inside the dumpster moments before the hydraulic lift snags the heavy metal container and tips restaurant refuse into the back of the trash truck, perfuming the air with the aroma of rotting food.

"Yes!" I cry out, performing a fist pump—a fitting end for that devil device.

"Well, that was exciting." Oralyn stands beside me, a lopsided grin spreading across her face. "I guess you didn't like the phone."

CHAPTER FOUR

Oralyn

The air of triumph after Ginny lobbed the phone into the dumpster dissolves quickly. She slumps against her car and gnaws on her lip. The light in her eyes flickers, as if the significance of her actions has just hit home. I know nothing of her struggles, but I have felt regret myself, and that is how she appears to me—remorseful. The kind of sorrow that sits deep in the chest and doesn't let go. Over what, I wouldn't know.

"Come on, Ginny." I tilt my head in the direction of the door. "The world always looks brighter on a full stomach."

She appears uncertain but follows me into the diner, gently cradling her baby in one arm and swiping away evidence of her crying jag with the other. We take the booth closest to the counter, and I holler to the kid with the serious acne problem to rustle up fried eggs, bacon—the works.

"If it's not too much trouble, I think toast might be better," Ginny says, rocking the baby in her arms. "I don't have much of an appetite."

"Of course. Anything you want. Remember, it's on me." I press on the table with both hands and hoist myself to a standing position. "Change that order to toast." The griddle kid salutes, and Ginny smiles, and I move on to greet my favorite customer, an old-timer with wisps of snow-colored hair that match his bushy beard.

By the time the last of the lunch crowd leaves a couple of hours later, my body and brain are exhausted. To my surprise, Ginny has not budged from the booth. She comes across as serene, more certain. The table before her is neat, almost too tidy, except for the book resting in the center, its pages slightly curled at the edges. When I approach her table, she glances up, her eyes steady and calm. A quiet focus seems to have replaced the desperation I saw earlier.

"I need some advice."

She closes the book—a well-worn Bible—and I wonder why she would need my counsel. What's her story? The license tag suggests she might be from Georgia. What's a cutie pie like her doing traveling alone with a baby? She interrupts my thoughts.

"Trashing the phone was a bit impetuous." A small smile plays at the corners of her mouth. "But what's done is done. Do you have any recommendations on where I can buy a new one? Probably need a map, too."

My niece, the one who's taking my job starting tomorrow—thank the Lord—handles those details for me. Since my sister passed, I have become Shannon's project. Allowing her to dabble in my affairs makes her feel useful, especially since her kids no longer require constant mothering. I don't, either, but she does spare me the hassle of learning things I don't want to know. I'm too old for that nonsense.

"Monty, would you come out for a minute?" I take a seat across from Ginny and sigh. My legs ache, and so do my feet.

Monty shuffles out from his hideout, eyeing Ginny with some curiosity. Given our location on historic Route 66, strangers aren't unusual. But she seems to have captured his interest. She looks like an innocent—someone he would want to protect.

"This is Ginny." I pause, waiting for her to offer her last name.

"Uh, Carmichael," she says, standing to take his extended hand.

"Monty Smitherman." He plops down next to me. His eyes are at half-mast—not surprising because he's been here since long before the sun peeked over the horizon. In my humble opinion, he should sell his stake. Both of us need to live out whatever time God has given us, doing something else. I can't imagine it would involve slinging burgers and deep-frying fries and tots or dealing with tardy employees who bury their heads in their phones.

"What can I do for you?" He caresses his temples.

"Ginny wants to buy a new phone. Where would she find one?"

"What kinda phone?"

"A burner," Ginny says in a firm voice.

"A burner? What's that?" My ignorance of technology shows almost daily. Television remotes, for example, baffle me.

"Woman, do you live under a rock?" Monty rolls his eyes. "They're prepaid phones. Didn't you watch *The Wire*?"

"Can't say that I have, Monty. Why would you need a prepaid phone?"

Monty stays up to date on the gadget front and tells me at every opportunity to get with the program and join the twenty-first century. He goes on to say that while burners aren't one hundred percent fail-safe, they can prevent unwanted callers from contacting you. He then pulls his phone from his pants pocket and starts scrolling through the missed calls. "Spam. Spam. Spam," he mutters. "Sick of these clowns bothering me." The corners of his mouth turn down. "Whatever happened to the good old days, Oralyn, before telemarketers?"

I shrug. Whatever happened to those little dials and knobs on television sets?

"It would work for me," Ginny says, resting her head in one hand while cradling her baby in her other arm. I have never seen a happier, more contented child. The light reflecting off Monty's readers, which are still planted on his forehead, seems to enrapture her. *Has he forgotten that they're up there?*

Monty crosses his arms. "You realize they have few features, and if you're like my kids and every other young person on this planet, I'd bet you can't go two seconds without checking social media or taking selfies."

She draws back and clears her throat to speak, but I interject. Based on what I've seen so far, something has gotten her overexcited, and her creased brow tells me she's debating whether to reveal more.

"Monty, that's none of your business," I say, comfortable in giving him grief. He's probably the only man I've ever mouthed off to, and he seems to enjoy it when he's in a good mood. "If the girl wants a burner—whatever that is—who are you to question?"

"Just wondering why she'd need one." Irritation registers in his voice.

"That's okay, Oralyn." Ginny touches my arm before cutting her eyes toward Monty, who has ordered the pimply teenager to clean up the food-prep area. "We...Laurel and I...left Atlanta three days ago. My fiancé, the baby's father, had become abusive." She touches two fading chin bruises that had gone unnoticed before. "And a friend—TC is his name—urged me to leave. He had experience with people like Jacob."

Ginny takes a deep breath and divulges the next in a rush. "I'm on the run, and now believe Jacob may know where I am." She presses her free hand to her temple, wagging her head back and forth. "I don't want to see him, talk to him, or text him. I don't want to hear his voice. I want Jacob out of my life."

With every declaration, I nod.

"Does he hit you?" Monty leans in closer, his eyes squinting as he studies the discolorations on her chin. The question doesn't surprise me. His oldest daughter and her two kids now live with him and his wife in one of the town's stately Victorians that his wife had inherited. For years, his daughter's ex-husband used her as his punching bag. Skeptical of court-ordered restraining orders, Monty installed a security system and resumed his martial arts training. A gun is likely at the ready.

She shakes her head. "He doesn't do that. He grabs my arms, face, and neck. Sometimes he bruises me."

"Honey, don't kid yourself. He's abusing you," I say, a bit bothered by her nonchalance.

She massages the discolorations before turning her head to study the framed photos of our town's war heroes, many now long gone. The baby starts to whimper, which draws her away from our memorial, and I feel bad. *Did my tone of voice upset the little one?*

"It's okay, baby girl." Ginny's voice is like honey. After several minutes of gentle rocking, Ginny calms her baby and continues her story, picking up exactly where she had left off.

"His abuse is mental, done in secret, and if you'd met him, you'd think he was the nicest guy in the world. Had me charmed." She looks at the table, fiddling with a turquoise-colored rubber wristband. "But he plays a game. One minute I'm worthless, and the next, I'm the love of his life. Around and around we go. My grandmother would've been horrified by the vulgar names he calls me." Her body trembles as she lifts her eyes to meet mine. "I can't let him prey on me again. I must protect myself and Laurel."

Everything adds up—the sobbing, shaking, and head-banging in her car, the reason her phone ended up in the dumpster. She's a victim of abuse like me. I didn't deserve it, either. But unlike Ginny, who's decided to run, I couldn't find the courage to do something about it. Living in quiet desperation, I pretended all was grand, behavior modeled by my mother, who would cower and shake when my old man came home drunk. He would thrash her first and then me and my sister before lighting into my younger brother, who had finally had enough. One cold-cock and Daddy's fighting days were over. He then avoided us. Easy since he moved out, never to show his face again.

No loss.

Monty doesn't say anything for a moment as he strokes his clean-shaven jaw. "Where are you headed?" His eyebrows lift.

Worry lines appear between her eyebrows. After a few beats, she speaks.

"Nevada."

I hold my breath waiting for more, but Ginny repositions the baby and starts patting her back, planting a tiny kiss on the top of the child's head. She says no more.

"Okay." Monty accepts this in stride. "How are you set up with money and lodging? Does the baby need anything?" His gaze turns to the now cooing baby, his eyes shimmering, as he angles his head in my direction. "What can we do?" We're on common ground. I want to help this girl, too.

"I'm set," she says, "but like I said, I need a phone, features or no features. I can't drive one more mile without some means of communication." She glances at the ceiling, as if looking for answers there. "I have to call my aunt and tell her where I am before—"

"Walmart is close by and has a decent selection." Monty caresses his chin. "You can get one there."

He reels off the directions. And for reasons I cannot riddle, his suggested route takes her through our downtown, where the tracks, forgotten scars bisecting the broad avenues, are the only remaining evidence of the town's once-bustling trolley system. Not so long ago (or have I completely lost all track of time?) bright red streetcars rumbled over them, ferrying visitors from the railroad depot to shops housed in buildings that also stand in stubborn silence, some boarded up like the long-abandoned motels and gas stations along Route 66. With their cracked windows and peeling paint, these derelict buildings offer little more than a ghostly reminder of better days. Ginny searches her cloth satchel for a pen and a piece of paper and asks him to start over.

"Monty, why would you direct her that way?" I ask. "Makes no sense."

"Why not? Everyone should get a feel for our little town."

Monty is the community's biggest booster, a proud Oklahoman who devours books about the town's history—the land rushes and lotteries on Indian lands, the cattle runs along the Chisholm Trail, and the railroad that employed hundreds. Others, particularly the young, are not as enthusiastic. After graduating, most head to bigger cities that offer better-paying jobs and brighter lights—a respite from a skyline dominated by a towering grain elevator. I get it. I wanted to leave, too, but life got in the way.

"How about I take her?" I interject. "I'm sure some young buck, a techie type like you, can help her at the store. Furthermore, my breakfast and lunch shifts are over."

He crosses his arms and laughs.

"How about we all go?"

My mouth opens.

"What's with the look, Oralyn?" He glances out the window and mentions his younger business partner, who slipped in without my noticing. "Your *other* boss is in the back getting ready for the dinner shift." Monty removes his apron and then glares at his watch. "Where's what's her name? Isn't she supposed to relieve you?" His eyebrows raise; he's referring to one of the third-shift waitresses. "That girl wouldn't know hard work if it slapped her upside the head."

He's dead-on in his assessment of her. In her world, work hours are a concept—a suggestion. The kid with bad skin may not be much to look at, and at times, he annoys even me with his stupid comments, but at least he shows up on time. Shannon will do likewise. When she starts work tomorrow, she will beat Monty to the door. The girl wears me out.

As if on cue, the now-tardy waitress breezes through the door. Monty gives her the stink-eye before doffing his Oklahoma Sooners cap and shoving his readers into his shirt pocket. "Let's go." He grumbles and stomps toward the front door.

CHAPTER FIVE

Jacob

Waiting for a return call from Adele has put me on edge. Needing to distract myself, I take a long, hot shower before heading for the office. My father is likely wondering why I haven't made an appearance earlier. He's one of those early-bird types, and it's already past noon. I poke my head into his office.

"I was about ready to call you." His deep, cultivated Southern accent sounds from across his spacious office space, the one I hope to inherit one day. He sits at his leather desk chair as if it were a throne. Behind him, a towering wall of windows offers a sweeping view of downtown Atlanta, a city he's long considered his domain. Today, he wears a crisp white dress shirt rolled at the sleeves—just enough to suggest he isn't above hard work—but the silk tie stays knotted tight at his throat, a reminder of the order he imposes. Even his meticulously groomed hair—now graying at the temples—

is deliberate, lending him an air of seasoned authority. He exudes power and wields it with the confidence of an old-time plantation owner.

"Where've you been? I haven't seen you in a few days." He leans forward and glances at his Rolex, a gift from my mom, who lives for him and *pretends* to live for me. Where she's concerned, I will always play second fiddle to him. "If you were working from home, you should've called. Lest you forget, I depend on you and expect you to work as hard as I do."

"Well, I did. Remember? I took a last-minute trip to the coast." I cannot recall the specifics of our phone call before picking up Red for our getaway a few days ago, but that was the general upshot. "I just got back."

He does not respond and appears no more aware of me than I am of the child I fathered. Straightening a stack of folders on his desk, he picks up a memo and begins to read. My jaw clenches, but if I expect an apology for his implied accusation of shirked responsibilities, I'm wasting my time. He glances up and does a double take.

"Anything else, Jacob?" He starts rolling down his sleeves and snaps his monogrammed gold cuff links into place, never taking his eyes off mine. "I have an appointment. We can talk later." He swings his suit jacket over his shoulder and strides toward the door.

I follow in his wake, wondering where he's off to.

My assistant hands me a few messages and asks about Ginny and the baby. "Fine, fine." Personal questions often go unanswered, and my assistant has learned to avoid those social niceties with me. Why would she bother today? "Please hold all calls for the next hour or so. No interruptions." I give her my no-nonsense mien and close my office door.

After dropping the messages on my desk, I spent several minutes lost in thought, scanning the Atlanta skyline. The grandfather clock—chosen by my mother to lend my space a touch of panache—chimes twice, pulling me back to the present. *Two o'clock?*

Time to check on Ginny. I chuckle, marveling at my planning and foresight, as well as my ability to exercise control over every situation. Leaving nothing to chance, I had also hidden a GPS tracker inside the Honda without her permission. If she decided to tamper with her phone's settings, I would still be aware of her comings and goings. The tracker app says the car hasn't moved an inch from a restaurant in Podunk. I wonder if she has gotten wise to the phone. A tap of that app tells a different story.

It's on the move.

Hmm. Interesting. Could she be taking a bus or a taxi? Sightseeing? Although that's unlikely. What is there to see in Oklahoma?

My phone rings.

"Adele, I had gotten worried. Have you gotten in touch with Ginny?"

"Since we last spoke, I've sent multiple text messages," she says in a matter-of-fact tone. "I also tried calling several times, but her phone just rings and then goes to voicemail." My questions about her mother, Audrey, go unanswered, and I can't help but wonder why. Has she learned something that I should be worried about, or does she want to end the call?

She sounds distracted, so it doesn't surprise me when she wraps up the conversation, promising to stay in touch.

My fingers start tapping, unsure of how to interpret that interaction. I shake myself and remind myself that the driver's seat is still mine. After all, I hold a couple of trump cards—the GPS tracker, of course, and a possible destination. Ginny might not visit her mother in Nevada, as Adele has suggested, but it would be foolish to overlook anything so early in the game. Mind made up, I scroll through my contacts and tap the call button.

"Bill, Jacob Hudson here. Any news on the woman I hired you to find?" I ask. "Yes, Audrey Carmichael." His hemming and hawing aggravates me. He's offering all manner of excuses for why his investigation of her has come up dry. I speak over him. "Well, Bill, I just got some interesting intel. She may live in Vegas and probably goes by her maiden name—Smith. Confine your search to Nevada and investigate both surnames. Send your invoice."

I then resume my scan of the Atlanta skyline, already thinking three moves ahead.

CHAPTER SIX

Ginny

Monty is a serial lane-switcher with a heavy foot as he heads west along Route 66 toward the Walmart and its choice of new phones. Oralyn yelps and grips the overhead handle when he makes a sharp left turn, roaring past a golf club, community college, a handful of restaurants, and housing developments. We are both on edge by the time he parks his late-model Chevy truck in the parking lot across the street from where Laurel and I bunked the night before. It was not the nicest accommodation; it smelled like wet dog.

"Remind me not to ride with you again." Oralyn gives Monty the death glare but settles down as soon as she spots a metal bench next to the doors. "I'll take the baby. You shop with Speed Racer."

Although I have the necessities, we stroll down the baby aisle just in case I have forgotten something. Monty grabs items out of reach for me and insists that I take advantage of the sale on baby diapers. A portable infant seat, like the one left behind on Jacob's kitchen island, captures my attention, but I move on. It's a convenience, but my car is already packed to the brim. I will make do without.

"If you need it, buy it." Monty notices my gaze. "I'll make it fit inside that little ride of yours." The box gets tossed into the cart, along with powdered formula and disposable baby-bottle liners. "Packing is like putting a puzzle together," he says, with the knowledge of King Solomon. "I learned how in the military. Learned to cook there, too, and a whole lot else."

His rubber-soled shoes squeak as his long legs carry him down the aisle, pushing the shopping cart, forcing me to increase my pace to keep up.

"Never again will I take orders from anyone other than myself," he says. "After my honorable discharge, I moved back to Oklahoma and married my high school sweetheart. We had a bunch of kids and worked hard to buy the diner." He takes a break from his machine-gun-style dialogue, letting out a sigh. "My kids aren't interested in running the place. So, I found a partner. Now that Oralyn's retiring, I suppose my wife will start hassling me again." He glances at me. "She wants me to sell my share, buy an RV, and travel, but that's about as appealing to me as having a boil lanced."

Stopping in front of a clothing rack, he examines the labels. "Is anything made in this country anymore?" He shakes his head and resumes his stroll. "How about you? What's your story? You said you were going to Nevada? Do you have people there?"

Before meeting TC, I never felt comfortable confiding in others. Childhood experiences and my innate shyness were to blame. I viewed most people as potential threats and kept them at arm's length. At the festival, TC picked up on my reticence at once. He suggested that I lighten up a bit. Not everyone was untrustworthy, he said.

I'm so conflicted. I am straddling a fence, holding tight because I cannot afford to land on the wrong side. Jacob is likely hot on my trail, yet I have made myself vulnerable to Monty, who has commandeered the shopping cart. Oralyn is looking after Laurel. While they seem like salt-of-the-earth types and remind me of Granny's friends, I should be more careful. What would TC say? The internal debate continues.

"Not sure if I'll stay in Nevada," I say, thinking that is a safe response. "At some point, I'll find a job, which won't be difficult given staffing shortages in my field, but I'm not making any major decisions yet."

"What do you do for a living?" It's a typical American-style question, often asked when meeting someone new.

"I'm a nurse and had plans to attend medical school." That detail could have gone unmentioned. My backstory should be revealed on only a need-to-know basis. *Be careful, Ginny. You don't know Monty.*

A quizzical expression crosses his face. "Impressive." But other questions, if any, go unasked. When we arrive at the electronics counter, the associate is attending to another customer, who appears to be Native American. Monty leaves me at the counter to examine the merchandise displayed on the shelves.

"What can I do for you, ma'am?"

The associate's question pulls Monty from the shelves. He takes two giant strides toward the counter. "This little lady wants a disposable phone." He raps the glass with his knuckles. "What can you show us?"

Since I won't be making many calls and have no intention of logging into social media, taking pictures, or watching videos, I select a super-cheap model after listening to Monty debate the pros and cons.

"That should do it." Monty then pulls out his wallet, selects a credit card, and hands the plastic to the salesperson.

I grab the card and hand it back to him.

Allowing Jacob to cover my expenses gave him power over me, and he exploited it. At every opportunity, he reminded me that I would be nowhere without him. He bought my clothes, let me live in his stunning home, and provided entrée to Atlanta's moneyed class. I can't believe that once impressed me. I can't let my guard down; I must take care of myself and be more cautious about whom to trust.

"Don't you think you've done enough for me, Monty?"

He rubs his jaw. "Didn't mean to offend. It's just my way."

Chastened, I touch his arm and hand the associate cash, hidden inside my satchel's zippered pocket. "No offense taken, and I do appreciate your generosity."

The bagged purchase joins the rest of my bag's contents, including my Bible—the one Jacob once tossed into the trash—and the little memento of my time with TC the night before deserting Jacob.

And then it happens. The spiritual guidance that I had once relied on.

It would always come the same way. First, a wave of energy would course through my body, manifesting as a physical warmth, and then God would speak. I had started to ignore His voice. Jacob's constant ridicule of my faith, coupled with his accusations and name-calling, made me question everything Granny had taught and modeled for me. It reached the point where I, too, began to question His very existence, agreeing with Jacob's point of view—much to his delight.

"A big, powerful God doesn't exist, Ginny, and neither does Jesus or that Holy Ghost, Holy Spirit—whatever you want to call it," Jacob would say. "Glad to see you're using your head… for a change." He'd shake his head and then ignore me for the rest of the day.

But this time, I take notice. "*Fear does not come from me. Why then are you afraid?*"

Walking through the store next to Monty, the fortress walls begin to fall, row by row, revealing a foundational truth. Monty adheres to a different code of ethics. He would no more hurt me than one of his own. An anvil lifts off me, and I let go of the fence railing, my muscles unwinding as I drop to his side. For the first time in a while, the tension evaporates, and I feel lighter, surer of myself.

"Did I say something funny?" Monty gives me a sideways glance and grins to himself. "You remind me of the cat that ate the canary."

"Feeling happy, that's all."

This brusque-but-kindhearted Oklahoman came into my life only because I had gotten tired of chain restaurants and wanted to sample local eateries. The hotel's receptionist recommended Monty's Diner, saying it was a landmark and a big deal in town for locals and travelers alike. I would be lucky if I got a table, but I did.

A stroke of luck?

Coincidence?

That's unlikely. Nothing is happenstance.

I stand on my tiptoes and wrap my arms around Monty's neck.

CHAPTER SEVEN

Oralyn

By the time Monty and Ginny return, I'm still planted on that metal bench at the front of the store, at my wits' end. Laurel's high-pitched screaming has broken my eardrums and everyone else's. The poor kid is burrowing her head into my well-endowed bosom, smacking her lips, angry tears rolling down her cheeks. Comforting her is impossible because I cannot give her what she wants.

"My, my, my, baby girl." Ginny runs toward me, takes Laurel from my arms, and starts rummaging through her oversized cloth satchel. "Oh no." She finds a baby bottle hidden amongst the jumble, but it is empty, so she tosses it back into her bag. Her search resumes until she unearths a bright pink binkie inside a plastic sandwich bag. "It's the best I can do for now, sweet pea," she says, plugging Laurel's mouth with the inferior alternative—the baby quiets, contented for now.

I'm astounded once again by the little one's good nature, reminded of my baby, Katherine, so many years ago. A lump rises in my throat as moisture gathers at the corners of my eyes. I brush it away, but the ache settles in my chest. How I wish to reexperience the blessings of raising a child.

"Monty, we need to get going. It's getting on suppertime for Laurel—and me," I say, glancing at my trusty timepiece, which has left a deep imprint on my wrist. Out of the corner of my eye, I notice Ginny's vigorous head shake. Monty nods, and we pile into his truck. The return trip is a white-knuckle affair. He races into the parking lot and comes to an abrupt stop, my seat belt strap digging into my chest. Before turning off the ignition, Monty turns his head to talk with Ginny, who is sitting in the back.

"Ginny, don't tell me you're hitting the road. It's getting late."

She chews her lip—a gesture I noticed earlier when she became frazzled or doubtful. "That was my plan. I want to get closer to Texas before stopping for the night. If Jacob is on his way, I don't want him finding me here and taking it out on you." She purses her lips. "Trust me, he can get nasty if things don't go his way."

Monty cannot, will not, abide bullies. He'd neutralized his daughter's abusive husband in short order thanks to his training in Krav Maga. I'd taken a class once, but gouging out eyes even on a rubber dummy turned my stomach. Those self-defense guys mean business.

"I may give the impression of being an old man, but no one, and I mean no one, intimidates me. Let him come. He'll wish he hadn't."

A half smile forms on Ginny's face, like he has confirmed a notion in her head.

No one speaks. What's to say? *You can take a horse to water, but you can't make it drink.* I stare out my window, praying she will listen to Monty. So lost in these thoughts, I am startled when she speaks.

"You're right, Monty. Traveling has discombobulated Laurel." She moves quickly to unlatch the baby's seat. "A normal routine, if only for one night, would do her a world of good." For the first time since we met, I see her dimples. "If Jacob is tracking me, he'll end up at the dump. Right, Oralyn?"

Monty's brow furrows as he scratches his head.

"She threw her old phone into your dumpster, and it's trash day," I clarify. "That's why she needed a new one."

Monty's guffawing erupts and fills the cab. Had we had the windows down, the entire town would have heard Monty's signature laugh. "Smart thinking, Ginny. That'll keep him guessing." He slaps the truck console a few times before pulling himself together. I'm not about to correct his impressions of Ginny's motives. Emotion drove that girly-girl toss, not scheming on her part. A calculating nature does not seem to be one of her personality traits, but then again, how would I know? I just met her a mere eight hours ago. "Great," Monty enthuses. "One more night here and you'll be on your way tomorrow."

A feeling, the move of the Spirit, comes over me, and that is when the idea pops into my head.

"Why don't you and Laurel spend the night with me, Ginny? The guest bedroom is plenty spacious. I have a homemade casserole in the freezer and a fresh pie on the counter. What do you say?"

Ginny stares at the tall black-and-white Route 66 monument across the street. The town erected it after the mayor saw throngs flocking to the corner of Winslow, Arizona—a place I'd love to see. Today, no one is taking part in a photo op, latching locks onto the metal map of Oklahoma, or investigating the old railcar, the central attraction in this small park. Except for the distant murmur of trucks on the highway, it is quiet. No breeze. Even the weeds sprouting up in patches between cracks in the sidewalk look wilted and worn out.

Just like me.

Moments pass. Has she forgotten my offer?

"Well, I'd love to have you." I prompt. "It is no fuss, if that's your concern."

"Perfect." She squeezes my shoulder and blesses me with another show of her dimples. "Where are you parked? I'll follow you."

CHAPTER EIGHT

Ginny

The calm I experienced at Walmart has become a blessed relief. Why not spend the night at Oralyn's and keep her company? Widowhood is lonely, Oralyn said before climbing into her passenger van. Yes, I do understand the feeling and could use some adult companionship myself.

Oralyn drives slowly and obeys traffic rules—no rolling stops for her. After taking several turns, driving past bike-riding kids, we finally arrive at her street, one of many arranged in a grid pattern. We pull into a short driveway, and I am astonished by what I see.

Flowers of all varieties, perennials and annuals—tended with care and purpose—line the front and back walkways, and a vegetable garden, with its judiciously hoed rows, takes up a small patch next to a stand-alone garage. I park behind her van and turn my head to take in the riot of color. It's something to behold—a bit of heaven here on earth. Everything feels rooted, secure, and alive.

The gardens remind me of Granny. She would wear a floppy straw hat and a baggy house dress to tend to her petaled beauties, working on her knees, plucking and pruning until she achieved perfection. Gardening, Granny often told me, was her happy place where she could do her part to showcase God's creative majesty.

"Oralyn, you've created a masterpiece." My eyes sweep her property. "I love your gardens."

She shrugs. "Keeps me busy." She opens the back door of my Honda and leans over to unbuckle Laurel's safety straps. "I'll carry some of the baby's things."

"Please don't. Why don't you go in and put your feet up?" I eye her legs.

Oralyn gives me a small smile and hobbles up the back porch steps to her gray clapboard bungalow, trimmed in white. I spend a moment or two basking in the sweet floral scent before grabbing Laurel's diaper bag and my cloth satchel, which is getting heavy with everything stashed inside. Juggling them and Laurel, I climb the stairs and enter Oralyn's kitchen situated in the back of the house.

"Oralyn?"

"In here."

Stretched out on a floral sofa—her legs propped up on pillows—Oralyn looks tired. Almost as exhausted as the furnishings in this time-worn living room. Cherrywood end tables cluttered with ceramic knick-knacks flank the couch, and a more temporary club chair sits close to the front door, kitty-corner from a wingback that occupies the corner next to the fire-place. Jacob would shudder at this modest home, where nothing matches, but her home brings me comfort. A wave of nostalgia washes over me, and I hug myself to keep the feeling close.

Laurel, who has sucked on her pacifier since we left Walmart, spits it out and lets out an ear-splitting shriek. Where her belly is concerned, she goes from zero to sixty in sixty seconds when the hunger pangs become intolerable. She will not wait a minute longer. "Would it be okay if I sat over there to feed Laurel?" I point to a wingback. "Or do you want me to go into the kitchen? I don't want to disturb you."

"Make yourself at home." Oralyn closes her eyes despite Laurel's ruckus. "I'll thaw the casserole in the microwave and then throw it in the oven. But I need to rest first." Within minutes, a snuffling sound carries across the room.

I hate to wake Oralyn, so I decide to get dinner started after filling Laurel's belly. Passing through a small dining room between the living room and kitchen, I spot the refrigerator in the corner. A foil-covered glass casserole dish sits in the freezer, surrounded by frozen peas, corn, ground beef, and bags of sliced white bread. Salad greens are in the fridge's crisper. I wash my hands and begin supper preparations, Laurel watching my every move from a play mat on the kitchen floor.

"Thank you, Ginny." Oralyn's voice startles me. My back toward the entryway, I hadn't heard her come in. "Must've needed that nap." She yawns and extends her arms over her head.

"No problem. The least I could do." Heat blasts my face as I open the oven door and pull out the bubbling chicken-and-rice casserole—the type of food Granny cooked for church socials and dinner. Her specialty. A lump forms in my throat. I never took Granny for granted, but had forgotten the simple pleasures of a home-cooked meal shared at the kitchen table. Jacob, of course, turned his nose up at meals like this, preferring more refined fare. Sushi, quinoa bowls, or kale salads—foods that felt cold and overly crafted—made up his diet. I fought his culinary pretension for weeks after meeting him, but then gave up, tired of his insults about my "corn-pone upbringing."

I had also given up the habit of offering thanks for my daily bread. Within seconds of Oralyn taking her seat, I am once again reminded of my former life before Jacob.

"I'll say grace." Oralyn bows her head, her hands clasped, and begins to speak in a soft, reverential tone. "Sweet Jesus, you've blessed me today. You introduced me to this lovely young woman and her precious child. Thank you for allowing me to serve them in this troubled world. In your name, I pray."

"Amen." I don't want to lift my head—not yet. Her words roll through my mind, reminding me of how far I had strayed from Granny's influence.

"Well, dig in, Ginny. It's getting cold, and Lord knows you need to eat. What have you had all day? A couple of pieces of toast?"

I nod and pick up my knife and fork, still processing my impressions of this Granny-like woman. Deep down, I know that I'm exactly where I should be. God had put her and Monty into my life, just as He did with TC. They are the special people Granny often mentioned. To Oralyn's delight, I devour the casserole and help myself to a second helping. She does most of the talking, one story leading to the next, as if she is eager for a connection.

She tells me about her now-deceased husband, whom she had met at Monty's Diner. Many years older than she, her husband, then a childless widower, proposed, and she accepted not because she was in love with him, but because he offered something she hadn't experienced until then—stability and respect, a refuge from the hardship that had followed her around like a bad penny.

"I'll never forget the day Charlie came in." Oralyn's face glows. "He was a regular and said he'd been watching me… liked my style." She screws up her face as if chasing after an elusive fact. "I was in my mid-thirties. Or was it my forties? Doesn't matter." She waves a dismissive hand. "Charlie and I got married in a small ceremony out there." A wistful expression crosses her face as she points to the backyard.

"At night, sitting here on this very chair, he'd massage my legs and tell me I was a good girl. He always called me *Brown Eyes.* Never Oralyn. Can you imagine?" She points to her wide-set eyes that reflect the warmth of rich molasses. A little smile forms. "Enough of my silly old stories. It's getting dark. How about I clean up while you bring the rest of your bags in?"

By the time I get Laurel bathed and dressed and her portable crib set up in the guest bedroom, Oralyn has moved to the front porch, which is filled with rocking chairs and potted geraniums. An American flag hangs from a porch post. Fresh air is good for the body and soul. Laurel and I join her there.

"Would you mind if I rocked her?" Oralyn's eyes shine. The crow's feet around her eyes have mellowed.

"That would be great." I nestle Laurel in her arms. "She'll be conked out cold, and if we're lucky, both of us will get some sleep."

That's when I remember Aunt Adele and pull the phone from my back pocket.

"Oralyn, do you mind watching Laurel for a minute?"

"Heavens no," she says, waving her hand. "Shoo."

Sitting in the wingback chair, I dial Aunt Adele's number. It keeps ringing until it goes to voicemail. Will she bother listening to a message from an unknown caller?

No other choice offers itself, and I leave a voicemail, asking her to call me as soon as possible, praying the whole time that Jacob hasn't gotten to her first, polluting her mind with trumped-up stories about me and my failings. *Don't worry about that now. Count your blessings.* Oralyn has offered a haven if only for a night, and I am humbled by her hospitality, tendered without reservation to someone she barely knows.

CHAPTER NINE

Ginny

Oralyn's rocking has lulled Laurel into a deep sleep. I carry her to the guest room and glance at the bed, almost tempted to pull down the sheets and call it a night myself, but I think better of it. If Aunt Adele calls, the ring will likely wake Laurel, and she doesn't need any more disruptions. She needs to sleep in a crib, not in a car seat, and spend more time exercising her arms and legs, like any growing baby.

What am I doing to my kid?

These worries run through my head as I turn off the overhead light and close the bedroom door, tiptoeing to the tiny hallway linking the two bedrooms. A strip of light beneath Oralyn's door leads me to her, and I gently knock.

"Oralyn, could I trouble you for a moment?"

Dressed in striped pajamas and a cloth robe, she opens the door wide. "Girl, you're no trouble at all. Come in." She points to an armchair in the corner and removes her readers, still attached to the rhinestone lanyard. "I'm just catching up on some reading." She shows me a dog-eared paperback, written by a humorist who writes about half-crazy people living in the Florida Everglades. "Love this guy's writing. Takes my mind off the real nuts in the world."

"I read a few of his books myself." I lean against the door jamb and tug on my earlobe. "Would it be okay if I took a shower?"

She sighs and shakes her head. "You interrupted a rip-roaring read for a question like that? Of course, you can take a shower. And when you're done, eat the rest of that pie. You need the calories; I do not. Now go." She points to the bathroom door.

Even the bathroom reminds me of Granny's house. Black-and-white ceramic tiles wrap around the walls and bath enclosure. A basket-weave design covers the floor. Spending the night here feels like a luxury, a much-needed respite from the road. I'm leaning over to turn on the shower when the phone rings, making me jump. Not wanting to disturb Oralyn, I speed-walk through the kitchen and out to the back porch.

"Hello?" My heart hammers, wondering who might be at the other end, praying it is not Jacob. Paranoia is setting in.

"Ginny, where are you?" Aunt Adele demands, her voice clipped and brisk. "I've texted and can't count the times I've called and left voice messages. It's not like you to go incommunicado." She pauses to bring her breathing under control. "Unknown phone numbers are ignored."

"I'm so sorry. I should've called days ago, but kept putting it off because…" I sit on the porch step and search my brain for the right words. "I need information, and I'm worried you might not give it to me and try to convince me against doing what I must do."

"Well, if running off with the baby is part of that plan, you would be right. Jacob is out of his mind, wondering where you are. So am I."

If my life could become more complicated, it just has.

"Whoa. Whoa. Whoa." I remind myself of TC, who used that expression when he wanted me to clarify myself. "How do you know I've run off and taken the baby?"

"Because Jacob told me…twelve hours ago." Her voice amplifies. "I'll ask again. Where are you?"

"What did he tell you, Aunt Adele?" I glance over my shoulder and see Oralyn standing behind the screen door, bathed in the warm glow of the kitchen's ceiling light. She does not speak, but her steady presence anchors me. I muster a smile. She nods slightly and walks away from view.

"He also said that you're drinking and abusing painkillers. Is that true?"

Shaken by the accusation, I stutter. "Do you believe that?"

"Well, Ginny, I'm not sure what to believe."

She drones on about substance abuse, how it runs in families. "You're well acquainted with the effects of addiction—better than anyone. You had a front-row seat, thanks to your father and, by extension, your mother and her poor choices. Now you're making your own." She pauses, as if weighing whether to say more. She throws caution to the wind. "I never thought I'd say this, but right now you remind me of your mother. She always ran from her problems instead of facing them head-on, and that's what you're doing now."

"What did you just say?" The words come out in a blast as my hand balls up into a tight fist. Who does she think she is, comparing me with my mother? For one, the comparison couldn't be more off base. I am running *toward* a resolution, not away from one. I stand and start pacing, the porch boards creaking with every step.

"I'm sorry. That was out of line." Aunt Adele sounds somewhat contrite. "But this behavior is so uncharacteristic for you, and you know it. Does this have anything to do with Mom's… Granny's death?" She asks the question with renewed vigor, but it's clear she's not interested in my response. She continues talking over me. "If you're struggling with depression and using drugs and alcohol to cope with the pain, you're approaching it the wrong way. Go home and get help."

Jacob's performance must have been masterful.

"Please call Jacob and tell him where you are." She keeps talking. "For the baby's sake, make the responsible decision."

"No, Aunt Adele, I will not call. I will not go back to him, and I will not tell him where I am. More than likely, he's hot on my heels. That's why I bought a new phone."

Silence.

"You haven't bothered asking why I would leave." My voice is sharper now, edged with something I have not let myself fully feel—anger. "You bought his cockamamie story and immediately assumed the worst of me." I tear my hand through my hair. "Have you ever considered that Jacob might have the problem?"

More silence.

I lob a few more harsh truths. "And for your information, Aunt Adele, Jacob is *not* my husband. He never was, and he will never be. If you prefer to believe him over me, go right ahead." My voice lowers, coming out like a snarl. "Don't even think about sharing this number with him. He is *not* who he pretends to be. Oh, and one last thing… Granny hated Jacob's guts."

I end the call, my body shaking all over, wishing she had ignored my message.

Moonlight casts shadows in the backyard. Not ready to face Oralyn or answer the questions she is sure to ask, I head for the middle of the yard, past the vegetable garden, and drop to my knees. I notice a sturdy-looking concrete structure hidden behind the garage. A storm shelter? Probably. April and May are always the worst in Tornado Alley, and I can only thank God it is early June. But with my luck, a vicious twister will probably materialize out of nowhere and swallow me whole.

If that happens, I want to land in Oz.

I shake my head, trying to dislodge the negativity. But the thoughts persist. I think about my aunt, who is probably on the phone with Jacob now. She will never question his lies. He fits every category on her attractiveness checklist: looks, money, and career. If I managed to sow some doubt, he would do what he does best—gaslight her. He would tell her that I exaggerate and never remember events as they happened. He would call me crazy, just like he did every chance he got, until I questioned my own sanity. Then, he would charm and coax her until she revealed how to get in touch with me.

Getting damp, I stand up and brush grass clippings from my knees, wising up to a truth I should have learned long ago. The same blood may course through our veins, but Aunt Adele is not family to me. Neither is my mother. Both are strangers.

I turn toward the back porch, where the glow from the kitchen spills out onto the worn wooden steps. Oralyn stands just inside, picking at the pie on the counter. When I get closer, she looks at me not in judgment, but in quiet reassurance, an expression that says, "*You don't have to explain yourself here.*" How I wish she were kin.

CHAPTER TEN

Oralyn

Like clockwork, my eyes pop open at five o'clock. I don't need an alarm—I've been rising before the sun for more years than I can count. After showering and getting dressed, I listen at Ginny's door, but all is quiet—no rustling bedsheets or squeaking bedsprings. As I walk toward the kitchen to start a pot of coffee, I notice Ginny curled up on the couch. She's dead to the world, cocooned in the burgundy-colored chenille throw that my niece, Shannon, gave me one Christmas.

Huh. What drove her there?

Last night, I wandered out to the kitchen to check on Ginny when I didn't hear the water pipes clanking after she went to take her shower. I found her sitting on the porch steps. Not wanting to intrude, I spotted the apple-crumb pie sitting on the counter, grabbed a fork from the drawer, and dug in. Just as I was about to bring the fork to my mouth, Ginny opened the screen door.

"You caught me red-handed," I joked, but her facial expression told me I would be eating that pie alone. Her unblinking eyes were unfocused and dull. I placed the fork on the counter and took a few steps toward her. "I'm here if you want to talk, Ginny."

"Not tonight." She looked at me but didn't see me. "I don't want to think or talk about anything."

She trudged off to her bedroom, and I finished the rest of the pie—my way of dealing with stress, whether it is mine or someone else's. Glancing at the time on the wall clock, I saw it was past my bedtime, my stomach in turmoil because I had committed one of the world's seven deadly sins. But I slept like the dead thanks to the little pink liquid I keep close at hand. Pepto-Bismol is my cocktail of choice.

The coffee machine beeps. I pour a cupful and breathe in the aroma. *Aww, nothing like a cup of joe. This is the best time of day.*

"Good morning." Ginny stands at the door, yawning, still dressed in the clothes she wore yesterday. Black smudges of mascara line her bloodshot and swollen eyes, confirming my suspicion that she had a good, long cry. Yet somehow, she seems well-rested, even chipper. "I slept on the couch," she says. "Hope that was okay."

"Was the bed lumpy? I haven't slept in it in years."

"I wouldn't know." She gives me a sheepish grin and pours herself a mug of coffee. "I never even pulled down the comforter… I had a rough night. I hope you didn't hear me or Laurel." She gazes at the steam rising from her cup. "Poor kid. Her mother is barely keeping it together, and my meltdown woke her up."

"I didn't hear a thing. I guess your aunt's not happy with you?" I ask, assuming the phone call was the cause of the upset.

"You could say that." She takes a seat at the kitchen table next to me and fiddles with her memory bracelet. "Jacob got to her first. She thinks I'm deeply depressed and need professional help. She urged me to go back to Atlanta." She sucks in her top lip and narrows her eyes. "That won't happen, and I will be okay—with or without her. The problem is she has my mother's phone number and address."

"Your mother's address?"

"Yeah. My mom lives in Las Vegas, but I'm not sure where she lives. I haven't seen her in at least two decades." She stares at the ceiling before continuing. "We both suffer from a bad case of unforgiveness."

Ginny had not revealed the endpoint of her journey, and I hadn't pried. She kept things close to her chest, dribbling details when she thought it was prudent. Or at least that was my impression. The news did ease my mind. If restoring a broken relationship was her goal, she would have my support. I give her a reassuring pat on her tiny hand.

"Ginny, I wish I had more time, but I promised Monty that I'd train my niece, Shannon. She's taking my job. We can talk later, after the breakfast rush." I lift my eyebrows, wondering how she will respond.

"Great! That gives me time to shower, feed Laurel, and find a laundromat." She counts the chores on her fingers.

"Save your shekels. Use my washer and dryer." Rising from the table, I point to a set of double doors in the kitchen.

"Oh, Oralyn, are you sure?" She glances at the laundry closet, then back at me, chewing her bottom lip.

I sigh and shake my head. Can she still be asking for permission? "Like I said for the fifty millionth time—make yourself at home."

I grab my purse off the counter and am ready to open the back door when she takes two quick paces toward me. Her arms come around me, pulling me closer in a hug that makes me want to cry.

"You've been so kind to me." Her voice is soft and rich with emotion. "You're like my Granny Smith and that's high praise." She pulls back, and our eyes lock. "Through you, Oralyn, God has extended a tender mercy."

I then hug and squeeze her against my chest. She feels like family.

* * *

Driving to Monty's, my daughter, Katherine, occupies my mind. What would she be like today? Would she be a woman like Shannon, who made decent choices? Or would she be someone like Ginny, who dared to stand her ground and change her situation before it was too late?

Or would she be like me?

What is done is done. I wasted my youth with a man of no account. He got me in the baby fix and then blamed me like he had no part in it. People talked. Of course, they talked. No one had an ounce of sympathy for me. To them, I was just stupid Oralyn, who didn't have the smarts to avoid becoming a notch in his belt. In those days, the only path to redemption involved a trip down the aisle before evidence of the transgression began to show.

Oh, he married me, all right, begrudging every minute of it. He berated me about my weight, my hair, everything, before slipping off to a bar in the city to sample someone less plain. When Katherine's medical issues became too much for him, he filed for divorce and left town, only to return years later with a new missus. I am sorry that he died the way he did; I also regret that I didn't leave him first. Courage was a trait in low supply then.

But in the end, Charlie came into my life. I had made the right choice with him.

I pull into the parking lot and realize the drive happened on autopilot. The diner's rooftop sign hums softly in the cool morning air, its steady, yellow glow contrasts against the gray sky. Two vehicles—Shannon's and Monty's—are parked in the lot. I pause for a moment, letting the quiet sink in before stepping out of the car. It's a place I've come to know well, but after all these years, I'm ready for a change.

Shannon greets me at the door, whistling, head held high. She gives me a peck on the cheek and rattles off all the work she has done waiting for me—inserting knives and forks inside paper wrappers, reloading salt-and-pepper shakers, stacking jellies, and starting coffeemakers. I am breathless watching her dash from the back kitchen to the counter and booths and then back again. Monty hides in the area behind the griddle, probably afraid he'll end up as roadkill.

"Here we go," she shouts as she flips the door sign from *Closed* to *Open* and positions herself next to the door. She's a natural and didn't need me to acclimate her to her new job.

A couple of hours later, the morning rush ends, and Shannon and I claim seats at the counter. We nibble on biscuits and gravy, which isn't a wise choice for me, given the previous night's excess. My doctor has warned me about my consumption of white bread and sweets and how I'll end up in a diabetic coma if I don't start pushing away from the feed trough. I take another bite and lick the sausage gravy from my fork.

"Getting out of the house is long overdue," Shannon chatters. "I started feeling sorry for myself because my room-mother days had ended. The extra money won't hurt, and I'd bet a paycheck that I start losing weight because of the running. A win-win." She, like me and other women in our family, carries weight around the middle.

"Not unless you ditch the fattening foods." I raise my eyebrows.

"Aww. You're no fun, Aunt Oralyn. A girl can dream."

The doorbell chimes, and, in a snap, Shannon leaps off the stool. Maybe a little weight loss isn't out of the question.

"Hey, there. My name is Shannon, and I'll be serving you."

"Oh no, I won't be staying..."

Recognizing the voice, I spin around and see Ginny.

"Just here to say goodbye to Oralyn and Monty." Ginny scans the room and spots me. "There you are." But before she can say another word, Shannon, aka Old Mother Hubbard, does what she does. She goes ga-ga over baby Laurel and relieves Ginny of her bundle.

A lump forms in my throat as I struggle off the stool. I have begun to see her as a daughter of sorts. And it makes me sad that she is leaving. How many times have I compared myself with the other women in this town? I attended their weddings and baby showers, all while pouting because I would never experience those milestones. Did those brides and mothers-to-be ever count their blessings? It's so easy to take good fortune for granted when life goes your way.

I walk around the corner and yell for Monty. "Ginny's here. She probably wants you to load her car."

As in the movie *Groundhog Day,* Monty moseys out of his culinary hideout and wipes his hands on his apron. As always, his reading glasses sit on his forehead—his self-described "third eye," which he claims is the source of his wisdom. Nothing changes about Monty. But right now, he is frowning.

"Are you sure you're still up for this trip?" he asks, pressing his lips together and placing his fists on his hips. "Don't you have a friend…someone to travel with?"

Ginny draws back from Monty's barking voice but recovers. She shakes her head and pulls herself taller, throwing her shoulders back. To my eye, though, she still looks tiny and vulnerable. "I'll be fine… I have a burner, a full tank of gas, and plenty of supplies and cash. Better yet, I have reinforcement from two people who've done so much to help me." She counts the items off on her fingers and beams. "And I promise…no unnecessary stops."

Monty groans, and I can only assume his thoughts now that he has had a night to think about Ginny's determination to continue her trip solo, toting a helpless baby. His neck gets a vigorous rub as he mutters, "I don't like it, not one little bit. Young women shouldn't be traveling alone with all the nutjobs out there." He stomps toward the door and lets it slam behind him.

"Yikes," Ginny says. She and baby Laurel, now reclaimed, follow him out the door.

"What's that all about, Aunt Oralyn?" Shannon's forehead is wrinkled with worry lines. "Why is Monty so upset?"

I heave a sigh and go to the kitchen. My feeling of foreboding, which I had tried to suppress, has returned with a vengeance. Monty is right. Too many dangers lurk out there. Ginny should have a travel mate. I close my eyes and send a silent prayer.

CHAPTER ELEVEN

Jacob

Red, my sultry paramour, sprawls on my bed. She is playing the sex kitten to make up to me and restore herself in my good graces. She had overstepped her bounds with her nonstop questions about Ginny, imploring me to go gentle when I broke off my relationship with her—something I promised to do soon. Funny, Red didn't give a fig about Ginny when she took up with me.

Red has gotten on my nerves.

"Oh, come on, Jacob. Don't be a poop." She pats the mattress, her lips curling at the corners.

Instead of accepting her invitation, I give her a long glare and wordlessly leave the bedroom. As I stride down the hallway, past the kid's never-used nursery and the spare bedroom that stores my clothes and mementos, Red shouts that she is going home. She's sulking. Like I should care. I want to be alone.

Sitting at my desk in my downstairs study, I hear Red's footsteps as she descends the stairs. She gently tries the doorknob and finds it locked. "Jacob, call me later." She sounds small now—so meek, as if she has remembered who calls the shots. No response is forthcoming, and within seconds, I hear the front door open and close. I wonder what the neighbors would think—especially those old coots next door—if they saw her slinking out so early in the morning. You have memory issues, I would tell them, if they said something to me. That's the thing with people. You can make them believe whatever you want.

I stare at my wristwatch. Hours have passed since I spoke with Adele, who promised to keep calling Ginny, but I haven't heard back from her. I scroll through my contacts and almost tap Adele's number when a better idea comes to mind. This morning, I checked Ginny's phone. It had no signal. No biggie, though. The hidden GPS tracker revealed that her Honda hadn't moved an inch from a residential area since last night. Ginny, so it seems, isn't in a hurry.

Why not make a surprise visit?

I am perusing airline itineraries from Atlanta to Oklahoma City when my phone trills.

"Hey, Dad, what's up?" I lean back and spin my chair to regard the photos lined up in rows on the wall.

"I need you to change your plans, if you have any," he says. So typical. The world revolves around him. True to form, he doesn't wait for an answer before informing me of a black-tie affair. The Georgia Secretary of State has called a special election to fill a vacancy in the state Senate. Dad's consultant has arranged informal discussions with donors and opinion leaders who are still undecided about backing him. If they do, they will reach deep into their pockets to select the best politician money can buy.

"Dad, how long have you known about this?" I interject.

"What does it matter? I need you and Ginny to make an appearance… You know, to present a strong family front. I thought you'd be interested."

"Given a heads-up, I would be. But Ginny is out of town and wants me to join her in Oklahoma. I'm flying out this afternoon; I'll be back Sunday night or Monday morning—"

"Not happening," he interrupts. "I guess we'll manage without Ginny, as disappointing as that might be, but you must be there." My fingers flex. Has he forgotten our discussion from before I had left for Savannah with Red? I had told him about Ginny's jailbird daddy and her potential problem with booze and pills. As I told him, she was unfit to care for my child. Either Dad's losing it, or he wasn't listening. Likely the latter. Or is it? He seems a bit distracted these days.

"Give Ginny an excuse and meet me and your mother at the country club. Seven o'clock sharp." He pauses, and I can practically feel the weight of his expectations in the silence that follows. "I almost forgot—you also need to take a meeting for me early Monday morning. I have a conflict, but I can always rely on you to help advance our interests."

"I learned from the best, Dad." The words come out a little smoother than he deserves, but it's a reflex. Of course, I will take care of it. I always do. Still, there is something about hearing those words—*I can always rely on you*—that pleases me more than it should. It's been this way for as long as I can remember.

No matter what I do, I'm never sure if it's enough for him. Even my mother would raise her eyebrows when he criticized me, but, of course, she refused to go to bat for me.

I spread my arms wide and perform a few neck rolls, unworried about a delay in my travel plans. Little mouse cannot hide from me. I hold the cards.

I turn off my laptop and decide to call Red. I may apologize for my short temper and bad manners.

CHAPTER TWELVE

Ginny

Monty huffs and puffs, mumbling under his breath, as he studies my Honda parked in front of his diner. "That fiancé isn't the only jackwagon out there. Whatcha gonna do if your car breaks down?" He gives me a sharp look and shakes his head. His protectiveness touches me. I've always longed for a father figure and seem to have found one in him. I will take it, along with Monty's disapproving words.

They mean he cares.

He keeps his promises, too. Heat radiates off the asphalt as he unloads his truck and the stuff I had packed when I said goodbye to Atlanta. In a snap, he has piled everything, including yesterday's Walmart purchases, in a jumble next to my car. Scratching his sweaty head, Monty studies the trunk and then opens the back door to scan the floorboards and seats before leaning over to examine the front. How he's going to cram that mound of stuff inside my car is unfathomable to me.

But he is the master packer. I am not. I go back inside, the size of his generosity settling over me. I'm not sure what I have done to deserve this level of kindness, but I know better than to take it for granted.

I sigh and hum softly to myself—the gift of air conditioning. My feet burn through my sandals, and Laurel's hair lies in a sweaty mat beneath her large, floppy hat. She starts to fuss. "Baby girl, you want a drink of water?"

"I'll take care of it." Shannon slides off her stool, rifles through the baby bag, and finds a bottle and liner before sprinting to the back room to fill it with filtered water from the cooler. Laurel starts cooing as soon as Shannon takes her from my arms and nuzzles her neck. Nothing like two mommies. And it would be nice to have a second set of hands on this road trip. I do understand Monty's point of view.

Taking the barstool next to Oralyn, I notice her mood. "What's with the gloomy look?"

"Time is flying, and we're short on help this morning. The griddle cook called in sick, and Monty's partner is out of town. He needs to fry onions before the lunch crowd shows up," Oralyn says, consulting her silver Timex, which seems too small for her swollen wrist.

I raise my eyebrows.

"It's nothing, Ginny. I'm just an old woman who worries too much."

"Aww, Oralyn." I wrap my arm around her shoulders and draw her close. "I can fry onions. Just show me where they are."

The doorbell chimes, and we all turn our heads. The look on Monty's face is hard to decipher.

"Were you aware of this?" He extends his open palm. Resting in the center is a small, black device, no larger than an ice cube. A tiny blinking light winks at me, steady and unassuming—innocent—as if it is not responsible for a creeping dread slithering through my body.

"I've never seen it before." My heart pounds. "What is it?"

"A GPS tracker." His eyes bore into mine. "Whoever put it in your car can keep tabs on you, even to the point of figuring out how fast you're driving. Everything. Just tap an app, and the information loads like that." Monty snaps his sausage-like fingers. "I found it beneath the dashboard."

Jacob—no doubt in my mind. No wonder he told Melinda that I could run but could not hide.

My mouth goes dry, and my tongue sticks to the roof of my mouth. The nausea twists in my stomach as the import of Monty's discovery settles in—the invasion, the control, the fact that he will not let me be. I take a sip of ice water, but it does nothing to wash away the sick feeling crawling up my throat. I need to step outside.

Leaning against my car, now packed and more cluttered than ever, I let myself feel an emotion I rarely show—hatred, a deep, consuming loathing. What gives Jacob the right to hunt me down like an animal? Why couldn't he disappear for good? For a few minutes, I even fantasize about how I might make that happen. However, those thoughts are quickly replaced by disgust. I wouldn't be able to pull the trigger, even if I wanted to. Only God has the right to deal with him.

But that doesn't mean I should play the victim. Choices exist. Granny, for example, never wallowed in self-pity. She showed grit, raising two kids and then me alone, always holding her head high even when town gossipers tittered about my mother's escapades, suggesting Granny was to blame. Enough is enough. No more anxiety attacks every time Jacob pulls another surprise from his box of tricks. No one promised me an easy road, and the one I'm on will be tough; so, I'd better get used to it.

I draw in a giant breath of air and exhale, throwing my shoulders back. I can and will do better.

Monty, Oralyn, and Shannon are sitting at one of the free-standing tables when I reappear, mopping my brow on the hottest day so far this year. Shannon, who is bouncing Laurel on her lap, must have gotten the inside scoop because she gives me a weak, sad smile. Though you can't know what goes on behind closed doors, she carries herself like someone who has always had a safe place to land—no wary glances over her shoulder.

Does she understand her blessings? In my imagination, I can see her running toward her husband—not away—when she goes home this afternoon after her shift. She'll prattle on about her day as he nods and asks questions, telling her that he's proud of her. She can do whatever she wants as long as she's happy.

Me? That hand is unknown to me. But that's okay, too. The thief in the night *will not* steal my joy, my life, or Laurel's. A bubble of mirth rises in my chest, and before I can stop it, I start laughing. Hard. The sound bursts out of me, raw and jarring. My shoulders shake. It's been so long since I've laughed like this—not since TC and I gripped our sides, hooting because Jacob had abandoned me for hours at the festival. The whole situation had become absurd and should have served as a warning. But I, of course, chose to ignore it.

Oh yes, Jacob, I can run, and I will hide. Your torment ends this second.

"Whew. I needed that," I say, cupping my face with both hands. Silence. Three sets of eyes fix on me. The expressions on their faces bounce between concern and curiosity. Will I get a grip or completely unravel?

I exhale sharply and grin. "Monty, what's the best way to throw Jacob off course? Send him down a few bunny trails? He's not the only one who can play cat and mouse."

And together, sitting around that table before the lunchtime rush, we devise a plan.

CHAPTER THIRTEEN

Adele

Twenty-four hours have passed since I quarreled with Ginny about Jacob. It's not the way I would have preferred to celebrate my early retirement and the generous buyout, but that's how it played out—a nasty fight. The sting of our exchange is still sharp in my mind. I still don't know where Ginny is or where she's headed.

I pour myself a nightcap and make myself comfortable on the living room sofa. The soft light of the table lamp reflects off the glass. I take a sip and study the room: the coordinated art on the walls, the precise arrangement of throw pillows, and the gleaming surface of the coffee table—all are deliberate, each element in its place. While creating this sanctuary, I left nothing to chance.

Just as I take another sip of the golden liquid, my phone rings.

"Everyone is here, waiting for the woman of the hour." Robert Berry, my companion, best friend, and soulmate, has joined our friends at our favorite Manhattan watering hole. We're supposed to be celebrating my retirement, but the sounds of laughter in the background confirm that my presence would only dampen the mood.

"Robert, I'm tired and out of sorts."

"What happened?" Robert asks, concern creeping into his voice. He understands me better than anyone. When I commit to things, like meeting friends, I follow through and show up on time. Glancing at my watch, I realize I'm already an hour late. No wonder he called. "Yesterday, you were raring to go."

"Family issues... My niece left her husband and took the baby. He called, upset. He claims she's drinking and has no idea where she would go. When I finally talked with her last night, she sounded sober, but she made some wild accusations. Anyway, he's at his wits' end, and I am worried."

"Start from the beginning because I'm not keeping up," Robert says. Despite the background noise, I hear him telling our friends in his melodic Southern dialect that something has come up, and that I will not be joining them tonight—a merciful gesture. "Save a seat for me," he shouts over the din. "Okay, Adele, I'm back. When was the last time you saw Ginny, and what did she say on the phone?"

"I saw her at Mom's funeral a few months ago...she was a mess. She couldn't stop crying. I don't know what to think. Now, she's angry with me."

"Why would she get mad at you?"

"Well, I suppose I didn't handle the situation well."

Robert has the patience of Job, but my vague answers seem to be annoying him.

"Good grief, Adele. What happened?"

The next part comes out in a rush. "When we spoke on the phone, she called Jacob a liar and then said they weren't married. I was shocked."

"Why would that shock you? These days, people don't get married. Look at you and me."

I don't want to talk about us. Robert has proposed to me, but I keep pushing it off for reasons I do not fully understand. "Because Jacob approached me at the funeral and introduced himself as Ginny's husband. Why wouldn't I believe him? Furthermore, he seemed deeply concerned for both Ginny and the baby. My gosh, that baby never left his arms. Frankly, he impressed me."

Robert does not respond, giving me a moment to catch my breath.

"But as I sit here, rehashing everything, something isn't adding up," I say, swirling my glass and inspecting the amber-colored tears as they roll down the sides, the phone wedged against my shoulder. "Mom told me about Ginny's pregnancy, but she never mentioned a wedding. That seems strange now in retrospect."

"Hmm. You'd think your mother would have mentioned it. But then again—and I mean no offense—you're not close to your family."

He is spot-on, as usual. Before his mom and dad passed away, Robert took every opportunity to visit his family and help on the farm in Mississippi. I can't say the same for myself, and I have only myself to blame for that. Aside from flying down for Christmas each year and the occasional Easter, I spent as little time as possible in Georgia. Only out of duty did I call Mom once or twice a month.

My family embarrassed me. After our father died in a construction-site accident, my sister turned into a hellion, getting involved with losers and deadbeats and sleeping with every boy in town. This provided plenty of fodder for the town's gossip mongers. Her sins became my sins in the eyes of others. Throughout it all, Mom held her head high, deepening her connection to her religion and urging me to show some compassion toward Audrey.

I wanted none of that. Pretending Audrey never existed was easier. If Mom wanted to pray to a God that did not exist, let alone listen to her Almighty, she could do so. As for me, I would take my chances in unbelief. I packed my bags and boarded a bus to make my fortune in the canyons of New York.

Robert's honey-sweet voice brings me back. He asks a few more questions, which I answer, before he says, "Adele, you sound upset. Perhaps we should talk in person. I can be at your place—"

"No, I'm alright. I appreciate your offer, but I want to be alone. Please understand."

"Are you sure? How about I call later tonight or tomorrow?"

"I love you, Robert."

"I love you even more."

I set the phone on the coffee table and take a small sip. My eyes wander across the room to the bookshelf where a framed photo of my mom and me sits. My father snapped that picture—a moment frozen in time. It shows us posing on the front porch of my childhood home, Mom's arms wrapped around me, both of us smiling ear to ear—a sweet moment, one of many…if I'm being honest.

A tidal wave of guilt washes over me. I never appreciated my mother's steadfastness and sacrifice after Daddy died. She didn't complain, either, when Ginny, then six years old, moved in with her. She accepted her responsibilities and did her best. Where was I? In New York. My heart had turned to stone, and I felt no obligation to either Mom or Ginny, and certainly not to Audrey.

I shudder at these thoughts.

I walk to the glass doors, giving myself a panoramic view of Central Park. My reflection stares back at me, forcing me to confront what I have become: a selfish, middle-aged woman who turned her back on her mother, her niece, and her sister because she didn't embrace their values and couldn't find a way to love them without judgment.

My eyes become unfocused, and a picture appears. It's of Ginny sitting on my mother's well-worn sofa, sobbing, lost in her profound grief. Jacob touches her shoulder.

And then I see it.

The flinch.

Fool me once, Jacob, but don't fool me twice.

I swallow the last of my whiskey and go to bed, vowing to uncover the truth.

CHAPTER FOURTEEN

Jacob

I do as Dad instructs. I attend the political shindig instead of flying to Oklahoma. Before entering the country club's grand ballroom, where Atlanta's movers and shakers and hangers-on have already begun to congregate, I stand before a gilded mirror to check my tie—deep red against a navy suit, almost too perfect—and adjust my cuffs, crisp and precise, before running my hands through my hair.

I look good.

It does not take long to spot Dad and Mom across the room, standing near the massive stone fireplace, champagne flutes in hand, surrounded by a small cluster of well-dressed guests. Dad is holding court, of course, commanding attention in his usual way. Mom, who reminds me of a Holocaust survivor with her protruding clavicle and barely visible breasts, gazes up at him, her doe-like eyes fixed on his face.

"Oh, there you are, Jacob. I thought you were lost." Dad has affixed his nice-guy smile on his cleanly shaven face. In his rush to begin the schmoozing, he had not noticed my pit stop at the mirror—so much for a grand entrance and the united family front. "Let me introduce you to my son, Jacob," he says to a man I've never met. "Before too long, he will be running Peach State Holdings."

"Leaving it in capable hands, no doubt," the man says, pumping my arm before changing the topic to his own son and his ambitions to study law. "Hey, I could use a favor."

His florid face swivels between Dad and me as he moans about his kid, a rising senior at one of the city's more prestigious universities. His son has not yet secured a summer internship and risks failing a class, which could potentially harm his GPA. The man sighs, giving us a "you-know-kids" kind of look. He adds, "I was just wondering if you might help us out."

It is not a question. It is a command—tit for tat. We make sure his kid doesn't spend the summer playing video games in the basement, wrecking his chance at law school and a future with one of Atlanta's white-shoe law firms, and he will reward us with a contribution.

"Our pleasure. Right, Jacob?" My father tilts his head and raises his eyebrows. Finding a job for this spoiled brat is falling on me.

"Consider it done." I give both a warm smile.

"Great." The man claps me on the back and offers his business card. "Call me on Monday."

My mother appears bored with the conversation. She scans the room until her gaze lands on a woman who is as thin as she is, also wearing a glittering, floor-length gown. Mom gives her a small wave and then extends her bejeweled hand toward the man. “It was lovely meeting you. You boys have business to discuss; I’ll go mingle.” She strolls across the ballroom, pausing to chat with gala-goers before moving on to the next assembled gaggle. Working the crowds is Mom’s exceptional talent.

No wonder Dad chose her as his wife. Despite her bony, sharp features, the result of decades of strict dieting, she is an attractive woman—in that social x-ray sort of way. Like my dad, she is skilled at navigating social situations, knowing what to say and when to say it to create an illusion of benevolence. If only her friends and acquaintances understood her true nature. Her main passions are my dad, money, and power.

“I need a refresh.” I hold up my empty glass and then nod to the man, who is still talking about his offspring. “Sir, we’ll get your son set up.”

The room is packed and buzzes with voices, the occasional laugh echoing above the din. Affairs like this aren’t new to me. Most faces are familiar, including one owned by a builder who collaborated with us on a condominium project a few years ago. Though completed, the project had not gone well—and neither have his business fortunes since then.

I wonder why.

Oh no, he’s headed my way. Shoot. He’s the last guy I want to see.

“Heard your father is considering a run for office.” The erstwhile business partner offers no businesslike grasp of hands. No greeting. He rambles on about a proposed piece of legislation that has irked the land-development community. So far, it hasn't made much headway, but a new crop of up-and-comers has vowed to hog-tie development along the coast.

"It's good seeing you, too." I extend my hand and put on my most expansive smile to counter his lack of manners, his poor attempt at a snub to put me in my place. "You can bet my father will do everything to kill that bill should he be elected to the Georgia Senate." I then clasp my hands behind my back and bounce on the toes of my Italian shoes. "We need to stick together, right?"

The one-time business partner narrows his eyes and sputters. "Do you think I'd vote for a Hudson? After how your company treated me?"

I decide to defuse the situation with the poise of a diplomat. There is no point in embarrassing my dad or me with an unsightly confrontation.

"As far as my father and I are concerned, we have settled our differences and are interested in doing business with you in the future," I say, my voice smooth and measured—striking the right balance between sincerity and authority. An effortless smile spreads across my face. I know how to make people feel like they are part of something special, that my attention is a gift. I let the moment linger before sharing the inside scoop on an ambitious development project we are working on. "If you're interested in bidding, give me a call."

In the corner of my eye, I notice a woman I have not seen since meeting Ginny and hooking up with Red. I want to catch her before she disappears into the crowd. Thankfully, our eyes connect, and she acknowledges me with a devilish grin.

"Look, I gotta go." His back receives a hearty clap. "Let's do lunch. Until then, reconsider your support for my dad." Before turning to catch up with my one-time lover, I see him nod.

I handled that well.

"Long time, no see," my ex-girlfriend says, eyeing me up and down as I approach.

"We need to fix that." I lean over and bite the crab puff pinched between her thumb and forefinger. Giggling, she snatches another from a silver tray on the food table, hiding the pastry behind her back. The role of a coquette suits her well.

"Come and get it," she purrs.

And I do.

* * *

What a night. Dad texted this morning to report that he had secured the necessary support and planned to announce his candidacy shortly. And me? Well, my success did not involve Red. Instead of waiting until the party ended, my ex-girlfriend and I crept out a kitchen side door, and we ended up spending the night together at her condo. When she suggested that we hang out today, of course, I begged off. I slipped out of bed minutes after the sun rose and didn't bother to write a note or send a text.

I do not need further complications. Red has been calling me nonstop. Furthermore, it's Sunday morning, and I have too much to do.

But first, a man must eat. I finish my eggs Benedict and sip a latte before unlocking the door to my private study. Last night, Dad filled me in on the details of the Monday morning meeting and what I needed to do to prepare. I power up my laptop and settle in. Research is one of my strengths, and hours slip by unnoticed. Finding a job for a college student with no known skills and only a vague desire to become a lawyer isn't in my wheelhouse. One quick phone call, and that chore goes to our in-house attorney; I then move on to the next item on my Sunday morning checklist: straightening my desk.

Hmmm. I didn't notice anything out of whack yesterday while I searched for a first-class ticket to Oklahoma, but then again, I was a bit preoccupied. Dad's demands that I drop everything for him made me mad. Now I see the evidence. Someone has rifled through my papers. The pamphlet for the Savannah getaway is not where I left it, and my other papers, which I had neatly stacked, look disordered. *This is not how I keep things.*

My eyes narrow, and questions blitz my brain. I had banned Ginny from ever entering my office without my permission. Possibly, I had gotten sloppy and forgotten to secure the door before heading out with Red the night Ginny guzzled bottles of wine and started slurring her words. The laptop isn't passcode-protected because it stays behind locked doors. Now I question the wisdom in that. *Did she search my laptop and review the browser's history?*

If she did, she wouldn't like what she discovered.

Before leaving that night, I had conducted another search—one of many into how I could gain custody of a child in a state where unmarried mothers receive more favorable treatment than fathers, unless an aggressive lawyer can prove the mother is unfit.

Did she flee because she discovered what I had considered doing?

The wheels turn. Maybe she did, or perhaps she didn't. Regardless, the loss of custody would drive Ginny to her knees—a practical tactic when I finally find Ginny and persuade her to stop her reckless behavior and return to me. And I do need her back. The members of Atlanta's aristocracy reminded me of that fact last night. They all inquired about her well-being and praised my good judgment in choosing her. They called her gorgeous, brilliant, and sweet—an asset to the Hudson family dynasty.

Blah. Blah. Blah.

If a silver lining exists in this situation, it's that she's making it easy for me. A quick check on the app shows her car still parked in a residential area of some backwater burg west of Oklahoma City. Did she move in? Who lives there? Why encamp there? Answers to those questions can wait until tomorrow. I roll my neck and shoulders to relieve the tension from hours in front of a computer, then head for the theater room. Right now, watching a thriller could be the perfect diversion.

CHAPTER FIFTEEN

Oralyn

We came up with Ginny's travel plan before the first of the lunch crowd showed up yesterday. Shannon is not the type to color outside the lines, but she seemed to relish the chance to play by a different set of rules as we fleshed out the scheme. Or would *caper* be a better word?

No matter. My excitement has been growing ever since.

I've never challenged convention, either. I stayed rooted in this little town, dreaming in my younger years of opportunities to prove myself, spread my wings, and one day travel across the country, maybe even the world, to see how other people lived. But that chance never came between caring for Katherine and scrambling to keep a roof over our heads. Charlie restored me, but he had no interest in adventure; he was content with his well-worn habits: eating breakfast at Monty's, ushering at church, and fishing with his buddies, until ill health robbed him of his simple pleasures.

Me? I forgot my dreams and found pleasure in being with him.

Later today, I will begin writing a new chapter in my story. I've agreed to join Ginny as her travel mate. *Whoop! Whoop!* I can barely control myself. To say that I'm eager to get started would be an understatement. I've already taken care of my flowers and vacuumed my rugs. The place is in order.

But it's Sunday, and church is what I do.

Ginny offers to drive us in her Honda since my legs are aching, and I match her kindness by chatting with Laurel to keep her occupied. We take our seats in the pew behind Shannon and her crew, and I notice sideways glances from several longtime parishioners, many of whom I met in Sunday school when we were just kids. They've never seen Ginny and are probably wondering how she fits into my predictable life. What am I going to tell them? I shouldn't lie, but my gut tells me to keep some information close to the chest.

After the blessing, we file outside and are struck by the intense heat.

Our young, unmarried pastor stands outside the two double doors to greet his flock. Since taking over, he has lit a fire under this little old church, starting with his own attire. He looks like he's going to the Cracker Barrel or Walmart instead of a house of worship. No clerical collar for him. His jeans-wearing style stuck in my craw at first, as did his desire to start broadcasting services online. I won't judge. I'll keep to my habits and show up in person. I wouldn't know how to tune in even if I wanted to.

"Oralyn, I understand you've retired. Congratulations." The pastor takes my hands in his.

"Indeed, I have." I babble about this and that, mentioning my first vacation in years. His eyes wander—past me, beyond me—until the message registers inside my thick skull. He isn't listening to me. He's looking at Ginny. "Oh, my apologies… Let me introduce you to Ginny, my—"

She had been shifting from one foot to the other, as if eager to join the meet-and-greet.

"Insightful message this morning," she says, thrusting out her hand. "I would wager you stepped on more than a few toes this morning." She seems unbothered by, or perhaps overlooks, his lingering handclasp and smile that widens with unmistakable attraction.

His sermon this morning was a barn burner for sure.

Heads started nodding when the pastor discussed adultery, but they went still when he switched to a different transgression. Even baby Laurel quieted. "Which is worse?" he roared from the pulpit. "Adultery or gossip?" He waited a beat. "The Bible mentions adultery thirty-eight times. Anyone want to venture a guess on gossip?" His eyes swept the flock. "More than fifty times…slander, dishing the dirt, rumor mongering, backbiting…whatever you want to call it. Sin is sin, and don't think one is worse than the other. Both are ugly in the eyes of the Lord. We all need the saving grace of Jesus Christ."

I wonder if the old biddies, the church ladies who've made careers in slinging gossip, got the message.

My young, unmarried preacher continues to act like a lovesick puppy, happy to jibber-jabber about his message. He won't let go of Ginny's hand.

"Sometimes we all need a little reminding, regardless of whose noses get out of joint," he agrees, giving her a goofy grin before asking the question he may have wanted answered minutes ago. "Are you new to the area, a visitor, or—"

"Just traveling through." Ginny extracts her hand to search her enormous bag. *Gracious sakes, that thing must weigh a ton.* "I met Oralyn yesterday at the diner, and she invited me to join her at church this morning." Despite Laurel's growing crankiness, Ginny smiles like an angel and inserts Laurel's fuchsia-colored pacifier into the child's turned-down mouth. "Well, we'd better get going. The baby is hungry. Again, great message."

Within seconds, a loathsome voice assaults my ears.

"Oralyn, you brought a guest."

The chief biddy.

She is out of breath, running to catch up with us, determined to meet the stranger. It's not because she's the welcoming type, but because gossip is her stock and trade. God forgive me, I struggle to remain civil. She has talked about me for as long as I can remember, starting decades ago when I became pregnant before I was married. Back in those days, unwed mothers were treated as pariahs, labeled as Jezebels. She would never associate with someone like me and, through her tongue-wagging, suggested others shouldn't either.

She gets a curt nod from me.

"Well..." She waits, looking at me, the corners of her mouth curling into her signature sneer. Good manners matter in these parts, and I have no other choice. *Bless her heart.*

"This is Ginny..." Sweat gathers along my hairline, caused by the compression stockings that Ginny insisted that I wear, and the fib I am ready to tell. I know nothing about technology or genetics, but a story on TV has popped into my brain bone. "She found me through one of those little DNA test kits… Uh, I can't remember the name." My head nods more than necessary as Shannon joins our confab. "We're kin. Imagine our surprise when she contacted me," I say, giving Shannon a sideways glance.

Oh, Father, forgive me, for I know not what I do.

"Is that right?" The biddy's eyes narrow and her dentures flop around, and I fear they might fly out of her pinched, lipstick-smeared mouth. "How are you related?" Her eyes glint. How I loathe that woman.

"Ah, yes." Ginny fumbles around for an answer and then gives up. She sighs.

"Yes, ma'am," Shannon pipes up. "A cousin, a few times removed, but to me, she is the sister I've always wanted. I'm so glad she found us. Anyway, we gotta run. Have a blessed day." Yes, indeedy, Shannon sure enjoys coloring outside the lines.

"What was that?" Ginny asks under her breath as we beat a retreat for her car that is parked in front of a chain link fence, which separates church property from a peeling, clapboard-covered bungalow like many in town. Shannon giggles and covers her mouth with her hand.

"I got a little carried away, I guess—just a little white lie to keep that old crone satisfied," I say, raising my eyebrows. Shannon nods. My dear, sweet niece is aware of that woman's wicked tongue and her holier-than-thou attitude toward me.

"Oralyn, it's not a little white lie," Ginny says with surprising intensity. "It's an untruth. Period. Little fibs lead to bigger ones, and before you know it, you've lost your soul."

"You might be right, Ginny, but I meant every word I said," Shannon says. "You are like the sister I've never had."

Ginny's voice quiets as she climbs into the driver's seat. "I didn't mean to criticize, but my whole life is based on one huge lie. TC, the friend I've mentioned to you, also warned me. Had I come clean about my trainwreck parents, Jacob would have never pursued a relationship with me. He doesn't consort with white trash, and because I fudged the truth about my background, I am paying the consequences now."

I know nothing about these falsehoods or the details about her parents. Ginny starts her Honda and waves goodbye to Shannon. Silence hangs in the air, both of us deep in our thoughts, until she pulls into my driveway. Monty is already there, sweating like a glass of iced tea on a hot day. Our bags are loaded into my van. Bless his big, old heart. He washed my van, which now shines—except for the rust spots—and loaned us his storm alert radio, just in case.

"Okay, ladies. You're all set," he announces. "Your rig is gassed up, and I've changed the oil and checked the tires. Shannon's supposed to stop by the house to water the plants, right?" I nod. He steals a peek at Laurel, who is nestled in her car seat, and then he opens the passenger door to help me into the seat. Ginny is already behind the wheel.

Monty takes a few giant steps toward Ginny and exchanges keys with her. "Don't worry about your Honda. It's in capable hands." He taps the hood with his open palm and salutes as Ginny backs out of my driveway, not yet sure of her mother's specific location.

"We'll find her. I know it," Ginny told me this morning as we got ready for church. "I will find her with or without my aunt's help. Miracles happen, but I do understand if you decide to back out."

I'm not sure about what she meant by miracles, but I am sure about this: I'm not about to walk away. I am a sixty-nine-year-old retiree with little to do. I can offer an extra set of hands in baby care, and she can keep me company. The time has come to step out of my comfort zone, take risks, and see the world for a change. This little gal dropped into my life for a reason, and I'm anxious to find out what the future holds.

However, the feeling of dread that started yesterday continues to simmer within me. Will the old biddy cause trouble? Or will the weather beat her to it? In the distance, I see dark storm clouds gathering.

CHAPTER SIXTEEN

Ginny

Oralyn and I cheered when the wheels started rolling, but the excitement has since faded inside the no-frills cabin—just a radio, air conditioning, and hand-crank windows. Now, the only sounds are the rhythmic drumming of overworked windshield wipers and the wind battering Oralyn's unwieldy vehicle. I bite on my lip and grip the steering wheel. My hands ache. Oralyn seems either lost in her thoughts or, like me, worried that the downpour will turn into something far more ferocious and unforgiving.

I've never seen a twister, and I have no desire to see one now.

"When do I start getting worried?" I ask, straining to make out the ribbon of road that will take us to Amarillo, Texas, which is four hours away under normal conditions.

"Of what? Don't you have thunderstorms in Georgia?" Oralyn holds Monty's storm alert radio in one hand and a peanut butter cracker in the other. Nature's fury doesn't appear to faze her. "This, sweet girl, is nothing."

She goes on to tell me about the most powerful tornado ever recorded—the one that touched down briefly southwest of her hometown, only to strengthen and behave more erratically, before growing into a two-point-six-mile-wide monster. The weather service clocked wind speeds of nearly three hundred miles per hour.

"That beast and the subsequent flooding killed a mess of people, including three professional storm chasers," she says in a matter-of-fact tone, taking a bite from the cracker before wiping her hand on her stretchy slacks. "The news said you could see its path from space. Charlie and I bit the bullet and got a storm shelter after that. He was too long in the tooth to run to the community shelter every time the siren screamed."

Her narrative makes me uneasy.

"And then six years later, almost to the day," she continues, "another biggie tore up a motel and a mobile-home park. My ex-husband and his woman died in that one. I guess he decided to ride out the storm in that tin can of a trailer. Not smart. Rescue workers found them buried beneath a heap of twisted metal."

"What?" My head swivels in her direction, but I cannot see her face because she's looking out the window.

"See, nothing to get worked up over." Oralyn points to the hints of azure peeking through gray-tinged clouds billowing above an endless plain of farmland, gigantic wind turbines, and ramshackle trailers. "Like I said, nothing to get too excited about. We should be okay from here on out." She reaches over and turns off the now-squeaking wipers. The storm-alert radio gets stashed between her seat and the console.

I realize then that I don't know much about my frizzy-haired co-pilot with a passion for carb-laden foods, a bad case of varicose veins, and a long-suppressed craving for adventure. A great deal has happened since I left Atlanta five days ago. When I waved goodbye to Melinda, I never could have predicted meeting someone like Oralyn, someone who, I suspect, has weathered her own share of hardships in her many orbits around the sun.

"You told me about Charlie, but I had no idea you were married before."

"I don't want to speak ill of the dead, but my daughter, Katherine, was the only positive that came from that relationship." She shifts in her seat. "He's a story for another day, and we have plenty of time to talk about him. I'd rather not, though, because it makes me feel bad." Her words are delivered in a rapid-fire manner. "But I'll tell you this: He was good-looking—too pretty for the likes of me. I should have known better, foolishly thinking he liked me. It didn't take too much convincing on his part to get me between the sheets. He got me in the family way and then left me high and dry when life got hard. Now, Katherine is another story. I don't mind talking about her."

I suppress my amusement. Even though Oralyn didn't want to talk about him, she ended up giving a detailed account before gliding into a happy dialogue about her daughter. She shared the little moments: the exact months Katherine smiled, babbled, rolled over, crawled, and began reading—all before other kids her age. Katherine's easy nature was a blessing, particularly when Oralyn became a single mother and had to battle for child support. With her resources drained, Oralyn gave up and moved in with her mother.

I listen, feeling the warmth in her voice like sunlight slipping through a window. I catch myself smiling along, a slight ache blooming in my chest—not sadness, exactly, but something tender and aching all the same. Somehow, without even meaning to, perhaps, she had let me into her world.

"We lived in a house like that." Oralyn points to a disheveled ranch-style house situated among others on the other side of the guardrails. It seems the occupants have no need for landfills.

"Where is your daughter now?" I ask.

The mood changes as quickly as the post-thunderstorm Oklahoma sky.

"You're a nurse, right? Do you have any experience with tetralogy of Fallot?"

I have never cared for kids suffering from the disease, but I know a little about the rare, congenital condition. A bad feeling comes over me.

"The docs diagnosed Katherine after her birth. Poor little thing. Her skin turned blue within seconds of her saying hello to the world. She struggled to breathe and gain weight. What did they call it?" She rubs her jaw. "Failure to thrive."

"Did she have surgery?"

"Of course, I did everything the cardiac specialist recommended. I was so desperate for her to live a normal life. It broke my heart watching her sit on the sidelines as the other kids played dodgeball, jump rope, and hide-and-seek. A weak heart denied her the best parts of being a kid." Oralyn dabs her eyes. "A few days after one of her many operations, an awful bacterial infection set in, and my sweet little girl couldn't fight it."

Oralyn glances at her lap and takes in a deep breath. "She would've been close to fifty years old, a decade older than Shannon, who, of course, doesn't remember her. Katherine was twelve when she passed. I was young myself—thirty—and at that point divorced. My only reliable income came from the waitress job at Monty's." She pauses. "Sometimes I think she plumb gave up."

"I'm so sorry." I reach over and touch Oralyn's arm, wondering how she managed to survive on a waitress's income while caring for a very sick child. My question is answered.

"I had a little government aid. So did Mama. She was sick, too. Mama would watch Katherine if I worked the evening shift. We made it work. She was a good woman and put up with her fair share of garbage, too. My father was a drunk, a mean one. Mama followed her mother's example, and I followed hers."

The moment passes. Oralyn blows her nose. "I've been thinking about what you said." She scrutinizes a billboard advertising a roadside restaurant and then turns to face me. "About telling lies… How I misrepresented our relationship. But you *do* feel like family, and what's funny is that I don't know you that well. We kinda fell into cahoots. I'm wondering why that happened. What am I supposed to learn, if anything?"

"I guess we'll find out." I give her a sideways look.

"Girl, you gave a pretty good speech this morning about being honest." She points her finger at me. "Your delivery had me on the edge of my seat. Don't you think I should know a little more about you? Look at it from my point of view: I've thrown in with a twenty-something mother who has a sick fiancé. Gee, I don't know; maybe I am asking too much." She touches her lips with her pointer finger and gives me a lopsided grin.

She is teasing in that flippant way of hers and has no idea just how much we do have in common. While I am young enough to be her daughter or granddaughter, the generational distance makes no difference. She and I, and her mother and most certainly mine, allowed others to use us. We cleaved to generational patterns, regardless of their harm, and allowed the brokenness to dictate our lives. I am not the only person looking for a do-over. I am on the road to redemption, and I suspect Oralyn is, too.

But will she believe the story that brought me to this moment?

CHAPTER SEVENTEEN

Ginny

I'm not sure where to begin in telling Oralyn my story. Should I start with the otherworldly encounter that launched this trip, or should I focus on something more mundane? I don't want her thinking I'm off my rocker—at least, not yet.

"I wanted to be a doctor… Jacob had encouraged me, but I suspect his support had more to do with enhancing his image than any interest in what might be best for me. Anyway, I applied, the medical school accepted me, and then I deferred enrollment because of her." I nod in the general direction of Laurel, who seems content in her car seat in the back. "I was supposed to start this fall."

"Medical school? Aren't you the smarty-pants? What kind of doctor?"

Oralyn gets the CliffsNotes version of how TC had urged me to pursue child psychiatry after I had told him about myself at the festival. "As a kid, I saw things no kid should ever see, and he thought I would do the greatest good by helping kids who also saw the uglier side of humanity. I could make a difference in their lives."

The worry line between her eyebrows grows deeper. "What did you see?"

Do I want to go there? I gulp a lungful of air and blow it out in one noisy exhale. Keeping my eyes laser-focused on the road ahead, I reveal in bits the details about my drug-addicted father and his Vesuvius-like temper. I tell her how he had stilled my older sister, Laurel, with one well-aimed kick to the head. Like Katherine, my sister never experienced the milestones of life.

"You witnessed that?" Oralyn's mouth hangs open.

I nod. "After that, Mom and I moved in with Granny. But within a year, before the sun even rose one morning, my mother walked out—whether she couldn't take responsibility for me or simply wouldn't, I never knew." This quiet, tangled hurt had been festering unnoticed, despite years of counseling, until TC laid it bare. I am awestruck by how God had put him in my life.

"Who's this TC fella? You've mentioned him a lot."

"TC is… Well, he *was* exceptional. We met because of a thunderstorm." I look through the windshield. The periwinkle sky dotted with billowing masses of puffy clouds takes my breath away. A promising sign, and I continue, feeling more comfortable sharing my story with her. "To be precise, we met at a music festival just before a thunderstorm."

The next part embarrasses me because it reveals just how much Jacob had controlled me.

"I was pregnant, and I didn't know it. I wasn't feeling good that morning, but as usual, I agreed to go to the festival with him anyway. I would do anything to please him." My eyes narrow. "Within an hour of getting there, he ran into an old friend, a redhead, and took off with her even though a storm was brewing. TC watched it happen. He took pity on me and invited me to his campsite to wait out the rain. Jacob would remain missing for at least eight hours."

"You took off with a stranger?"

"My goodness, Oralyn. Jacob ran off with that woman, unconcerned about me. I didn't know a soul. What would you have done?" I peek at Oralyn. She's staring out the passenger-side window, but swivels her head to look at me.

"I probably would've bawled like a baby."

TC gave me a good feeling, like God had arranged our meeting. And I tell Oralyn as much. He was funny. Outgoing. He had the most entertaining friends, to say nothing of his gut-ripping stories about his big family and the off-the-wall people he seemed to attract. In almost every way, the short-statured, boisterous TC was the opposite of me and drew me out of my shell.

Before I knew it, I had jumped into the deep end and started sharing details about my childhood—things that even Jacob didn't know. Even then, Jacob had begun telling me what to wear and how to speak at social functions. Foolishly, I interpreted his comments as signs of his love and affection, thinking he wanted a shy, inexperienced woman like me to shine before his circle. However, after meeting TC, doubt began to creep in. TC accepted my flaws and imperfections; why couldn't Jacob? Why was he always insisting that I change to suit him?

"Do you know what is sad?" I steal another glance at Oralyn and see her shrug. "Despite everything, TC kept beating himself up, comparing himself with others. He saw himself as a screw-up and hid his doubts behind that big laugh, the ready joke. I tried convincing him otherwise, but sometimes we believe the lie."

This sentiment hits me hard, and I shudder as my eyes fill.

"You and Granny would have loved him. Everyone loved him because he was authentic, even in his self-doubt."

"What happened to him?" Oralyn's voice is soft. Perhaps she senses the way this story ends.

I try to blink away the tears, but the dam is springing leaks. Until this moment, hurtling toward the unknown, I had not processed the experience, afraid of telling even Melinda. But why keep my time with TC hidden? It is my miracle story. The pent-up waters cascade down my cheeks as I reach for my cloth satchel.

"Go ahead, Oralyn, peek inside."

Frowning, she hoists the bag onto her lap and finds an empty wine bottle amid all the clutter.

"Why would you have this?" She examines the label and then gazes at me.

The night TC came, I had not seen or spoken with him in a year because neither of us had exchanged our phone numbers or our last names. In retrospect, it was a regrettable mistake. We had no time. Jacob finally showed up and told me it was time to go. I rub my arm, remembering Jacob's firm grip as he started tugging on me. In that moment, I stood up to him, turning away to face TC. As we hugged, TC whispered for me to stay with him. He knew precisely who Jacob was.

"Anyway, on the night he visited me," I continue, my nose now running, "I'd drunk a lot of wine and figured I'd go to sleep and never wake up if I swallowed a fistful of painkillers. But TC came before that could happen." Chill bumps cover my arms because the next part still leaves me incredulous.

"Oralyn, hours earlier, he had drowned in Tennessee… Do you understand? He died."

Oralyn stutters. "I don't understand. If he died in Tennessee, how did he visit you in Georgia?"

"Oralyn, TC came to me in a dream. But it wasn't an ordinary dream. It was supernatural."

The vividness of the experience has not faded. I can still picture TC demanding to know my intentions. Suicide was never a part of my future, he insisted, as he showed me how my inability to let go of the past had prevented me from moving toward my destiny. He bent down, picked up one of the empty wine bottles off the floor, and placed it on my nightstand—in the exact spot where I found it the next morning, sober and clear-headed.

"He then told me his last name, which I didn't know, and urged me to look up his name when I woke up. The story about his accidental death checked out." I wipe the tears from my eyes. "How would I have known these facts otherwise? That bottle proved he had visited. God himself had sent TC to save me from myself."

Oralyn puts the bottle back inside my bag and covers her mouth with her hand. I'm shaken, too—over many things. As a nurse, I had patched up all types of people living on the fringes. Many of them were strung out on drugs. I understand their despair. Who, after all, had considered swallowing painkillers to end her pain? Allowing myself to reexperience TC's unexpected visit makes me realize how far I had fallen and then gained. Nothing happens by coincidence. Different people come into our lives for a reason. Granny was right.

"Do you think I'm nuts?"

Oralyn shakes her head but doesn't speak for several minutes. "I never experienced anything like that, but that doesn't mean it didn't happen. The Lord works in mysterious ways. Your TC stopped you from doing the unthinkable."

I nod—feeling entirely certain. Just then, a song that disc jockeys never play on the radio, but one I discovered on YouTube after Granny's death, begins to play through the speakers: "Dancing in the Sky." The lyrics are haunting, poignant, and relatable. With TC gone, I, too, feel like everything good is missing.

I find myself sobbing—for my special friend, for Granny, and for myself.

My vision is too blurred to continue driving, so I pull off the interstate and park in the first lot I can make out. My tears burn my cheeks as Oralyn squeezes my shoulder, encouraging me to let it go. To grieve. Her soothing words remind me of Granny's when she would hold me tight after my mom had abandoned me, telling me that God did not make junk. The song ends, and oddly, I am consoled just as I was the first time I'd heard it. The angels do know what they have. Heaven is nicer now that TC has arrived, singing in the angel's choir.

Hearing that song feels like a gift.

"We've had a tough day," Oralyn says, giving my shoulder another squeeze with one hand, blotting her eyes with the other. "Are you still aiming for Amarillo today? Because I won't complain if we call it quits and find a place to stay." She then gives me a crooked smile. "Or are you wanting a go at the slots?"

Huh? I glance at the building in front of us—a sleek, neon-lit casino owned by one of the many tribes here in Oklahoma. I let out a hearty laugh, grateful for her well-timed attempt at lightness.

"How about you, Oralyn?" I sniffle. "Feeling lucky?"

She tilts her head. Her eyebrows arch. "Nope. My ex-husband did enough gambling for both of us."

"Okay then, let's keep going. Amarillo is about two hours away, give or take." I give her a small smile, feeling depleted, though lighter and renewed somehow. "We'll find a hotel and have a nice meal. I figure we can reach Vegas in a couple of days. Does that work?"

Oralyn winks.

I couldn't have asked for a more agreeable or understanding co-pilot. She was the shoulder I needed to cry on. But another worry rears up miles from the Texas state line. Can Jacob get access to my credit card account? The thought had crossed my mind a few days ago, but with all the excitement, I had put that worry on the back burner.

"Oralyn, I don't think it's smart to use my credit card." I twirl the memory bracelet. "I should've thought about this before. May I use yours to pay for our hotel room? I have plenty of cash and will pay you."

Oralyn rolls her eyes the way she did when I asked if I could shower in her bathroom. "It all works out in the wash, honey. No worries. I know where to find you."

She leans down to remove her phone—an older iPhone—from her faux-leather handbag, which sits at her feet. "I have a feeling Monty might need to talk with me. He may have news." Her eyebrows draw together as she taps his name in her phone.

I shiver at her words. No more surprises, please.

How, in God's name, did I think I could do this alone?

CHAPTER EIGHTEEN

Adele

Finding the truth about Ginny and Jacob was not hard. Marriage records are public, and most jurisdictions make them available online. After a brief conversation with Robert, I spent Sunday checking records in every county in Georgia before expanding the search to a few neighboring states. My head ached by the time I shut off the computer and went to bed, thankful my commuting days in the Big Apple had ended. The crowded subways, the push to get to work on time, the grind of it all—it was all behind me now. I had joined the rest of the Baby Boomers who could sleep in from time to time.

But that did not happen this morning. Jacob started calling before I climbed out of bed, and he hasn't stopped. His messages are polite, but I detect a growing irritation in his voice. "It's important that I talk with you, Adele. Please call… Why haven't you gotten back to me? Is something wrong?"

On it goes.

He won't be hearing from me.

He is no more married to my niece than I am to Robert. How many other falsehoods has he told?

The digital clock on the stove shows that it is not too early to call, regardless of the time zone. I select the stored number in my phone.

"Hello?" A hesitant voice answers after several rings.

"Ginny?"

"Yes."

"Uh, this is Aunt Adele." I hear tires rumbling over asphalt and Ginny's muffled voice.

"My aunt…" Ginny is speaking to someone, a woman who has a Southern accent much like Ginny's, Robert's, and mine. That is, until I hired an accent-reduction tutor. This was yet another attempt to distance myself from my family and heritage, convincing myself that no one could judge me or question my intellect based on my manner of speaking—another mistake.

"What do you want? Haven't you already taken sides?" Ginny's voice interrupts my thoughts, and I cannot blame her for the hostility. "Aunt Adele, I owe you nothing."

"You're right. I *owe* you." I am eating crow and deserve it, but fear my apology has fallen on deaf ears. I can only make out boisterous laughing and the woman's voice.

"Phew, baby girl just had an accident…a big one."

"Aunt Adele, I'll call you back." Ginny's line goes dead.

I straighten the kitchen and then make myself comfortable on the sofa to scan financial news online. Inflation has gone stratospheric. The market is in negative territory, and I can only imagine the panic on the street. Another vital bridge has collapsed. More banks have closed. Supply chain issues persist, and a large Midwestern food-processing plant has exploded.

Meanwhile, retailers continue to shutter their brick-and-mortar stores due to widespread shoplifting and now looting. Something is very wrong. I am grateful I took the buyout and cashed in my shares, giving myself a comfortable margin to withstand a potential collapse. At times, I feel like I'm watching Nero fiddle as Rome burns.

The trill of my phone shakes me from my doomsday thoughts.

"Sorry about that. I had to make a quick stop. What were you saying?" Only thirty minutes have passed, but I am hearing a different Ginny—the even-tempered version that I had always known. Perhaps I can mend the fence that I broke.

"I called to apologize." I gaze out over Central Park and wonder how much longer I can stay here. The excitement of living in Manhattan has faded, and it no longer feels like home. Did it ever? Why hadn't I noticed the increasing homelessness or the overwhelming stench of garbage piled high on the sidewalks? City life amplifies social ills, but it also offers anonymity. I could ignore the desperation, looking away as I hurried past the needles and strung-out people. Now, however, I yearn for a slower-paced lifestyle among people who genuinely care about their neighbors and know them by name. Does such a place even exist?

"No point in making excuses," I continue. "I *did* believe Jacob over you."

"Which part?" she asks in a neutral tone. "The part about my alleged drug and alcohol abuse or the bit about me being married to him and how he would lay down his life for me and Laurel?"

"The marriage, Ginny. Based on what I could find, or did not find, no marriage license has ever been issued to a Jacob Hudson and a Virginia Carmichael. That's one problem. The other involves your grandmother. She never once mentioned Jacob by name or your marriage to him. Certainly, she would've said something about that." I sit on the sofa and consider the photo of Mom and me. "If a man can lie about that, what else is he capable of?"

We talk for about forty-five minutes, a conversation that is not obligatory but rather enjoyed as we get to know each other. I am certain my mother is smiling down on us both.

I am just as sure that Ginny made the right decision in leaving Jacob. Examples of his duplicity and need to control and diminish erase my admiration of him. My gosh, he had even doubted his paternity and accused her of stepping out on him. Toxic is too mild a word to describe him. If I believed the stories learned in Sunday school, I would think he was Satan's spawn.

"Where are you now?"

"We're at the *Cadillac Ranch*. Oralyn found it online now that she's learned how to use a browser on her iPhone." Ginny laughs. She had already filled me in on this Oralyn woman, and I'm not quite sure what to think of it all. "We were on our way to the hardware store to buy a can of spray paint when you called, and the baby needed an emergency diaper change."

I ignore the latter. "Spray paint? Whatever for?"

"Because that's what people do. It's sanctioned graffiti. People come from all over to spray paint ten Cadillacs buried nose-first in the desert… Oh shoot, Oralyn almost tripped over a chunk of paint that fell off one of the cars." I hear more laughter, and I am envious. Whimsy is alien to my serious-minded self. "We're off to see the second-largest canyon in North America, a place called Palo Duro, provided baby girl cooperates."

Ginny's words trip off her tongue, bubbly and carefree. My niece is having a good time. Has this woman influenced her, or has her newfound freedom thrown off the usual reserve?

What Ginny hasn't revealed is her journey's end and why. Impatient, I ask point-blank.

"Oh, that… Oralyn and I are driving to Nevada to see Mom. I would appreciate any information you have on her whereabouts. If you decide not to help, we'll handle it ourselves. I have full faith. I will find my mother, with or without you. I mean no disrespect, but finding Mom is that important to me."

By the time we hang up, I've decided to pack my bags, ignore the barrage of Jacob's voice and text messages, and fly to Albuquerque, where Ginny will meet me tomorrow afternoon. Although I feel better, questions still linger.

Is Ginny making a mistake?

CHAPTER NINETEEN

Jacob

It's only Monday, and already my week has gone down the tubes. Adele hasn't returned my calls, and now Dad has taken a dim view of me because I pushed too hard, and the owners of two thousand acres north of Atlanta withdrew from negotiations this morning. This was *his* deal—*his meeting.* Not mine. But he pawned it off on me because he had better things to do. I run my hand across the back of my neck and glance out the window, the skyline blurring in the midday haze. The clock chimes in the background, taunting me. Because I had to attend Dad's oh-so-important meeting, as well as the gala on Saturday, I delayed flying to Oklahoma to surprise Ginny.

And now I have lost track of her.

Ginny's car, which had been parked in the same general vicinity for the past few days, gave me a false sense of security. This morning, it began to move. The last time I checked, it was following a winding route, generally in a northeasterly direction. *Where is she going? New York?* Why isn't Adele returning my calls?

I sit motionless at my desk, my free hand drumming against the wood. The sharp taps of my fingers are the only sound in the room. The longer the silence stretches, the hotter my blood runs. I scan my desk, my gaze landing on the half-drunk mug of coffee beside my laptop, the liquid now cold. Without thinking, I grab it.

The mug flies across the room.

Crash.

Glass splinters across the face of the grandfather clock. A jagged web spreads before the shards fall, and the ticking hands stutter before freezing altogether. The pendulum survives, but barely. It wobbles before coming to a halt.

"Are you okay?" My assistant pokes her head inside the door. Her eyes are as big as saucers.

"Of course, I'm fine. Shut the door. Cancel everything on my calendar this afternoon and tomorrow."

She hesitates, biting her lip. "Your father is holding a media event tomorrow. He wants you and Ginny in attendance." She ducks out before I can throw something at her.

I tap the app again. And again. And again. *Damn you, Adele. You're as useless as Ginny.* I take a few deep breaths. Inhale. Exhale. I call Dad's cell.

"Dad, Ginny can't attend your announcement tomorrow." My voice sounds tempered, but it is a struggle. I want to wring his neck for putting me in this situation. I continue quickly. "Ginny's out of town. I told you that."

My pronouncement does not faze him. He's blathering about his chances of winning his election and the need for a strong family front. He tells me that I need to book a flight pronto and get Ginny home tonight. I tell him what first pops into my mind.

"She can't. She has a family emergency and has left for the Northeast. She sends her regards."

He hangs up in a huff. He will get over it. My eyes scan the office and zero in on the shards of glass glittering on the floor. The janitor will clean it up. My fingers thump the top of my desk. What to do? What to do? I call Ginny's friend, Melinda, leave a message, and then contact Adele again. That, too, goes to voicemail. My fingers twitch. The app is screaming my name.

Tap me.

Tap me.

Tap me.

A quick head shake breaks me out of my obsession. *Get a grip. Take command.* I tap another number.

"Bill, I'll pay triple your hourly rate and all expenses if you'll fly to Oklahoma and investigate my girlfriend, Ginny Carmichael."

I give my PI the lowdown, or at least most of it—the part about how she left five or six days ago, and I haven't heard from her since. He's full of questions and wants to know her last known location and whether I suspect a felony. The GPS locator goes unmentioned; he is not a stickler about the law, but you never know. I will bring that up with him later, if necessary. "No, nothing like that. It's unlike her to keep me in the dark, and I wonder if she's been truthful about why she might've gone there. Snoop around."

Dollar signs must dance inside Bill's head. I give him carte blanche to fly first-class and to stay in the finest hotel. He may rent a luxury car, for all I care. He thanks me profusely for the assignment, but more likely, he is relieved I hadn't dressed him down. The investigation into Ginny's mother, despite the intel I imparted a few days ago, has yielded nada so far. Disappointment isn't my thing, and he promises to keep looking.

"Oklahoma takes precedence over the mother," I say. "Fly out today and report back as soon as possible."

There is no need to get excited. Bill can be my arms and legs. *You can run, Ginny, but you can't hide.* I lean back in my desk chair, link my hands behind my neck, and take in the view of Atlanta—my phone jangles.

Dad.

What does he want now?

"Jacob, meet me in my office in ten minutes for an emergency video call. Some of our investors are getting worried."

"Why?" I ask, gently rocking in my ergonomic office chair. Given all the fires I have stoked or extinguished over the past few days, the larger world around me has gone ignored. I have no idea why they might be spooked. Our projects always make money.

I don't even pretend to focus on Dad's urgent meeting. My eyes stay glued to the screen, tracking that little dot creeping along the interstate. Five minutes pass. Then ten. Every mile she travels fuels the fire in my chest, but I can't look away. Not yet.

Finally, I force myself to stand, smoothing my shirt as if that might press the tension from my body. I must attend a meeting—no doubt, a pointless one.

As I stroll past my assistant, seated at her desk, I notice the news headlines on her computer monitor. She shakes her head and bites her lip. As I said, if my day could get any worse, I would be surprised. Little did I know that chaos was unfolding all around me.

CHAPTER TWENTY

Oralyn

We've been on the road for two days, and we aren't making great time. I'm to blame.

Quirky roadside attractions and tacky mom-and-pop stores spark my curiosity, especially those tucked along Route 66, weaving alongside or merging with Interstate 40. I've driven past Monty's Diner in my hometown more times than I can count, never giving the historic byway much thought. But out here, it feels like a gateway to something bigger—like adventure, reinvention. Fun. For many, the *Mother Road* opened the door to fresh starts, and I get it. The old me has taken a leave of absence, and the new one is embracing possibility.

Even little Laurel is having a big time. She coos and waves her arms whenever someone stoops over her stroller to tickle her belly or caress her fat, rosy cheeks. They give Ginny and me furtive once-overs, possibly wondering if we're related. *That old goat couldn't have possibly spawned such beauties.*

Let 'em think it.

"She's a flirt," I tell Ginny as I fill my plate at the hotel's complimentary breakfast buffet somewhere west of the New Mexico state line, delineated by an eye-catching stone gateway welcoming travelers to the *"Land of Enchantment."* Golden waffles drenched in syrup, buttery croissants with flaky layers, and a slice of warm banana bread fill the plate; my carb load has elicited mild scolding from Ginny. She's a yogurt-and-fruit kinda gal.

Traveling with a nurse has its disadvantages.

A frown crosses Ginny's face as she listens to my keen observations about Laurel's flirty nature, and I figure thoughts of her mother have prompted the expression. Last night, stretched out on our hotel beds watching *Family Feud*, we shared more details about our lives. I told her about my early years with Katherine's father, and she told me more about TC before putting flesh on the outline she'd drawn of her mother—a troubled woman with a real talent for hooking up with good-for-nothing men.

Sort of like me—before Charlie.

I can't understand why this woman would have no interest in her daughter. It makes no sense. Ginny is a keeper. This morning, for example, she massaged the ropes of twisted veins on my tired and misshapen calves and helped me into the compression stockings.

Without complaint, she does all the driving and stops whenever I ask. Which is a lot. My bladder is working overtime. My only job is spinning the dial, looking for country music stations—an easy job in these parts. We sing. We talk. Or I crawl into the back seat to comfort Laurel when she pitches a fit—a suitable arrangement for everyone. I guess we'll soon discover the whys and wherefores of her mother's inattention.

We reload my passenger van after breakfast. Suitcases and baby gear go in the back, and the bags of souvenirs go beneath the seats—T-shirts for Shannon and her family and a little doll for Laurel. At my suggestion, Ginny bought a map of historic Route 66, and I settled for a floppy straw hat and a cheap pair of sunglasses.

Pulling down the visor to assess my new hat and shades in the mirror, I can't believe it's me—an old gal incognito. I grin, a lightness spreading through my chest, the kind I haven't felt in years. I have a reason to smile. The warm sun filters through the windshield, and for the first time in a long while, I feel unburdened—like I have shaken off a piece of baggage I didn't realize I was carrying. Unfortunately, we have no time for sightseeing today—we're on a tight schedule.

Ginny's Aunt Adele is arriving in Albuquerque this afternoon. I'll have to pass the time riding shotgun and staring out the window at countryside that looks a lot like parts of Oklahoma and Texas. All I see are endless plains dotted with empty billboards, cattle ranches, and outcrops of rock embedded in bone-dry dirt. How settlers navigated this largely featureless terrain is still a mystery to me.

I notice something else, too: boarded-up hotels, restaurants, and service stations. Debris litters the side of the road. These are things you expect to see on Route 66, of course, but on Interstate 40, too? Has it always been like this? I scratch my head and let it go. Staying on the sunny side and burying my head in the sand are easier, especially since I roll past talk radio and the hourly newscasts. If the world has begun to spin in the wrong direction, I would rather not know.

Furthermore, why burden Ginny with my Debbie Downer observations? Why spoil her cheery mood? Her dimples have become permanent fixtures since Monty—bless his big old heart—reported Sunday after we had left that an Army buddy had picked up her car at my place. It was now on a leisurely joyride to Chicago, where his buddy would park it in his used-car lot until we figured out what to do next.

Then her spirit soared still higher when she spoke with her aunt yesterday. That meeting of minds, I am happy to say, happened in part because of me. You can choose your friends, I advised as she cleaned and rediapered Laurel inside a ladies' room after the baby's gastrointestinal upset, but you cannot choose your family. You are stuck with them. So, why not try to get along? She is whistling now as we pull out of the hotel's parking lot and merge onto the interstate.

That's when my phone rings.

Monty.

We've been in regular communication since hitting the road. With all this travel, time has gotten confused in my mind. Are we on Central or Mountain Time? I imagine those time-zone maps to keep it straight in my head. Yep, he is two hours ahead—noon his time.

"Where are ya?" he asks, without emotion.

"New Mexico, east of Albuquerque. Why?"

Sometimes you wish you had not asked, and this is one such moment. Monty spends the next few minutes telling me about a private investigator who dropped by the diner this morning to inquire about a missing woman. He arrived in style in an expensive Mercedes with Oklahoma tags. The man was a bit cagey, but he showed Monty his credentials. He refused to say who hired him, only divulging that the woman he was looking for had left Atlanta days ago and she hadn't been heard from since. Her car was last seen in the area, more precisely in front of his diner.

"That doesn't mean he's looking for Ginny," I say. As Ginny taps her fingers on the steering wheel in beat to a Chris Stapleton tune, my breakfast starts to work itself into an indigestible lump. With the mention of her name, Ginny glances my way. Her brow bunches up, just like it did the morning she showed up at Monty's, discombobulated by Jacob's unhinged hunt for her.

"I would say it does." Monty is quick to dispel my delusion. "He showed me a photo of Ginny and the baby and asked if I'd seen them," Monty says with bewildering practicality before dropping the other bombshell. "He also hinted that Ginny might be with you."

"What?" My shouting prompts Ginny to make a last-minute exit off the highway. We are careening on two wheels into a vacant, weedy parking lot that once served a roadside motel before it bit the dust. I fumble around with my phone, trying to put it on speaker, when Ginny grabs it.

"Monty, Ginny here. Back up a bit." She runs her hand through her hair, again pulled back in a messy updo, her usual style. "What happened?"

I could strangle Monty. He acts like this type of thing happens every day. Now on speaker, he repeats what he told me and then fills in the details.

"Before hassling me, he visited that little church of yours, Oralyn, and spoke with your pastor," Monty continues, sounding unflappable. "The PI is as greasy as petroleum jelly and must have played the young rector hard."

"How do you know?" Ginny asks, leaning in closer.

"Because I called the pastor after the dude left."

Despite our detailed planning on how to throw Jacob off Ginny's scent, we had overlooked a simple precaution. After Monty discovered the tracker, he reinstalled it on purpose, knowing the car would end up in Chicago. However, we forgot to take it out before we went to church—a big mistake. If I were Jacob, of course, I would dispatch the snoop to my church because that is where we were for a couple of hours on Sunday.

Oh my gosh. Hadn't I made a huge deal about my retirement and vacation? Wasn't the biddy within earshot? Did the detective interview her? Jacob likely knew my address, and of course, the diner's. But why leave more breadcrumbs? You would have to be a dimwit not to get a little suspicious about my potential participation in her disappearance.

"Your pastor had himself worked into a dither," Monty continues, of course unaware that my face has turned the color of talcum powder. My sweet, trusting pastor would become bothered by Ginny's missing personhood. He is that kind of guy. "I set him straight and urged him to say zippo if the gumshoe comes around again," Monty says in that take-charge voice of his.

"What did you tell him about us?" I turn my head to make sure the cavalry hasn't arrived, guns drawn, to return Ginny to a man who makes my ex look like a choirboy. Ginny and I are like matchy-matchy twins. Both of us got pregnant by men who didn't deserve us. While mine wanted nothing to do with me, Jacob won't give up. He is dogged, and this worries me. What else has he hidden up his sleeve?

"The truth, for the most part." Monty chortles, sounding pleased with himself. "I told Sherlock Holmes that you hadn't absconded with Ginny. You were in Arkansas visiting your brother, and I had no idea what had become of Ginny. She hadn't cleared her travel plans with me. There is no need to alter the plan at this point, but you may need a different ride. I'll be in touch."

The phone goes dead.

* * *

Ginny says we will decide our next steps—including whether to ditch my rusty old van—when the time comes, like when Adele joins our girl party once we reach Albuquerque. Ginny isn't worried, and I should take her example. Who cares if the detective interviews the old busybody? She doesn't know much anyway.

Radio static starts plucking my last nerve. I turn the knob and find a crystal-clear country station on the FM dial. We warble until we reach Albuquerque, with its salmon-colored highway overpasses, in plenty of time to pick up Adele from the airport. To kill time, we decide to pick up a few items at Walmart, but, shockingly enough, discover it is shuttered. A Walmart? What has this world come to? I check my wristwatch. Adele's come-fetch-me call should be coming soon. My sense of direction has gone haywire as we head to the airport. I don't know where I am, and send up another silent prayer thanking

God for Ginny, who finds the passenger pickup parking lot with ease. She pulls into an open space and shuts off the ignition.

My phone rings. *Uh-oh. Monty. What now?*

"Another update on the private dick," he says with no introduction, as Ginny climbs into the back seat to keep Laurel company while we wait for Adele's call. "He stopped in for another interrogation and got into my face. He made threats. He knows your vehicle and tag number." My heart skips a beat, and my mind spins, trying to make sense of this bizarre turn of events. I grip the armrest to steady myself. "I ended up tossing the scumbag out on his ear, making threats of my own. He won't be visiting me again."

His blow-by-blow confirms what had been gnawing at my craw. The detective had run into the most detestable of women.

The biddy.

My skull box can see the twinkle in her eyes as she settles the detective in her living room, offering him cookies and coffee, all too happy to confirm my name, address, and the vehicle I drive. How I—a person with sketchy morals—had shown up at church with a pretty stranger, a baby cradled in her arms, both of us claiming to be relatives. This old bat would flap her lips even if Jesus himself padlocked them shut. We are supposed to love all of God's creatures, including our enemies, but un-Christian-like fantasies run through my mind.

"He said he's going to focus his search on you since you're related and will involve local police if needed. Cops do not take missing-person reports lightly, he said, and neither did he," Monty says, interrupting my thoughts of delicious revenge. "He may be blowing smoke, but you never know. Time to change your wheels." He waits a second or two before asking, "Are you related to Ginny?"

"No! I fibbed…" I smack my forehead with my open palm and remember Ginny's warning about the peril of fabrications and how they will bite you in the butt. Mine have left fang marks in my big behind.

Monty guffaws. He sounds like he's enjoying himself.

"Monty, this isn't funny. What would I do without my van? I can't afford to get rid of it." Ginny, who had been bouncing Laurel on her lap—"baby aerobics," as she calls it—must have heard the panic in my voice. She pokes her head between the front seats, wanting answers. I hold up my finger before rummaging through my purse for a pen and a piece of paper.

Monty, the king of the griddle, has saved the day. Or at least he has done his part. While we cruised the streets of Albuquerque, he called in another favor, which ensured we would reach our destination undeterred by a bona fide, game-playing psycho. We had no intention of raising the ante, but Jacob has forced us to redefine the rules of the game. The trophy will go to the team that outwits the other.

Game on, provided Aunt Adele agrees to play.

CHAPTER TWENTY-ONE

Adele

The flight from JFK to Albuquerque went off without a hitch—a relief given the chyrons running across the bottom of the airport TV screens. In my nearly six decades, I have never seen anything quite like it. Not even the 2008 economic meltdown compares with the current collapse. Perhaps it is a New York thing, but most people at JFK kept their eyes glued to their devices, many likely wondering if they would be the next to lose their jobs.

The scene is different in New Mexico. People appear unbothered by the catastrophe that began yesterday, only to grow worse since the markets opened this morning. Sports channels reign in the bars, and the drinks keep flowing. All bread and circuses. They will learn soon enough. I hope the economic downturn is short-lived.

Ginny and a middle-aged woman wearing a silly hat and aviator-style sunglasses—Oralyn, I guess—roll up to the passenger pickup area in an old white van pocked with rust spots. Ginny hops out of the driver's side, moving with an energy I do not quite recognize, and pulls me into her arms, laughing. Her hug is firm, but something about her feels overly wrought.

Still smiling, Ginny pulls away, and I get a good look at her face. I had forgotten her endearing dimples and her uncanny likeness to her mother. "Aunt Adele, this is Oralyn Strumpf. Oralyn, Adele Smith." She makes our introduction as she sprints to the back of the van to load my bag. Before I can shake Oralyn's hand, Ginny peers around the open back doors, biting her lip.

"We're in a bit of a fix. We need to rent a car, and I, of course, can't use my credit card, and now we're wary of using Oralyn's." She clasps her hands together and bows her head like a little girl saying her bedtime prayers.

When I booked my flight, I had no intention of accompanying Ginny on this expedition to Nevada. The sole point, as I told Robert, was to fly out and make sure Ginny was not under the influence of anything or anyone, including this Oralyn woman.

"Ginny, what's going on?" I rub my face with both hands. I am tired. I peek into the window and spot baby Laurel, chubby and content, sitting in her well-padded car seat, sucking on a pink pacifier. As for my sister's kid? She is behaving as if she's on an adrenaline rush. The direct opposite of the lethargic young woman I spent time with four months ago.

Again, I wonder. Is this just the thrill of the road? Or is something else driving her? Is she using drugs like Jacob had claimed? I pull up the strap of my Louis Vuitton bag and smooth the wrinkles on my cotton top with the quarter-length sleeves. "What has changed since yesterday?"

"Whelp, the cops are after us," Oralyn says from her perch inside the van, her dimpled elbow resting on the open window.

Ginny slams the back door. "We don't know that, Oralyn."

Oralyn shrugs. "Not the way I see it." She mutters something about a nasty old woman with a motor mouth and a private detective snooping around to find them.

What have I just stepped into? I close my eyes and sigh. "This is insane, Ginny. What is she talking about?" I tilt my head in Oralyn's direction. "Why do you need a rental?"

Ginny moves in my direction and takes my shoulders with both hands. Seeing her in her ripped jeans and form-fitting tee, I am again reminded of Audrey, who loved the latest styles—so different from Mom, and even me back then. Ginny draws back her shoulders, and a calm comes over her.

"Aunt Adele, I will admit to being a little jacked up—not in a bad way, mind you. I owe you an explanation because our situation has changed since yesterday." She glances over her shoulder to see Oralyn, who is massaging her lower extremities. I do not need a pain chart to know she's in misery. A tight grimace pulls at her face.

"Let's find a restaurant to talk things over," Ginny continues. "Oralyn, you can prop your legs and order a bite to eat. We can rent a car later, provided Aunt Adele agrees to help us out." She faces me. "Would that work for you, Aunt Adele?"

Of course, that would work for me. I gravitate to the calm, the well-reasoned. Mistakes happen when emotions take over. I make a mental note to call Audrey, whose number is now stored in my phone—something I did before leaving my apartment—and squeeze into the back seat next to Laurel, not sure of what to expect. One thing is certain, though. A reunion with my sister is not on my life list.

As Ginny navigates the busy roadways, directed by a navigation app on what I assume is Oralyn's phone, I take in the metropolitan area. Edged to the east by the Sandia Mountains, it then sprawls across an open plain in every direction, the terrain covered with tile-roofed houses, Pueblo-themed shopping centers, and big-box stores. Oralyn gripes about the congestion, and I smile to myself. I suppose she has never been to New York City.

We find a bistro close to the center of town, my attention drawn to a large television positioned above the bar. The talking heads are referring to today's market plummet as "Black Tuesday." Most do not have a clue, and neither do the so-called financial experts spouting their nonsense. They seem to be celebrating the bad news, painting worst-case scenarios that would panic anyone.

Including Oralyn.

From the corner of my eye, I notice that the wall-to-wall coverage also transfixes her. She does not strike me as someone who would follow financial news, but her mention of a small pension corrects my first impression. The economic experts, including me, had expected the slippery slide that is the New York Stock Exchange. But that doesn't temper the sting for millions of Americans on fixed incomes. Her crow's feet deepen, and I try to mollify her unease. Like the change in seasons, I tell her, the stock market is cyclical. But no one can predict how long or how deep it will go before it corrects itself. All you can do is hang tight and avoid fear-driven decisions.

"You're right. No sense in worrying," she says. "I can't do a thing about it. Isn't that right, baby girl?" She takes Laurel from Ginny's arms and starts kissing the baby's neck.

"Oralyn Strumpf, you are a baby hog," Ginny teases, showing no interest in the happenings dutifully reported on cable news. Is it her age? More likely, she is overwhelmed by her other challenges. "I bet my aunt would love to get acquainted with Laurel." Ginny gently bites her lip. "Wouldn't you?"

"No. That's okay." I shake my head, but Oralyn catches Ginny's facial expression and places Laurel on my lap. I feel like a usurper of Oralyn's domain. She is good at this. I am not. I've never done kids…or husbands. My closest friends, like me, married their careers. Despite my clumsiness, Laurel soon snuggles in, chuckling, as Oralyn bugs out her eyes and contorts her mouth playing peek-a-boo with a napkin.

What was I thinking? Lulled into believing that baby care might be fun, I start bouncing the baby on my knees. Little Laurel seems to enjoy the ride until she doesn't. "Ugh," I yell, repulsed by what appears to be the regurgitated remains of a full bottle. It now soaks my lap.

"Just a little spit-up. Happens all the time," Oralyn says, pointing to a stain on her blouse before grabbing a rag from her purse. "I should have warned you. I go nowhere without one of these." Without invitation, she starts mopping my besmirched jeans.

"Please stop." I try to stand, pushing her hand from my leg. "Just… Take her." My words come out harsh and overblown, and the baby starts screaming. Before I can fully process what has happened, Oralyn takes Laurel from my outstretched arms and pulls the shrieking baby to her chest.

"Shh, baby girl. It's okay," Oralyn whispers, patting Laurel's back. Within moments, the baby's cries give way to whimpers until she sighs, now content to be in more competent hands.

Embarrassed by my histrionics, I excuse myself for the ladies' room to scrub my jeans properly. I glance at Ginny before standing and slinging my bag over my shoulder. The expression on her face is unreadable. She squeezes Oralyn's shoulder and gives her a small smile, perhaps to reassure her that she did nothing wrong.

"What would I do without you, Oralyn?" she says in a soft voice. "God sent you. Don't you forget it."

My eyes roll as I slip away for the bathroom. I heard enough talk about God growing up. If they want to believe in that nonsense, who am I to argue? One thing is sure, though. No one will upend Ginny's affection for the woman she just met at a small-town diner. And the same goes for Laurel. Oralyn makes that baby happy.

I have never felt so out of my element.

By the time I get back, the only evidence of what amounts to a minor milk spill—albeit processed—is a large, wet spot in an area that attracts attention. I take my seat and notice that Laurel is wearing a clean onesie, and our coffees have arrived, along with a Frisbee-sized cookie for Oralyn, who then regales us with stories about shrinking brains due to a lack of nutrient-rich foods. Ginny laughs but gently steers the conversation to Jacob and the detective whom she suspects Jacob hired to track her down. The update unsettles me. How Ginny stays so composed, I cannot begin to understand. I can't even handle baby vomit.

"Monty thinks we need to get the van off the road and rent a car," Ginny says. "Between Oralyn and me, we have plenty of cash, but don't car rentals require a credit card on file?"

"What would you do with the van?" I ask, fanning the laminated menu in my lap. It is a logical question.

Ginny has a solution for that, too—one of Monty's friends has agreed to garage the van for a few days. I enter his address into my app. He lives north of here in the hinterlands, a lucky break if Ginny is trying to avoid prying eyes. From there, it is just a couple of days of leisurely driving to reach Audrey's.

I take a sip of my coffee and consider the facts at hand. My niece's life has become a cinematic thriller, and she will not get far without a credit card.

"This is how I figure this playing out," I say, now secure in my wheelhouse. "I'll rent a car and make you a secondary driver." I glance at Ginny, who nods. "We'll drop off Oralyn's van and then come back here to spend a night or two." I search for hotels on my phone and book three rooms for two nights in a nice one not far from the bistro.

Ginny and Oralyn lock eyes. I cannot decipher their unspoken communication, wondering if they would prefer to bunk together. Having shared a bedroom with Audrey growing up, I cannot imagine they would mind separate quarters. The togetherness, at least for Audrey and me, made matters worse, and sisterly love went the way of the dodo bird.

"Are these arrangements okay with you?" I then ask, considering how my compulsion for planning and organization could come across as pushy. Oralyn shrugs. And Ginny gives me a thumbs-up. "Great. It's all settled then." I tap the table with an open palm. "I've been thinking, Ginny. Are you in a hurry? Let's take our time," I continue, trying to sound nonchalant, without an agenda even though one exists. "I've never spent time in the Southwest. Seems like an interesting area, and we're booked for two nights. How about you, Oralyn?"

I know why I made the request—I am stalling. I do not want to face my sister. What will we find once we land on her doorstep, and I am forced to confront my role in our estrangement? It is easier to pretend she doesn't exist or blame her for everything that happened. I've done that for years.

Oralyn tips her head to the side and massages her temples. "Sure, why not?" She grabs her fake-leather purse and starts pulling out tourist pamphlets for hot-air balloon rides, ghost tours of Old Town, and visits to the Indian Pueblo Cultural Center or the Sandia Tramway. "What do we do first?"

For the first time since planting both feet in New Mexico, I smile. Maybe this trip won't be so bad, after all. Again, if I believed in God, I might think my arrival here was meant to be. But I will leave those beliefs to Oralyn and Ginny.

CHAPTER TWENTY-TWO

Jacob

Dad is the man. I stand at the back of our Mom-curated reception area, watching him announce his candidacy. Grinning and slapping the backs of his most ardent supporters, he steps up to the podium, clears his throat, and says in his urbane Southern drawl, "We will survive the market crash, and we will emerge stronger." I am about to join in the spirited whistles and handclaps when I receive an incoming call.

Bill is on the line. While I would rather step away and get his update, instinct tells me to stay put. Dad's eagle eyes miss nothing. Why stir the pot and risk a dressing-down now that I have redeemed myself?

Today, he is pleased that I blew that agreement to buy several thousand acres north of Atlanta. Market downturns—as he reminded our investors yesterday afternoon—are a blessing to those who have the resources and wisdom to ride out the inevitable storms. That property and others will start going for fire-sale prices if this rout—so far, the massacre to beat all massacres, if you believe the pundits—continues. Hang tight, he said in that Churchillian oration. Never, never, never give in.

I was the first to applaud, for more reasons than one. Who wants to be poor, and who wants to disappoint Dad?

"You're one of the largest land developers in Georgia," one reporter says when Dad opens the event to media questions. "How do you read the situation?"

Dad seems to grow two inches as he throws his shoulders back. "Market corrections happen. If we keep our cool and make smart decisions, we'll weather the storm—and by that I do include the middle class." I chuckle. These rubes may care about the bourgeois, but people like my father and every other politician on the local and national stages could not give a rat's patoot. The monied aristocrats pull the strings to advance their self-interests.

It's a basic fact of life.

Although my fingers twitch, wondering what Bill has learned, I keep my impulses in check. My old man is a master. He is worthy of my admiration. Compared with his competition—a granola-crunching do-gooder—he has the business mojo to steer Georgia's ship of state. Not the other guy, or so says my dad.

Dad entertains one more question and knocks it out of the park, wrapping up with an outsized smile and humble gratitude. Most of the assembled shuffle out, including employees who were guilted into attending. Since the catered sandwiches and chips, soft drinks, and coffee are long gone, whisked away as soon as Dad took the podium, they have no reason to hang out.

Neither do I.

Before making my escape, I see him jawboning a few stragglers, including Mom, a human barnacle who has attached herself to his side. She must have had a tough morning or needs her eyesight checked. Her eyeshadow lies thick, and her hair looks mussed, like she just rolled out of bed. Interesting. We all have issues.

After walking back to my office, I sit at my desk and dial Bill's number.

"I was just about to call you again. I got a line on Ginny, and you should be pleased." Bill is on speaker, and the faint hum of traffic comes through in the background.

"Hang on for a second." I pull up the app on my phone. Ginny's car has stopped. I zoom in on the screen to check details. It shows a commercial establishment. Is this a car lot? Why would Ginny go there? "What do you have?"

"She's traveling with an older woman named Oralyn Strumpf, a former waitress at the diner you told me to visit. The owner…a guy named Monty Smitherman…didn't offer much, except that Oralyn had left town to visit a brother in Arkansas. He had no idea where Ginny went. But some old woman, you know, one of those nosy types, said she'd seen Ginny and Oralyn driving off Sunday afternoon in a Dodge passenger van. She also mentioned that the two were related somehow. Did you know this?"

How would I know? "Are you sure they're traveling together in a van?"

"Not one hundred percent. Why?"

"Because Ginny drives a Honda, and it's now parked at a car lot outside Chicago."

My jaw clenches so hard my molars ache. No one beats me—no one, least of all that ungrateful, conniving—

A snarl rips from my throat as I slam my fist onto the desk. One swift kick sends my chair skidding into the bookshelf, rattling framed photos until they crash to the floor. This time, my assistant, whom I sense is listening at the door, does not risk even a knock. My chest heaving, I take several giant strides and drop onto the sofa, pressing my palm over my forehead. I force myself to take a breath and then repeat the process. It does not soothe my jangled nerves. After nearly a week, I still have no idea where Ginny is. She is beating me at my own game.

"And you know this because?" Bill seems to be ignoring the commotion and my cursing, interested only in how I might have found the Honda. He waits a beat. "Never mind. Don't tell me; I don't want to know."

I swing my legs to the floor and sit upright on the sofa.

"Where are you?"

"I just pulled into Will Rogers World Airport to return the rental and fly home."

"Change your flight." The command sounds strangled. "I'm offering the same deal as before. Go to Chicago and find out how that car ended up at a car lot and why it's there." I search my brain. Is Ginny planning to sell it? She keeps essential papers, including the title to that piece-of-crap car, inside a cardboard box stored on the closet shelf. I scratch my head. I do not recall seeing it there when I tore through the house after she pulled her Houdini. "Your visit to Chicago shouldn't take long—no more than a few hours at best. You are to call me the minute you talk with someone."

"I think you're making a mistake," he says. "My gut tells me she's with that Oralyn character, in her van. If the diner owner was on the up and up, they could be in Arkansas. I have contacts there. In fact, I have contacts everywhere. Do you want me to call in a favor or two and put the van on their radar? I do have the tag. Or would you like me to focus on leads in Nevada? I'm making some headway there. You decide. It's your coin."

He may be on target, but I will never admit a mistake—a tactic my father has perfected. "I'm paying triple your hourly rate. Go to Chicago, and we'll go from there."

The rest of the day is a blur of tense phone calls, half-finished reports, and watching numbers on my computer screen tumble. I check in with our finance experts, who are running projections that shift minute by minute, recalculating how long we can hold out before making tough decisions. Our investors are jittery. Some dodge my calls entirely, while others give me clipped updates on what they are hearing on the news—contracts frozen, expansions scrapped, budgets slashed to the bone.

Dad, the keeper of the purse, claims we can ride this out, but the talking heads on cable news would drive anyone to question his calm. I call Red to relieve the tension.

I don't like to lose.

CHAPTER TWENTY-THREE

Ginny

Oralyn, who has filled my ear with happy talk since we waved goodbye to Monty at her house in Oklahoma, has gone quiet since my aunt arrived this afternoon. The shift is striking. She frowns and exhales sharply as we debate and settle on our plans, her lips pressed into a tight line. Even when asked her opinion, she keeps her thoughts to herself as we drive back to the city after dropping off her van.

Unusual.

But she sure has taken a shine to the rental, a jet-black Cadillac Escalade, equipped, of course, with satellite radio. For a woman who dislikes technology, it doesn't take her long to preprogram the stations, favoring country and bluegrass. From the rearview mirror, I see Aunt Adele raise her right eyebrow; I hear her deep sigh.

These two live in different universes.

Without asking for my input, Aunt Adele had decided which items to transfer from Oralyn's multi-seat passenger van to the Escalade.

"You don't need this, or these," she said, pointing to the baby seat that Monty insisted I buy at Walmart and Oralyn's plastic souvenir bags. "What's this?" She discovered Monty's storm radio that had been wedged between the seat and console.

"A radio."

"Do we need it?" I shrugged, and she took that as a no. "They can stay in the van. We need to make room."

She was right, of course. Aunt Adele thinks things through. She is a natural-born leader—traits that I can only assume led to her rapid ascension in the corporate world. Granny seemed to take solace in her success.

Other characteristics impress me as well. While not particularly attractive in the traditional sense, like my mother, Aunt Adele makes the most of what she has. Her hair, carefully styled and colored, suits her, and her makeup—subtle but deliberate—draws attention to her deep brown eyes. She dresses with the kind of awareness that comes from experience, choosing outfits that flatter without trying too hard. Time catches up with everyone, even those who take care of themselves. Aunt Adele knows how to meet aging on her terms.

Oralyn, on the other hand, is an unabashed coupon clipper and a lover of kitsch. She takes a fistful of pharmaceutical drugs and eats far too much processed sugary food. My style-conscious aunt would not be caught dead in the elastic-waisted stretch pants, flowered blouses, and comfy, well-worn sneakers that comprise Oralyn's wardrobe, likely bought at Walmart.

To say I'm concerned about Oralyn's change in mood, her withdrawal, is an understatement. I enjoy her whimsy, which became more pronounced with every mile we traveled. Just last night at yet another indistinguishable hotel, I had made a big deal about styling my hair. I threw my head forward, brushing my blonde strands over my crown before giving my head a good shake to let them fall about my face.

Oralyn watched, the corners of her mouth turning up. "Don't hold it against me, but I don't own a hairbrush."

"Well, how do you fix your hair?"

"With these." She wiggled her fingers before demonstrating her technique on her deep-gray, wiry coils.

All she wants is companionship, a chance to spread her wings far from the small town she never left. She revels in being useful, and Laurel and I seem to be satisfying those yearnings. Without fail, my sweet baby opens her mouth wide and giggles when Oralyn enters Laurel's space and stops fussing as soon as Oralyn picks her up, as shown by what happened at the bistro earlier. I can't picture this trip without Oralyn, who enthuses over the sights she sees and the people she meets. As Granny would say, the woman could talk bark off a tree.

She is good for me.

Will I ever feel the same about my aunt? I do not know, but I am certain of this: I will never tell her about my otherworldly encounter with TC. She seems to see the world in black and white. In her ordered world, there is no room for the inexplicable.

We arrive at the higher-end hotel, with the spacious, well-appointed lobby, gift shops, restaurants, and bar—a far cry from our budget-conscious lodgings so far. Aunt Adele checks in, distributes our room keys, and heads for the elevator. She has decided to order room service and catch up on the news, which I have ignored for days now. Snatches I've picked up have convinced me to keep my head buried. I have enough to think about between my mom, Laurel, and keeping my middle-aged travel pals on an even keel. Those two are like oil and water, and I'm the emulsifier. Without me, they wouldn't mix at all.

"Oralyn, how about you? Do you want to go to a restaurant, or would you prefer a night off from me and Laurel?" I throw my arm around her shoulder. "You won't hurt my feelings if you'd like a break. I need some downtime myself."

She gives me a funny look and limps to the bank of elevators. Huh. I should ask what is eating her, but I understand she's under stress, too. She seems uncomfortable around Aunt Adele, and Jacob's machinations have affected her, too. Thanks to him, we had to hide her van in a stranger's garage.

I get to my room and then lie down on the bed next to Laurel. I should call Melinda. She needs an update, and it is closing in on her bedtime.

She answers on the first ring. Her voice is as light as a gentle springtime rain as I fill her in on what has happened over the past few days. "Hey, you might be happy to know that Jacob has gone silent," she says. "But here's the interesting part: A private investigator contacted me with questions about Jacob. I gave him an earful." Melinda chuckles. "The plot sure thickens, doesn't it?"

That it does, and I wonder if the private detective is the same man who hassled Monty. If so, the plot *has* thickened. Although Jacob is the last person I want to think about, I can't help myself. He is now front and center in my thoughts. "What did you tell the investigator?"

"I mainly recounted how Jacob behaved the day he turned up at our place. I hope someone nails that good-for-nothing to the wall." Melinda pauses. "Hey, since when do you have an aunt? I had no idea."

That fast, the conversation turns to my family, and I file her news, figuring it might become important later in this unwanted game with Jacob.

Melinda is somewhat familiar with my upbringing. She has heard stories about Granny, but I never bothered to tell her much about the other two women in my life. What would I have said? One relationship is nonexistent—a source of shame—and the other is skin-deep, or at least it was in the past.

When my aunt would visit Granny and me in Georgia, she would make polite conversation, asking about school and my activities, but she did not ask the follow-up questions that would prompt a quiet kid like me to go beyond one-word replies. She made me think she was watching an hourglass, waiting for the sand to run out so that she could fly back to Manhattan—a place Granny and I had visited *only* once because big-city life had no appeal to Granny.

But as I tell Melinda, Aunt Adele didn't have to rent the car. Yet she did. She changed her plans and joined the brain trust—as Oralyn calls it—perhaps against her better judgment. So here we are. Three women and a baby, thrown together like a load of mismatched laundry.

I say goodbye to Melinda and start channel surfing when someone raps on my door. I glance through the peephole and unlatch the door.

Aunt Adele has scrubbed off her veneer. Her jowls sag next to a pinched mouth. *Oh boy, what's going on?*

"I know Oralyn has her heart set on seeing the sights tomorrow," she says, pushing her way through the open door. "But I think we should leave early." She leans over my bed to caress my sleeping baby and gives the faintest hint of a smile before snatching her hand back as if she touched a red-hot coal. She drops into the overstuffed chair in the corner.

"Why?" I sit cross-legged on the bed.

"Maybe I'm overreacting, but I have a bad feeling." She waves her hand. "Never mind. I should stop torturing myself and watch a comedy instead."

"Back up. What's the problem?" Any lingering thoughts of the detective leave my head entirely.

"I tried your mother's number several times. Her voicemail is full."

"From what little I know of my mother, that doesn't seem unusual."

She doesn't take her eyes off mine. "Your mother and I have had our differences. You're aware of that. But she's my baby sister, and I feel some responsibility for her." She rubs her face with both hands. "And right now, my instinct tells me something is wrong."

A change has come over my aunt. Earlier, she seemed ambivalent about connecting with Mom. Wasn't she the one who suggested that we take our time and see the sights? But I saw through the ruse. She wanted to postpone her reunion with Mom for as long as possible. What changed?

"I don't get it. You weren't in a rush a few hours ago. You know Mom is a flake, irresponsible," I say, and continue my scan of romantic comedies available on a streaming service. I glance at her. "Try again. Maybe she'll answer this time."

Aunt Adele sighs, taps Mom's number, and puts her phone on speaker. My mother's smoky voice, with an accent much like mine, floats across the room. *"Hey there, Audrey here. Leave a message. I'll be sure to get back."* Her voice curls around each word like it has all the time in the world.

Memories flood my mind, one tumbling over the other. I think of the time she called me "sweet pea" and how she would create games for us to play while Jimmy was away, drinking and doing drugs with his irresponsible friends. She endured the beatings to protect my sister and me from the same kind of abuse. A voice, reminiscent of Siri, confirms what Aunt Adele has already concluded: My mother is either ignoring her calls or is too lazy to clear the backlog. I shudder at the third possibility.

Could she be in danger, or even worse…dead?

"Maybe you're right. Let's leave tomorrow morning."

CHAPTER TWENTY-FOUR

Oralyn

Something is wrong with me. I'm always hungry, even though I eat a lot. My face is constantly in the feedbag. So why do my pants sag around my once-formidable backside, and why don't my buttons strain at the midriff anymore? I make a cup of coffee with the in-room Keurig and stretch out on my king-sized bed with the fancy sheets. I could take a nap.

My eyes are drifting shut when I hear a tap on the door. I mutter, annoyed, but get up anyway, hobbling in my compression stockings to see who needs to see me so darn bad. We planned to rendezvous in the lobby at ten o'clock this morning. I glance at my watch. It's only seven-thirty, which means I still have time to get more shut-eye.

"Where's Laurel?" I ask, seeing Ginny standing alone in the hallway.

Ginny's brow bunches up. "Uh, she's with Aunt Adele."

"Harrumph. I know she's kin, but she doesn't give me the warm fuzzies. Baby girl is probably screaming her lungs out." I turn my back on Ginny and shuffle to my bed. Glancing over my shoulder, I see Ginny is hot on my heels.

"Okay, what's with the cranky mood?" she asks, taking a seat next to me, her face inches from mine. "I came to let you know we've decided to leave for Nevada this morning before checkout time, but you need to tell me what's going on. Something is bothering you."

I ignore her question. "Your aunt reserved our rooms for two nights. Are you telling me we're not sightseeing today?" I sound like a spoiled brat. "She sure knows how to call the shots—the bossiest woman I've ever met. She's worse than the biddy."

Ginny looks at me through narrowed eyes, but concern is written all over her face. "I couldn't agree with you more, but that's Aunt Adele's way." Her hand covers my forehead. "How are you feeling?" I shrug. "Back in a second."

I gulp down the last of my coffee and snatch a bottle of water from the nightstand, only stopping when the crumpling of plastic tells me it's empty. *Why am I so thirsty? Why do I want to rip someone's head off?* I understand my anger toward my chief nemesis, whose flapping lips landed my van in a garage. But what about Ginny? Her aunt? Well, I'm not so sure about the aunt; she always seems to wrinkle her nose as if she's smelling poo when I'm around. Forgive me, Lord.

When Ginny returns with a blood-pressure monitor—one of those manual thingamabobs—I am still sprawled on my unmade bed, my feet propped on a pillow, seconds from going back to sleep. From my window, I can see clear skies dotted with puffy clouds, making it a perfect day for taking in the sights. However, I don't feel like my usual, eager self, and I'll admit it.

Today, sightseeing would be akin to having your molars pulled without local anesthesia.

"Have you been taking your meds?" she asks, velcroing the inflatable cuff onto my upper arm.

"Of course, I'm taking my meds." Air fills the cuff, biting into my arm. I can feel the blood pumping through my veins. "Where did that come from?" I point to the blood-pressure gadget.

"My satchel."

"That cloth bag you carry around? My gosh, girl, what else do you have in that thing? Where's the wine bottle?"

"Rolled up in a T-shirt inside my suitcase. Now hush." She doesn't indulge my complaints or peevish observations; instead, she turns her attention to the pressure gauge, her movements sure and steady. When she slowly loosens the valve, I catch the way her eyes flick between the gauge and my face, measuring something beyond blood pressure. The cuff fully deflates before she delivers her verdict.

"Your pressure is okay. But you aren't yourself this morning, Oralyn. You haven't been yourself for a day or so."

She tilts her head sideways, waiting for my response, and then spies the empty water bottles jammed into the trash can. "I'm glad you're drinking water, but your consumption seems excessive." Ginny scans the rest of my now prone body. She sucks in her top lip. "You've lost some weight, too."

I shake my head to her other questions about blurred vision, tingling, numbness, and unexplained sores that refuse to heal.

"Oralyn, you need a blood test."

"For what? I feel fine," I lie.

"Your blood sugar. You're showing signs of diabetes, and you don't want to mess with that." She takes my hand. "I'm taking you to an urgent care. If something is wrong, we need to deal with it now."

In my mind's eye, I see myself tucking into cookies, pastries, and fried foods—the stuff I crave—and my own doctor's stern warnings when I crossed into diabetes territory some time ago. I can imagine Adele's looks of disgust when Ginny informs her of her suspicions. My poor choices have gotten me in this pickle, and instead of being a help, I have become a burden. Will they send me packing? I do not want to go home to my empty house.

"You said you and Adele wanted to saddle up early. We don't have time for a blood test. And what's more, it usually takes days to get lab results if this place is anything like home."

Ginny had been standing but took a seat next to me, covering my hands with hers. "You just don't get it." She gives me the tiniest of smiles. "You're important to me. We're not going anywhere until you see a doctor. Furthermore, you will be making significant changes starting today—and I will be Nurse Ratched."

I swallow hard, not quite sure what to do with this—this steady, unwavering care that comes without conditions or condemnation. My first instinct is to pull away, crack a joke, and act like her concern doesn't fill some hollow part of me. But I don't. Because it does. Instead, I nod at her and grab my purse with hands that feel clumsy and not quite my own.

How will Adele react to this change in plan? Will she raise her eyebrow and look down her nose at me, the frumpy, unsophisticated rube who has complicated her well-laid plans?

I can't believe that woman is related to Ginny. *Why am I so thirsty?*

CHAPTER TWENTY-FIVE

Adele

Baby Laurel and I have reached an understanding. Although I don't engage in baby talk like Oralyn does, I have what she loves best. Laurel is gulping her bottle and making happy sounds when Ginny and Oralyn show up at my door. Ginny's tight-lipped expression tells me something is wrong. I can confirm this just by looking at Oralyn; her skin appears clammy, and she seems short of breath.

"I'm taking Oralyn to a clinic," Ginny says. "Would you please watch Laurel? It could take a while."

"Absolutely." I do not dare interrupt Laurel's mealtime and use my chin to keep the bottle in place as I walk over to the nightstand, grab the key fob, and hand it to Ginny. I look up and down the carpeted corridor. "Let's not have this conversation in the hallway." I open the door wide. "What's going on?"

Oralyn squeezes past me and drops onto the edge of my bed without even stealing a glance at the baby.

"Go on, tell her," Oralyn snaps. "I don't have the energy."

Ginny tilts her head to the side, as if she is unsure of what to think or say.

"Tell her."

Ginny and I exchange looks. Although I haven't spent much time with Oralyn, you would have to be deaf, blind, and dumb not to detect a change in her.

"What do you think is wrong?" Glancing at Oralyn, I notice her shooting daggers at me. *What have I done to her?* Getting on the road was my desire last night, but I am not that hard-hearted. Of course, her health concerns take precedence over my own desires.

"I'll explain later," Ginny says under her breath, her eyebrows arched in perfect half circles. She places Laurel's diaper bag on the floor and starts rattling off instructions, repeating some as if I can't handle basic childcare. Admittedly, my experience is limited, but not entirely nonexistent. It's just a bit rusty, like a tool forgotten in a shed. I *had* helped Mom feed, diaper, and take Audrey on walks in the stroller. She was my treasured doll, so pretty and sweet. That is, until Daddy died, and she turned into a little monster.

"Got it, Ginny. Don't worry."

She clasps her hands together and then drops them to her sides before glancing at Oralyn, who is studying her sneakers. "Okay, then. We'd best be going."

Laurel finishes her bottle, and, after a gentle thumping, she belches without incident. Even the clean diaper is straight and fastened securely—and it took only a few attempts. Her belly gets tickled, and her outfit is changed. The ruffled dress and matching pantaloons, found in Ginny's diaper bag, remind me of baby Audrey. Their resemblance to each other is striking and a little unnerving. My stupid sister. She should be here enjoying this sweet baby. Not me.

"It's belly time," I say, imitating Ginny and Oralyn's mothering techniques. Laurel is positioned on her abdomen, within reach of her rattles and stuffed animals, which are assembled on the play mat. She straightens her arms and begins to rock. Then, in one swift motion, she tips, teeters, and lands flat on her back. What do you know? The baby just achieved a developmental first, and Ginny missed it. I get down on my knees and clap like she's riddled an algebraic equation.

"You did it, Laurel. Won't your mommy be surprised? You're a big girl now." Laurel shows me her swollen, still-toothless gums, grabbing her feet and bringing them to her mouth. I am still clapping when the phone rings.

"You wouldn't believe it," I tell Robert.

"Wouldn't believe what?"

"The baby rolled over for the first time."

He laughs and tells me he would give up his theater tickets—Broadway shows being one of our passions—to see my maternal instincts in action. He is in a good mood, pleased that I decided to join Ginny on her road trip. "You need to settle differences with Audrey, too," he said when I told him about my plans. "Life is short." His call lifts my spirits, but I sense he has a reason for contacting me so early.

"Have you heard from your sister?"

"Her voicemail is full, and she's not picking up," I say. "I got a little dramatic last night, thinking the worst. But ignoring phone calls is Audrey's MO. Anyway, we'd planned to leave this morning, but Oralyn is sick. Ginny just left to take her to one of those walk-in clinics."

Robert is nothing if not polite. A native Southerner, too, he adheres to time-honored niceties. Even though no one could know the specifics of Oralyn's ailments, he asks anyway, urging me to give her his best, to feel better. His mother raised him right. So did mine. But unlike me, he has not forgotten his roots or tried to eradicate any evidence of his upbringing.

"Do you remember showing me a photo of your niece before you left?" he asks next, out of left field.

"Of course, why?"

"And didn't you say Ginny is a clone of her mother?"

"Why are you asking a million questions, Robert?" He is working up to something in that slow, drawn-out way of his, and I wish he would get on with it.

"Good grief, Adele, why are you so impatient?" He sighs. "I saw a video, something originally posted on Instagram yesterday by a woman named Peaches. *This* woman is a spitting image of Ginny—the hair, eye color, and the dimples. Everything. She looks older, of course, but if I were a wagering man, I'd say she is related. She sounds like a Southern girl through and through."

Instagram? When did he open an account? Furthermore, why would a woman named Peaches send him a video? My puritanical side rears up, or is it a touch of jealousy?

"Back up, Robert. You have some explaining to do."

"Ha. I bet you'd love knowing how the video came into my possession." He laughs. "Unfortunately, it's a dull story." His voice is melodic and comforting as he tells me about a buddy he had gone to lunch with after taking me to the airport. "He's a Vegas regular and follows a few female bartenders on social media. Just my mention of your trip fired his engines. This morning, he sent the video of Peaches. Want to see it?"

Within seconds, I hear the ping and put him on speaker before tapping the icon.

"Hey, guys. Peaches here," the woman drawls in a breathy voice, leaning closer to the camera to give her fans a close-up of her bountiful cleavage, unmistakably the handiwork of a plastic surgeon. "Get down to the Cork & Barrel. The jackpots are flying." Strands of her bottle-blonde hair fall across her eyes. She smiles seductively as she sweeps the hair off her face. "The machines are hot, in more ways than one." She winks. The video ends.

My sister—no doubt.

At first glance, an unknowing observer might think that the head-turning Peaches is decades younger, but I know better. Audrey crossed the half-century mark about a year ago, and no amount of foundation, eyeshadow, or false lashes can hide the relentless passage of time. I wonder what Daddy would think of his baby girl—his little "Pixie"—now. My mother would have buried her head in scripture, which was always her go-to response when it came to Audrey.

"Well?" Robert's voice drifts across the ether. "Your sister, right?"

"Yes, my sister—the Dixie-Pixie performing in Vegas."

"Whoa. Hide your talons; they're dangerous."

He is right, of course. I am too old to let old resentments simmer like a witch's brew. Yet, they linger. Bitter memories of my childhood flash through my mind: Mom and I clear supper dishes at night while Audrey dances in the living room, begging Daddy in her angelic voice to turn off the TV and tell her a story. I can still hear his deep chuckle as he sweeps her onto his lap… *"Once upon a time, in the land of Nod lived a peach of a girl named Pixie. She was a gift from God…"*

It was the same routine every night.

For him, it was easy to reserve affection and stories for my baby sister. God, or whoever runs the universe, had not made me cute and charming. He made me responsible, and it seemed so unfair. Skating through life, depending on my looks and personality to get by, would never be a possibility for me. Only beautiful people enjoy that privilege.

"Well, at least she's not hurt or dead," I say. "I can't believe that thought crossed my mind."

"Adele Smith, get over yourself," Robert says with force, which shakes me a little because he uses that voice rarely, if ever. "Your sister has nothing over you. We all have gifts. You're smart and attractive. She is gorgeous. Big deal. Like I said, lay it to rest." His ability to see my heart astounds me. "Call me later, okay?" The line goes dead, and I stare at the phone in disbelief.

Did he just hang up on me?

The baby gurgles from her play mat, and I sweep her into my arms before lying down on my bed—the little one snuggled at my side—to consider Robert's rebuke.

Even though I don't want to, I need to call my sister. I glance at my wristwatch. It is not quite noon her time, and maybe she will pick up this time. Then again, perhaps she won't. Audrey, Peaches, or whoever, probably screens her calls, and I should not blame her if she chooses to ignore mine. Growing up, she had gotten a full dose of my self-righteous moralizing and unsolicited advice—all rooted in jealousy. There you go—the truth. I enjoyed feeling superior to her.

I never thought retirement would dunk me headfirst into self-reflection, much less have me dusting off old wounds before I even had time to dabble in watercolor painting or join a book club. Taking personal inventory, which began in New York the night after my fight with Ginny, is tiring and unpleasant. I have made many mistakes. What did my mother always say? "Lamenting what you don't have, Adele, prevents you from appreciating what you do have. We all have talents to offer."

An overwhelming fatigue engulfs me. My eyelids begin to drift shut before I fall into a fitful sleep—the baby warm and cuddly against my body—only to be awakened several hours later by a harsh knock on the door.

CHAPTER TWENTY-SIX

Jacob

Bill, the investigator, has no one to blame but himself for lighting my fuse a day after Dad's announcement. "Why don't you have answers?" I shout, not caring who hears me. In the hunt for Ginny's Honda, Bill claims to have discovered the car lot in a derelict Chicago neighborhood, but he hasn't spotted the car itself. The lot is mostly vacant, surrounded by a tall chain-link fence wrapped in razor wire and posted with *"No Trespassing"* signs.

"Climb over the fence," I shout, pacing my office and venting my frustration with a few choice expletives I usually reserve for Ginny. "Her car is there. Find out who owns the lot; someone must own it. You have the resources—get to the bottom of my missing girlfriend. She could be in trouble."

The connection goes silent.

"Are you still there?"

"You know, I have a bad feeling about you," Bill says, his voice sounding like subdued thunder. "I did a little digging into your background. Made some calls. Your girlfriend isn't missing; she bailed on you, dude. And for her sake, I hope you never find her. Keep your dirty blood money. I'm done."

The line goes dead.

My head throbs as I lie on the sofa, massaging my temples while debating whether to call him back to apologize or hire another detective. I glance at the broken clock face, which seems to taunt me with reminders of my failures. A ceramic statue—yet another expensive gift from Mom—catches my eye. I hurl it, and my aim couldn't be more precise. The pendulum dangles for a moment before thumping to the hardwood floor.

Good. I hate that clock.

It reminds me of Mom. Instead of protecting me from Dad's relentless put-downs while I was growing up, she either sided with him or, worse, said nothing at all. Where was she when Dad sent me off to that well-known New England boarding school popular among wealthy northeastern elites? Good grief. I was barely out of diapers.

"Oh, Jacob, you'll be fine," she told me during a rare visit home when I complained, begging to attend a private school closer to Atlanta. I felt lonely living so far away. My family had money and social status, as did my classmates; however, I never quite fit in, no matter how much I tried to ingratiate myself. My accent, my manners, and my Southern ways set me apart, making me fair game to the northern bluebloods who rarely, if ever, ventured across the Mason-Dixon line.

Ruffling my hair, Mom, already dressed for one of her charity events, reassured me as she glanced at her watch. "I miss you, too, but your dad knows best. Think of the connections you can make."

The long and short of it? At school, I belonged to the wrong tribe, and at home, I was an unlovable pariah. On both counts, I felt powerless to change the situation. I had to learn how to survive.

As I step out of my office, I notice my assistant sitting at her desk with her head bowed, focused on the contents of a drawer. She looks up, pinching her lips, clearly wishing she could be anywhere but working for me at Peach Street Holdings. However, we pay her well, and those golden handcuffs have effectively shackled her to her desk. There's a sense of satisfaction in reminding her of this.

"Your annual review is coming up. Make sure that the clock is gone by the time I get back."

Rivulets of sweat have soaked my shirt by the time I dip into my favorite downtown eatery for a drink. Afternoon imbibing is not a habit of mine, but I down the shot of Grey Goose before ordering another.

The bartender raises his eyebrows.

"Wife problems," I confess, twirling the spirits before tossing them back. The alcohol has gone straight to my head, loosening my lips and sense of time. "She left me."

"Well, if I were you, bro, I'd call your wife's mother," the bartender advises. "When my wife left me, she hightailed it for Mommy. Mother-daughter relationships run deep." He wipes the counter and asks if I would like another shot.

"I don't have my mother-in-law's phone number. Hell, I haven't even met her. I think she lives in Las Vegas." The bartender crinkles his brow, probably trying to riddle why a married man wouldn't know his mother-in-law, let alone her address. Let him wonder. It is not his business. "As for the drink, no thanks. I'll take the check."

After paying the bill, I stumble toward the men's room, making a wobbly beeline for the sink. The tap water feels warm on my face as I lean into the mirror. My eyes are bloodshot, and my hair is disheveled. I do not like the man reflecting at me in the mirror. Maybe it is time to cut my losses. As I have reminded myself many times before, the world is full of women who appreciate what I have to offer.

Screw Ginny. She is an ingrate who does not deserve me.

The bartender is behind the bar when I walk past, headed for the exit. "Hey, Jacob. Before you go…"

I stop, noticing the restaurant has cleared out. I roll my eyes. Can't he see I am in no mood for conversation?

"Didn't you say that your mother-in-law might live in Sin City?"

"Yes, something like that," I say, crossing my arms. "Why?"

"I have a buddy, the operations manager of a Vegas tavern, with locations all over town." He pulls out his wallet and extracts a business card. "Give him a call. Please mention my name. He knows everyone. He might know your mother-in-law. You never know. It's worth a shot."

Curious, I close the space between us and accept the proffered card, emblazoned with the corporate logo above the manager's name and contact info. The flipside includes the insignias of its many properties. For some reason, my eyes fixate on a tavern called the Cork & Barrel. A feeling comes over me like the gods are smiling. I straighten my posture and pocket the card before shaking the barkeep's hand. "You're a good man. I'll give your buddy a shout tomorrow."

"Better yet, how about I make your introduction?" He grabs his phone from beneath the counter. His fingers fly across the screen as he texts. "Done. Let me know how things turn out. We men need to stick together."

"Right," I reply, with more sincerity than normal.

My watch says it's late afternoon. The sidewalk shimmers in the heat, and sweat collects along my hairline. I call Dad and give him a plausible excuse for my earlier disappearance, which had prompted a flurry of calls and texts. Anything related to work usually brings him down from his high horse, as do compliments. I congratulate him on his flawless performance during his press conference, emphasizing that no one is as skillful as he is. Blah, blah, blah. But it does the trick.

Driving is not an option, given the vodka shots I consumed, and I cannot run the risk of getting pulled over for drunk driving. I vow never to overindulge again. Under the influence of alcohol, it is too easy to surrender control of situations and people.

Even so, I could use a pick-me-up—something to take my mind off Ginny.

A skinny-dip in the backyard pool would restore body and soul, and so would the loving attention from the one woman who will do anything for me. I call an Uber and then an often-dialed number.

Red answers on the first ring.

The cloud has lifted. I am back in the driver's seat. If Ginny wins, I lose, and that is not happening. The pursuit of her resumes once more.

CHAPTER TWENTY-SEVEN

Audrey

My voicemail is full. I should have cleared it days ago, but I never got around to it. I was too busy—pouring drinks, playing Keno, and losing money. This is the story of my life.

I am lying on my king-sized bed, wearing a pair of shorts and a snug, deep-scooped T-shirt—the same clothes I had on yesterday. My head is throbbing, and I can't think clearly, but it's too early to mix myself a drink. I have promised to cut back on morning drinking and avoid the hair of the dog.

So, I do what I always do: I scan social media and read comments on the video I posted yesterday. Some make me laugh. Most make me sick. Men are pigs—but to my thinking, it is a small price to pay. The videos and attention from the men I serve at the tavern bring in business, as shown by the twenties, fifties, and Benjamins strewn across the nightstand like confetti on New Year's Eve.

This is a good thing.

My rent is due, and as usual, I am short.

The phone rings, jarring my nerves. Through bleary eyes, I make out the name: Angel. She is a young, very pretty coworker who lives up to her name. Unlike me and every other female bartender I know, she has not succumbed to the evil influences that make Vegas, Vegas. She keeps it clean—a bona fide *Rebecca of Sunnybrook Farm* in a town that worships money, sex, and rock 'n' roll. She hustles drinks only because the money is good—a means to an end that involves law school and her own practice. I don't expect her to hang around long. Good for her.

I swipe my thumb across the screen quickly to answer.

"What's up?" I ask, using my left arm to block the blindingly bright light pouring through the bedroom shades. What time is it? Better question: How did I get home? I only remember quaffing free shots after my shift ended at eleven o'clock last night. One of Cork & Barrel's regulars hit a six-figure jackpot and shared the wealth. "I think I'll lie low today."

"Probably a good idea," Angel says. "Things got a little wild last night."

"What did I do?"

"Do you want to know?"

"Hold on." I roll out of bed, thinking a cup of joe will clear my head. "I'm putting you on speaker. Need to make a pot of coffee." I weave down the hallway and spot the Kahlua and handle of vodka, like good soldiers keeping watch on the kitchen counter. Forget the coffee. With shaking hands, I mix a Black Russian and take a sip, ignoring my vow to hold off for a few more hours. *Ahh. Just what the doctor ordered.* "What were you saying?"

"I asked if you wanted to know what happened last night."

She is patient with me. For some reason, she has not given up on me yet, but that's just a matter of time. Before too long, she will bail on me…or I'll bail on her. More likely than not, it will be me who ends the friendship, especially if she starts pressuring me about my lifestyle choices. I am a runner.

Ask my family.

Ask Ginny.

Angel has no idea of Ginny's existence, and what would she think of me if I told her?

"Go ahead. Tell me what I did. You're gonna tell me anyway, right?" I laugh.

She does not share in my mirth.

"You threw a drink at one of the big spenders and then passed out. You fell off the stool, like Humpty Dumpty. All the king's horses and all the king's men couldn't put you back together again. And your timing couldn't have been worse. Danny stopped by to check on things and saw the whole thing."

She is referring to my boss, Danny Mason, who is known for his stealthy pop-ins to ensure employees maintain some degree of professionalism. While staff might enjoy a few cocktails and spend hours playing the *"Bartender Five"* on Keno after shifts, he will not tolerate sloppy drunkenness. An employee gets three strikes, and then they are out.

I rest my head on the counter for a moment and try to remember how many warnings he has already given me. One? Two? I take another sip.

"Was he angry?" I ask. I can't think of anything better to say because my phone, sitting on the countertop set on speaker, is distracting me. I hear the vibrations buzz against the surface as another call comes through. I lift the phone closer, squinting to focus my eyes. *Huh. What does Adele want?* She called yesterday. I snicker to myself. I do not know because my voicemail is full. The joke is on her. Another day without hearing her condescending voice is a tender mercy.

"Of course, he wasn't happy. You made a fool of yourself." Angel's voice wafts through the speaker. She does not mince words. "But Danny is decent. He scraped you up off the floor and then carried your dead weight to his car. We both tucked you into bed."

I can't remember any of it.

"Thanks, I guess." I don't want to hear more and change the subject. "It's Wednesday, right?"

She affirms and reminds me that it is my day off.

"You should expect a call from him. He wants to talk." Angel pauses, and in my mind's eye, I can see her biting her lip, debating whether to spill what is really on her mind. "I'm worried about you. This isn't the first time you've blacked out and gotten belligerent. Audrey, are you listening?" Her voice sounds thick with concern. "You might lose your job."

Only work colleagues and former boyfriends know my Christian name, which is a lesson learned two decades ago after driving across the country in my battered Chevy to try my chances in the land of make-believe. I was determined to reinvent myself and leave my past behind. Within a month, I was on my way, landing a job at a popular pool club. The job was easy, and the tips were even better. All I had to do was show up on time, wear a skimpy bikini, chat up the club's well-heeled male patrons, and ply them with drinks.

To my delight, I had talent. I was good at cavorting with these mostly married men who treated me to gifts and compliments. One even paid the plastic surgeon who had enlarged my breasts. This was a big mistake on my part. That guy started demanding far more than an occasional romp in bed. He hounded me and told me that I owed him. Who did I think I was? I was just a fresh piece of meat in a town that devoured girls like me. Scared, I quit my job and never heard from him again.

Even so, the experience rattled me, evoking memories of the bad old days with Jimmy. With him, my girls and I had been lambs led to slaughter—both literally and figuratively. If I wanted to become independent and reclaim Ginny, my goals at the time, I had to get savvier about working in the gaming industry, which seemed to be my only career choice. After all, where else could a high school dropout like me pull down a six-figure income by serving drinks?

Nowhere.

That's when Peaches came to life and Audrey Smith went into hiding. But as they say, wherever you go, there you are. My fictitious name did not change a thing.

"Of course, I'm listening to you, Angel." I put on my accent, which usually amuses this native New Yorker. "Thanks for the heads-up, but don't worry about me. Danny and I go way back. I'll get this straight. See you tomorrow."

My drink sloshes onto the tiled floors as I ping-pong off the walls back to my bedroom. I close the blinds and welcome the dark and the hum of the air-conditioning unit. Crawling into my unmade bed, I smoke a cigarette and polish off my drink while debating whether to return Adele's call.

Instead, my thoughts turn to Ginny. I do not know my child. I abandoned her to Mom's care, rationalizing that she was better off without me until I could get my act together, which, of course, never happened. That little voice inside my head—the one that reveled in reminding me of my mistakes—convinced me I would never amount to much. Mom never understood me, preferring Adele's company over mine, but I was certain she would take good care of Ginny.

Time marched on.

My one attempt to communicate with Ginny—a postcard a few years ago—probably made matters worse. She didn't write back, but who could have blamed her? And my shame deepened. When Adele called to tell me about Mom's accident, I gave her a lame excuse for why I would not attend the funeral. The truth was, I could not bear seeing my daughter. She was a living, breathing testimonial to my failures as a human being.

I burrow beneath the blanket and cry myself to sleep.

CHAPTER TWENTY-EIGHT

Ginny

On our way to the medical clinic, Oralyn grips her stomach.

"Pull over," she gasps. "I'm going to get sick."

I steer the Escalade onto the shoulder and lower her window. She hangs her head out of the window and loses whatever was in her stomach. Taking her to a walk-in clinic is a bad idea. She needs medical attention *now.*

Oralyn mops her mouth with a napkin I hand her, and I throw the car into gear—pedal to the metal. The tires scream. *Where did I see that hospital? Did we pass it?* I smack my forehead. *Think. Think. Think.*

"I'm so thirsty, Ginny," Oralyn mutters. Her skin looks flushed. "Why am I so thirsty?"

I have no time to waste. I can't risk getting lost in an unfamiliar city as Oralyn's condition worsens.

I take an exit ramp, spot a shopping center, and dial nine-one-one on my phone.

"What is your emergency?" a woman asks, her voice calm. I collect my composure and describe Oralyn's symptoms and our location. "An ambulance is on its way."

Oralyn has slumped over her seat belt, which has aggravated her tortured breathing. I sprint to the passenger-side door and lower her seat. Now she is reclined, and I take her hand. It feels dry to the touch.

"You're going to be fine, Oralyn," I whisper into her ear. "You've got this."

"Why are you sending me back home?" Oralyn's eyes look terrified. Her words are slurred. "Baby girl is crying. She needs me."

"Baby girl wants you to get better, and so do I." I kiss Oralyn's hand and close my eyes. *Please, Lord, heal this sweet woman.*

The wailing of a siren tells me help has arrived. Two broad-chested men bound from the ambulance and steer the stretcher toward the Escalade. The commotion attracts attention. The lookers gawk but keep a respectable distance.

"Did you call in the emergency?" the paramedic asks me. I nod and step aside to give the EMT room to do his job. "Dispatch said she's fatigued and agitated and complains of extreme thirst. Did she vomit?"

"That's correct." I wrap my arms around my midriff, mainly to give them something to do.

"Do you know her medications? Or if she's had an infection, pneumonia, a urinary tract infection, or sepsis?"

"She takes a blood thinner and medication to control cholesterol and high blood pressure. I've observed no signs of infection, but she has been under some emotional stress. Frankly, I believe she's showing complications of diabetes. Which type I don't know. I doubt she knows. I've noticed a frequent need to urinate, but the confusion, vomiting, and extreme dehydration came on quickly."

He raises his eyebrows.

"I'm an emergency-room nurse. I've dealt with this before."

He nods and turns his attention to the EMT leaning over the prostrate, unmoving Oralyn.

"Ma'am, Miss Oralyn, can you hear me? What's going on?" the EMT asks in a firm but soothing voice.

No answer. Has she slipped into a coma? My hand flies to my mouth. *No. No. No.*

"I'm going to check your blood sugar, okay?" He swabs her finger with an alcohol pad and performs a finger stick. Within seconds, he has results. "Her blood-sugar levels are sky high, and her breath smells fruity." He then uses his curled knuckles to rub her sternum, a technique that should elicit an immediate reaction from an alert, conscious patient.

Not a yelp. Oralyn is still.

"Get her on the stretcher." The paramedic moves fast, brushing me aside to help his partner load Oralyn onto the rolling cot. "Go. Go. Go."

For the first time, I am scared for Oralyn. Her varicose veins are the least of her problems. She should be at home under a doctor's care, not on a trip across the country to see my mother, who has never shown any interest in seeing me. As I run alongside the stretcher before they roll her into the back of the ambulance, I speak a prayer: *Please, Lord, don't let Oralyn die.*

"I'm sorry, ma'am, but I don't think you should ride with us and leave your vehicle unattended," the paramedic says, his eyes scanning the Escalade and then the surrounding neighborhood. "We've had a string of car thefts lately." He takes Oralyn's blood pressure, attaches EKG pads, and covers her face with an oxygen mask. An IV is already delivering saline to her fluid-depleted body.

"Oh. I wasn't aware of the car thefts. I'm unfamiliar with Albuquerque." I lift my hands, palms open, and glance around the parking lot. "Where are you taking her?"

"Presbyterian. Five or six minutes away," the EMT says. "Follow us."

He slams the doors, and I sprint to the Escalade. The sirens wail. Motorists get out of the way, creating catawampus configurations on and off the highway as we speed past. I feel like Moses and his people crossing the parted Red Sea. My foot presses down on the accelerator. I pound the steering wheel. *I* cannot *lose sight of that ambulance.*

Thoughts rush through my mind, and I feel an urge to throttle that stubborn old woman who likely ignored her symptoms and her doctor's advice. I am also upset with myself. Why didn't I see this sooner? The warning signs were there—agitation, unquenchable thirst, and a sudden loss in weight despite her eating more than usual. *How did I miss these signs?*

One thing is sure: Oralyn and I make a great team. Both of us think that if you ignore your problems long enough, they might go away, but they never go away.

They compound.

CHAPTER TWENTY-NINE

Ginny

Oralyn's belongings are in a plastic bag at my feet. I am waiting for an ICU doctor to update me on Oralyn's condition. The wait is *endless.*

I flip through a magazine, but I am too distracted to read the articles. Even the photos hold no interest. I stretch and roll my neck to work out the kinks, deciding to ride the elevator down to the cafeteria to get something to eat or a bottle of water—anything to break the monotony.

"Ginny Carmichael?" A balding, bespectacled man approaches, wearing light blue scrubs, a color popular in hospital settings because the hue promotes calmness and a sense of professionalism and cleanliness. I am anything but calm myself.

"Yes." I stand and offer my hand, searching his face for answers.

He smiles—a good sign. "Oralyn is doing much better. We want to keep her for observation for the next day or two."

I breathe a sigh of relief. "Thank God. When can I go in and visit?"

"Now, if you'd like." He glances at his watch. "But first, let's talk." He guides me to two overstuffed chairs in the corner of the ICU waiting room, illuminated by table lamps.

Nothing he says surprises me. Type 2 diabetes typically afflicts older, mostly sedentary people who lean toward obesity. Oralyn checks the boxes as memories of her habits invade my mind. *"Me, take a walk? Forget it. My legs hurt."* How many times did she say this as she stretched out on her bed after eating a big dinner?

"She's quite the character." The doctor raises his eyebrows. "At first, she claimed she hadn't been diagnosed, but then admitted she'd tipped past pre-diabetic levels some time ago and ignored her doctor's advice. Appears diabetes runs in her family."

He taps his top lip with his finger. "What is your relationship with her? Are you a daughter, granddaughter, or something else?"

I consider bending the truth, but I don't, recalling the fabrications I had told Jacob as well as those Oralyn had made up—another example of how we ignore our problems and hope they'll go away. "No, we're friends."

He rubs his jaw. "She arrived confused, but her mental acuity is improving. She keeps saying she's on a long overdue vacation, the adventure of her life, and has no intention of cutting it short." He cups his head in both hands. "Are you a nurse? She says you are."

"I am, but what do you think? We're driving to Nevada, but she lives in Oklahoma. Should she go home?"

"Let's visit that question tomorrow." He slaps his thighs before standing. "She keeps asking about you. Go." He points to the double doors leading to the ICU. "We don't need her getting anxious on top of everything else."

I exhale a breath I hadn't realized I was holding and nod in thanks. As I walk past him, I notice the young woman at the ICU desk watching me with a knowing look, as if she has seen this scene unfold countless times before. I offer her a small smile and step out into the corridor, searching my cloth bag for the burner. I need to inform Shannon about her aunt's medical emergency.

The phone rings twice before she picks up—a blessing. No one wants to repeat bad news twice—once in a voicemail and then again in an actual conversation.

"I think a come-to-Jesus is warranted, don't you?" Shannon's sentiments match mine exactly. "Did she tell you that her mother lost a toe because of diabetes? Given all that, I'm surprised she would ignore her symptoms."

"Shannon, she never even told me about her condition. My goodness—" Worst-case scenarios spin through my head.

"Whelp, she mentioned it to me in passing, acting like it wasn't serious." Shannon sighs. "I guess not. She's a mess… Look, I'm flying out tomorrow, and I'll talk to her then." Our goodbyes said, she hangs up.

The ICU's double doors open, and I am directed to a dimmed room across from the nurses' station. Except for the rhythmic whooshing and beeping of the heart monitor and IV pump delivering a fluid holding insulin and electrolytes, I only hear Oralyn's snuffling. She looks helpless, dressed in a hospital gown, her gray coils fanned out on the pillow, the covers pulled up to her chest. I don't want to disturb her, but she must sense my presence.

Her eyes open. "I bet you're wanting to kick me to the curb." Her voice sounds tired, defeated. "When are they springing me? And then what?"

"Let's get you better first, okay?" I lean down and kiss her cheek. "Shannon is flying in tomorrow. We'll talk then."

She nods but struggles to keep her eyes from drifting shut. "I owe Adele an apology. Tell her I'm sorry for being an old crank." She falls asleep.

* * *

By the time I park and ride the hotel elevator to Aunt Adele's floor, it is closing in on the dinner hour. I knock on my aunt's door. Moments pass before she unlatches her lock and opens the door. She looks frightened; her face is pale and drawn tight, as if she has seen something that has rattled her to the core.

"What time is it?" She ushers me into the room quickly. "I fell asleep." Her voice quakes.

"You look upset. What happened?"

She waves a dismissive hand. "Nothing." A puzzled expression must cross my face because she quickly adds, "Nothing to worry about, Ginny, honestly… What's that?" She points toward my hand.

Something happened while I was gone, but Aunt Adele refuses to talk about it. It's probably best to let it go for now. "Oralyn's stuff," I say, glancing at my left hand, which holds the plastic bag containing her clothes and purse. "She's in the hospital recovering from a diabetes-related complication."

"Diabetes?" Adele's hand flies to her mouth. "Is she okay?"

"If she's a good girl, her doctors will probably release her in a day or so." I squeeze past her and spot Laurel lying on her bed, surrounded by pillows as if she is penned in. Laurel's eyes twinkle, and her arms and legs twirl as soon as she sees my face. I swoop her into my arms and nuzzle her neck.

"This trip feels snakebit. Doesn't it, baby girl?"

Laurel has no answers. And neither do I.

The bathroom tap turns on, and I watch Aunt Adele splashing water on her face, then trying to tame her hair, which is flattened on one side from her nap. I lean against the doorjamb, watching her. "Umm, Oralyn asked me to pass along her apologies."

"What for? She's done nothing to me," Adele says, her eyes still unsettled as she casts her gaze on me, water dripping down her cheeks. Moving in double time, she mops her cheeks with a hand towel and gives her hair one last pouf before striding past me. She is on a mission, and apparently, it does not involve hanging out in her room. "Do you think they'll allow me to visit?"

"Who?"

"Oralyn," she huffs. "I owe her a visit and a whole lot more." Aunt Adele gathers her designer bag, then stops and extends her hand. "Need the keys," she says. "And one more thing. Don't leave your daughter unattended on a bed. She could roll off. She'll be crawling and walking before too long."

"She rolled over?" I gaze at my baby, squirming in my arms, marveling at how quickly she is growing, and pained that I missed her tiny yet monumental first.

"And, another thing, your mother..." From Aunt Adele's body language, it's clear she wants to leave, but she pauses for a moment to pull her phone out of her bag. She taps an icon and then hands the phone to me. "No need to worry about her. She's alive and well."

As I watch the one-minute video, painful memories resurface: I remember covering my head with my bed pillow, trying to block out Mom's screeching. She would demand that Granny mind her own business about the hours she kept and the people she chose to befriend, even if they were married men, drug users, or worse. As a child, I often blamed myself for Mom's disappearing acts. I thought she didn't love me, and that's why she stayed away from Granny and me.

However, Mom did that. Her choices in life were hers and hers alone.

Can I truly forgive her?

TC's advice crosses my mind. Yet, after seeing that video, I question whether I can let go of the hurts. She hasn't changed—not even a little.

CHAPTER THIRTY

Adele

The rules are lax at the hospital. Even though I'm not a family member, the ICU nursing staff allows me to visit Oralyn. A fake-leather armchair is positioned next to her bed. I move it closer and take Oralyn's hand, careful not to disturb the plastic IV tubing snaking from multiple locations on her bruised arms. She looks peaceful, deep in sleep.

"Oralyn, I need to get this off my chest," I say in a soft voice. She doesn't react, not even a twitch, and I wonder if I should wait until she wakes up. But I push forward, afraid that hesitation will swallow my courage whole. Since when do I hesitate? Since when do I feel this…this uncertainty? I am accustomed to taking charge and owning every room I enter. Yet here I am, grasping for boldness, as if it were foreign, something that does not belong to me.

"Ginny is right. You are like my mother…" I search for words that do not come easily or naturally. Aside from Robert, most people see the choreographed version of me. "You give and give and give and make few demands," I continue. "You are the direct opposite of me."

I feel foolish whispering these words and perhaps a little unhinged over what instigated them. While Ginny raced behind an ambulance, no doubt consumed by worry, the baby and I napped.

I slept fitfully.

I had a dream, more like a nightmare, and I doubt its intensity will ever fade.

I saw myself standing before a judge, whom I perceived to be God—not the grandfatherly Creator I was taught about in Sunday school, but someone far more fearsome. "You have turned away from me and worshiped the things of the world," the great adjudicator thundered from his golden throne, surrounded by angels singing their praises. "Most egregious are your arrogance, your condemnatory nature, and your ridicule of even me. Who do you think you are?"

"But—"

"Silence. I've heard enough of your excuses. You still have time to redeem yourself. The decision is yours."

The gavel slammed, and the courtroom erupted in raucous shouts. As I swiveled my head to see who might be cheering, I recognized Oralyn and my sister, along with former employees who had quit because I had condemned them for choosing a sick child over work. There were also the homeless, whom I had spurned because they smelled, set up camps in the park, and did nothing to help themselves. Mom and Dad were not among the celebrants, but they weren't shedding tears either.

I stood alone, convicted.

Surprisingly, Ginny wasn't among the jubilant mob, and then I understood why. The soul-searching begun in New York had produced a pleasing outcome. Instead of continuing my habit of playing judge and jury—a job that belonged only to God—I had offered my heartfelt apologies to Ginny for judging her. I put myself in her shoes and stopped long enough to get her side of the story.

Ginny's relentless knocking on the hotel room door ended the dream.

As I sit in the dimly lit room next to Oralyn, the vision plays on a continuous loop in my mind.

"I judged you, Oralyn. I thought you were ignorant, undeserving of even a smidgeon of respect. So blinded by my own perceived superiority, appalled by your choices, I rolled over you and ignored your opinions."

Thoughts of my mother play around the edges of my mind. She had tried so hard to show me the light, imploring me to treat others the way I wanted to be treated.

"Your job isn't to judge folks, no matter what they've done," she said. "Your job is to love the sinner, not the sin. Because you know what? You might need some grace yourself. Trust me, you're not perfect, and neither am I." She gave me a no-nonsense look before opening the screen door and skipping down the steps, headed for one of her backyard gardens—gloves in one hand and her floppy hat in the other.

Habits die hard, and so does pride. I feel like an addict working through a twelve-step program. Still unsaid is the most crucial part of my confession.

"I'm deeply sorry for how I treated you and ask for your forgiveness."

Minutes pass. The machines continue to beep. The blood-pressure cuff inflates, and a new reading appears on the monitor. Oralyn's chest rises and falls. The scene hasn't changed, but I have. A feeling of thankfulness comes over me. I still have time. My sister is alive. I can make amends with her, too.

"I bet you thought you were talking to the wall," Oralyn murmurs, her voice barely audible above the incessant bleeping. "I had you fooled." She squeezes my hand and opens her eyes, moving her head to the side to get a better view of me. "I accept your apology and hope you'll accept mine. I didn't think much of you, either. But you're the kinda gal I want in my corner. You're smart. You don't dither. You keep us straight." She starts nodding her head. "You know, Adele, we all have crosses to bear. But we don't have to carry the weight alone."

What she says next stops me in my tracks, knocking the breath from my lungs. I hadn't shared with her what prompted my apology—I hadn't confided in anyone.

"Dreams are just another way that God talks with us and shows us how we missed the mark," Oralyn says. "Ginny knows this well."

The slur in her voice does not dull the weight of her words or their mystery. She holds my gaze, something knowing and steady in her eyes, like she sees straight through me. A chill spreads over my skin. *How does she know about my dream? Did Ginny have one, too?* Within a snap, she falls into a deep slumber, and I don't get a chance to ask.

Though wary about this trip at first, my emotions have flipped. So full of myself, I had deluded myself into thinking that I called the shots, when something far larger and wiser had a different plan.

This trip has a reason.

I stay rooted in that uncomfortable chair until the sun rises over the horizon, creating a masterpiece of deep blues, yellows, and reds—the handiwork of the Almighty, the Creator himself. No one knows what will happen later today, tomorrow, or two weeks from now, but the path is clear for me.

I will change my heart.

CHAPTER THIRTY-ONE

Jacob

Dad is on the phone when I walk into his office one day after Bill quit. He lifts his hand in a vague gesture to invite me to take a seat, then turns his back on me. Huh? *What has crawled up his bum this time?* I take a breath, square my shoulders, and stride toward my usual chair.

"Yes, I've had a chance to review your report," he drawls in his cultivated accent, the product of his wealthy upbringing. "Thorough, if not unsettling. I'm grateful you brought these matters to my attention." He listens and offers a few "uh-huhs" before signing off and spinning to face me.

"What can I do for you?" He reclines in his desk chair, arms crossed, and I notice a tiny narrowing at the corners of his eyes.

"Umm." My lap gets my undivided attention. "I owe you an apology, sir."

He sits upright and tilts his head. "Oh… What prompts this apology, Jacob?" He sounds sarcastic.

"I've been absent, which, of course, isn't fair to you." I straighten my posture, planting my feet firmly on the floor and clasping my hands together like a man in command of the situation. But the heat creeping up my neck and the moisture gathering under my arms betray the effort. I feel like that little boy who could never please his father.

"On that point, you would be correct." He raises his eyebrows, waiting to see if I have more to say. I don't and stand to exit.

"Sit." He points to the chair. "I have quite a bit more to say to you." Never one to spout off, he takes his time formulating his words. The pause makes me squirm. While I am unaware of what has angered him, I know from past reprimands that I am in for another. His mouth looks like an angry slash, and his eyes are cold. "Your mother spoiled you and never held you to account, but the jig is up. You've dishonored yourself and my family name."

What? My stomach lurches.

He leans over to retrieve a manila folder from his desk drawer—the one he keeps locked—and hands it to me. It is filled with color photos of me and Red kissing inside hotel lobbies and frolicking naked in my backyard pool. One even shows her opening my front door with a key that I, of course, had given her.

"Where did you get these?" I stammer, arguing that the man in the photo is a doppelganger, a look-alike hired to set me up.

"Enough." Dad holds up a hand. "You're going to listen to me, not the other way around. You know how I feel about her." The photo of Red—Rachel, as my family knows her, the daughter of my dad's former business partner—has sparked his ire. "That woman is a tart. A harlot." A withering look crosses his pinched face as he points his finger at me. I almost laugh. *A harlot? In which century does he live?* "But do you know what bothers me more?"

He does not wait for a response.

"You're a liar."

My mouth drops open. I try to interject, but he shuts me down just by raising his index finger.

"Why did you tell your mother and me that you and Ginny had eloped?"

Another folder from the same drawer is placed on his clutter-free desk, and he starts scanning its contents. "Let's see," he says, running his finger down a sheet of paper. "Absolutely no county in the Atlanta metropolitan area or beyond has ever issued a marriage license to you and a Virginia Carmichael."

My mouth feels dry.

"Where's Ginny?" The corners of his mouth turn up as if he knows something that I do not. He pushes his chair back and begins to pace, like a trial lawyer setting the stage for a prosecutorial kill.

I lick my lips and debate whether to confess. His narrowed eyes suggest that I should, even though I'm reluctant, and a mostly honest account slips through my mouth.

"Uh… I told you that she's visiting relatives in Oklahoma, but she's not. She left me and took the kid. I don't know where she is now." I dab my forehead with my palm and try a gambit to take the heat off me. "Do you remember my mention of her suspected substance abuse?"

"I do remember that conversation, and I also recall telling you that as a family, we would get the support *your wife* needs."

More sarcasm drips from his mouth, one drop at a time. "At the time, I had no reason to distrust you. Now I do."

He shakes his head and locks his arms behind his back. "Your cock-and-bull stories were meant to deceive me, and for a moment they did. Congratulations." He shows his perfectly aligned teeth, but merriment does not register in his eyes. "But something didn't ring true, and I got to thinking. If you're capable of spinning a story about a fictional marriage—an unnecessary falsehood in today's world—are you capable of other fabrications? It didn't take long to find out."

The Rottweiler-like patrol of his office stops so that he can consult yet another folder lying on his desk.

Now what?

He opens the folder, pauses to glance at me, and then starts reading. "Let's see, Ginny's father is serving a life sentence for the brutal slaying of her sister, a crime Ginny witnessed when she was just a child. And then, roughly a year later, Ginny's mother ran off, leaving her in the care of her grandmother, one Alma Smith, a woman of high character. But you already know this."

His laugh sounds harsh.

"But you might find the next part far more interesting." More pages get shuffled before he finds the ones he wants, a puzzled expression crossing his face. But I suspect the look is an act. He pauses for dramatic timing. "Didn't you tell me that Ginny was unfit?"

It is a trap. How should I answer it? I cough and rearrange myself in the chair.

No comment forthcoming from me, he jumps right in. "Well, according to witnesses, you may have lied about that, too." He organizes the pages and walks around his desk toward me. "The detective you hired to track down your *girlfriend* had second thoughts about you himself. He interviewed Ginny's friends and associates. Every single person spoke highly of her. One even shared the reasons for Ginny's sudden departure." He tosses the folder onto my lap. "This woman disputed your accusations. She called *you* abusive." He taps the folder with his knuckle. "These interviews don't paint a pretty picture."

"And you believe them?"

Dad stands inches from me as I flip through the documents, already familiar with most of the information. Except for the interviews with Ginny's friends and former work colleagues, which Bill collected at an obvious quick speed, copies of this report can be found in my home office, safe behind a lock and key. *This can't be happening.* Who authorized Bill to interview Ginny's acquaintances, including that blasted Melinda? And why would he then hand his findings to my father? Just as important, who in God's name took those photos?

I want answers.

"Bill has promised his support, and as I just said, he got a bad feeling about you, Jacob." Dad takes the folder and walks over to his desk. He slides the desk drawer open and pulls the key from his pocket. The sound of the lock latching echoes across the room. "He thought I should know. As for the photos, that's none of your business."

My hands shake. "This is unprofessional, Dad. I hired Bill to do a job, which didn't include sharing the results with you." And then another thought crosses my mind. Has that SOB blackmailed Dad? Has someone else? It would not surprise me.

Dad shrugs. “Unprofessionalism isn’t my worry—your reckless, scandalous behavior is. If my opponent catches wind of your peccadillo, coupled with that damning testimony, he will dish to the news media. You can count on it. I have enemies, too.”

The spin, the hand-fed news stories about the privileged son of an ambitious politician who abuses a beautiful, deeply traumatized woman, only to betray her later, would make news along with the titillating details about her flight, her desire to save herself, and, yes, *their* baby.

Tabloid material for sure.

“I did not abuse Ginny. I swear. The last time I saw her, she was sloppy drunk, garbling her words. I saw her bag of pills.”

Dad takes the seat next to me and crosses his legs. “I don’t know if these interviewees told the truth, but that’s neither here nor there. Perception is reality. If this comes to light, voters, especially women voters, will view Ginny as the victim, and guess who they’ll see as the predator?”

His finger is aimed at me.

“In three months, the voters will decide if I am worthy of the state senate, and I need the women’s vote to cross the finish line decisively.” His voice lowers another notch. “I want a mandate, Jacob, and it won’t happen if this unpleasantness comes out and unravels everything I’ve built.”

He stands, looking down on me.

“I’ve been a distant father and haven’t always been there for you. Hindsight is twenty-twenty. I should have done better and put a stop to your mother’s coddling. Despite my failings, I’ve always wanted the best for you.” He straightens his posture, his hands finding their way to his hips. “I will give you a pass on this nonsense—I'll forget any of it happened—but I do expect something in exchange."

I lift my head. Our eyes connect.

"Number one, you will dump Rachel. Today. There is no question in my mind that she instigated many, if not all, of your recent behaviors. She is bad news—a siren who will bring ruin on you and me.

"Two, you will stop your harebrained pursuit of Ginny. Yes, I read all about it." He tilts his head toward the locked desk drawer. "You tracked her like an animal. It's unseemly, Jacob. If Ginny wants you, she'll come back. Have some self-respect, for goodness' sake. You're a Hudson, after all. Give her space and proof that she's better off with you.

"And three, steer clear of Bill. If I catch wind of any untoward behavior, you will be out on your backside. He did me a favor and has promised to keep this under wraps. Capisce?"

Maintaining my dad's good graces is my overriding concern. Although he ordered a cease-and-desist in my search for Ginny, he also suggested that I give her a reason to return to me. Wouldn't winning her back please him?

I stand and extend my hand, my eyes drilling into his. "I will make this right. You can count on me."

Although the bell has saved me, I'm not out of the woods yet. Nothing ever goes as planned. Now, I must contend with Red's latest trickery and the unwelcome news she delivered this morning with a cheerful smile.

My dad can't find out about this.

I extract the business card the bartender offered and make the call.

CHAPTER THIRTY-TWO

Audrey

Angel's heads-up about Danny wanting to talk with me was a gift. When he called yesterday afternoon, I was not blindsided. I knew a talking-to was coming and behaved accordingly. I didn't stay out late last night; I went to bed early and then spent the early morning hours making myself look presentable, dabbing on potions, lotions, and makeup to hide the haggardness.

By the time I arrive, he's already sipping a cup of coffee and studying the brunch menu at a restaurant popular with the locals.

"No morning cocktails? Poo." I smile the smile that puts my dimples on full display—a tactic that will disarm any curmudgeon—and slide into the booth across from him. "Orange juice and a little bubbly sound good to me."

"You must be kidding." He frowns and signals the waitress for a coffee refill. He is all business this morning. His eyes stay trained on mine, which is not unusual for this clean-cut farm boy. Plunging necklines and deep cleavages do not tempt him. After years in Vegas, the scenery all looks the same to him.

"Come on, Danny," I say, ordering an *unsweetened* iced tea—a heresy to my Southern-born-and-bred mother—before getting myself settled and deciding that a little light-hearted ribbing can only work in my favor. Even so, my insides perform backflips, which I try to allay with more false bravado.

"I need to be on the top of my game when my shift starts in a few hours, and a nice screwdriver assures me of that." I flip my hair, hanging loose and bouncy around my face, my vowels more elongated than ever.

"Well, Audrey, that's what I want to talk to you about." He places his hands on the checkered tablecloth and draws in a deep breath. His deep-brown eyes look watery, like those of a basset hound.

The server brings our drinks and takes our orders. I'm caught between gratitude and annoyance at the interruption. For now, I'm still employed. But once she's gone, what happens then? Maybe it's best to get this over with.

Danny doesn't pussyfoot around.

"I'm letting you go." He rubs his chiseled jaw. "And it's a decision I don't take lightly or enjoy. Do you remember the reasons why I hired you? What? Five years ago, when I'd just started my job?"

I have heard the story many times before, but I want to listen to it again because it helps dull the sting of losing the best job I ever had. While working for Danny, I never experienced unwanted groping, inappropriate comments, or the fear of being manhandled when refusing someone's unsolicited advances.

Danny was my protector. Anyone who harassed me, including the big spenders, was told to find a different tavern.

He ran a tight ship.

"I hired you because you *weren't* a fresh-faced twentysomething." He seems lost in that memory. "You were a professional. You understood the business and showed up on time. You worked hard and helped to grow our customer base. Because of your efforts, Cork & Barrel is the corporation's most profitable tavern. But above all else, you were loyal. I didn't worry about you dipping into the cash register."

He studies the ceiling and then fixes his eyes on me.

"You threw it away. Why?"

"I don't want to throw it away." My eyes are welling up, and I would rather he not see me cry. I'd rather not beg, either, but that is what I'm about to do. I have just enough money to cover the month's expenses. "Please give me another chance. I promise to straighten up and fly right, and I agree that I got out of hand the other night. I got caught up in the excitement."

Danny is unmoved. Although he is unhappy about firing me, he has a business to consider.

"You've drunk to excess before, Audrey." He rests his hands on the table. "Look, many of our employees drink and gamble too much. And some fraternize with customers, even though the company frowns on it." He is not alluding to Angel—the most disciplined person I know. "But most try to keep it under control, including you, or at least you used to. What's going on with you?"

I shrug and stare at my hands.

"Do you remember what you did?"

Angel told me, and I do not need a reminder. But he must think otherwise—maybe to put an exclamation point on why he is cutting the umbilical cord tethering me to the Cork & Barrel.

"You had already consumed several shots when your lover—or whoever he is—showed up with his wife." I try to explain that relationship, but Danny talks over me. "It probably wasn't the smartest decision on his part, but you had no business approaching him and then throwing a drink in his face. You made quite the scene, Audrey, especially after you passed out and fell on the floor."

Our breakfast arrives. I rearrange my scrambled eggs on the plate and notice he doesn't have much of an appetite, either. His omelet gets one taste before he pushes the plate aside.

Our waitress materializes out of nowhere and asks, "Is everything okay?"

"Everything is fine, but I'll take two carry-out boxes," he says, his words clipped. The "get lost" message registers, and she scurries off. He then turns his attention back to me, and sadness fills his eyes. "You have no idea how I hate doing this."

"Please, Danny, give me one more chance. I need this job."

Danny lifts his shoulders and rolls his head. Time passes in slow motion as he runs his hands through his dark, thick hair—another physical asset—and across the back of his neck. "As much as I want to, I can't. I'd be setting a bad precedent. We toss customers for doing less. Do you understand?"

A tear leaks out, and I brush it away. He is right, of course. I'm getting the boot because I deserve it. Good fortune comes my way, and as sure as the dawning of a new day, I will find a way to sabotage myself, only to then drown myself in self-pity with the ever-present bottle or something else. Little does he know, but I popped an antidepressant to get through this meeting.

"I understand, Danny." I give him a sad smile and pick up my carry-out box, even though it will end up in the trash.

We both slide out of the booth and face each other. He towers over me by several inches. I extend my hand, wanting to end this relationship professionally, with at least a shred of dignity left, but he ignores it and draws me into a brotherly hug instead. "Get help, Audrey," he whispers, slipping a business card into my bag. "When you're clean, call me. I will rehire you in a heartbeat. That's how much you mean to me."

I nod, all too aware that help will not be coming soon. I don't build bridges. I burn them.

CHAPTER THIRTY-THREE

Oralyn

The day begins early in the ICU, where I am recovering from my little episode. A nurse wakes me up to draw blood, check my IVs, and hang another bag of whatever she is dripping into my bruised, pin-pricked arm. At least she's chipper and seems happy that I'm still alive.

Rubbing sleep from my eyes, I glance around the room, noticing the furnishings and antiseptic smells. My gaze lands on the chair in the corner, where a slumped figure stirs. I blink, adjusting to the dim light. Is that…Adele? Her usually polished appearance is gone—her hair tousled, clothes wrinkled, not a trace of makeup. Did she spend the night here?

"Good morning, Oralyn," she says, rolling her shoulders before striding over to my bed. She positions herself next to the nurse, who has just finished her routine and now wants me to visit the bathroom. Adele, it would seem, wants to help. She presses the remote hanging from the bed rail, and the mattress moves into an upright position. "Much better."

The nurse rolls her eyes and manages to steer me to the toilet without Adele's aid. Minutes pass before I hobble out to my bed.

"Why are you here?" I ask, scratching my head. My brain bone needs a good dusting to remove the lingering cobwebs.

Her face falls.

"Because I want to be here," she says, sliding off the bed to make room for me. "I came to visit last night. Don't you remember?"

Of course, I remember, but recollection comes slowly, like the lifting of ground fog. Every word of her apology registered, and I hope my own contrition did as well. We are rewinding the movie and starting over—no need to give it another thought, but getting used to a solicitous Adele could take some time.

"Do you need anything? A book? Something to watch?" Adele grabs the remote again and turns on the television, just as my breakfast arrives, hidden beneath a metal dome thingamajig. Before I can get a word in edgewise, she lifts the cover. "Whole-wheat bread, shredded wheat, low-fat milk, and coffee. Looks yummy."

"I don't eat that stuff." I scowl. "For crying out loud, they could've at least given me white-bread toast."

"It's a new day, Oralyn," Adele says with a rare grin, glancing at her watch. "I need to hurry. Your niece is flying in, and Ginny needs the Escalade to pick her up." To my surprise, she lifts her arm and sniffs her armpit. "And I, my friend, need a shower."

It is a new day, indeed.

By the time Ginny and Shannon arrive a few hours later, I am bored senseless. My paperback is back at the hotel along with my readers, and none of the limited TV channels hold my interest. I watch the news for a few minutes and realize that going into a diabetic coma has its benefits. You're too out of it to worry about an economy in free fall or what you'll eat for the rest of your life. How will I ever manage without my bread and sweets?

A familiar voice invades my self-talk. "Aunt Oralyn, my gosh, you gave us a scare." Shannon rushes into the room, drags one of the armchairs to my bedside, and sits. "I don't want to lecture you, but you deserve one. What am I going to do with you?"

"Nothing. I got my wake-up call. Right, Ginny?"

"I hope so." Ginny pecks my cheek before positioning herself at the foot of my bed, which gives her a direct line of sight to the monitors. "How are you feeling?"

"I couldn't be better. When are they springing me?"

"Your doctor should be stopping by shortly," Shannon answers. "We'll discuss everything—"

The entrance of my thin-haired, wire-rimmed-glasses-wearing doctor puts a pause to her storytelling.

"You're doing great, Oralyn," he says, reviewing my file. His bedside manner is better than most doctors'. He speaks in a language I can understand and directs his comments specifically to me. "Your glucose levels are moving into the healthy range, which makes me think we can manage your diabetes with pharmaceutical drugs and a continuous glucose monitor, which means no insulin shots or finger pricks. But—and it's a big but—you must adhere to a strict diet and start exercising."

He pats my hand. "However, we'd like to keep you one more day. Your insurance will cover it. How does that sound?"

"Better than the alternative, I suppose."

"We'll talk more tomorrow." He smiles at me and nods to Shannon and Ginny.

The doc isn't two steps out the door before Shannon starts in. I know she means well and has grown accustomed to looking after me because I let her. But right now, I do not need or want her worried tut-tutting about what is best for me. This trip has been good for me, despite Jacob's antics and my hospital visit. Throughout my life, I've made decisions like a squirrel darting into traffic—pausing at the worst possible moment, second-guessing, and zigzagging in panic. And just like that poor, indecisive critter, I've ended up flattened more times than I care to admit.

No more.

"Aunt Oralyn, I want you to come home with me." Shannon is insistent, blabbing on about how she needs to keep a closer eye on me. "We can either fly home together, or, better yet, we can drive home in your van."

The old Oralyn would have done what convention dictated.

"You heard the doctor, Shannon." My eyes feel squinty. She needs to hear me and consider my point of view. "What's the difference? Taking meds at home or on the road? Plus, I have a built-in nurse. Unless, of course, Ginny opposes." I turn my gaze on Ginny, who starts coughing and fidgeting with her cloth satchel. I raise my eyebrows.

"Of course, I can help," Ginny says after a long beat, "but Shannon has a point."

"And the point is?" I ask in a firm voice.

Shannon starts sputtering. Ginny looks bewildered. But going along to get along isn't going to cut it for me anymore. Adele has indeed shown me that. Ginny sighs and taps her mouth.

"No one is forcing you to go home," Ginny says. "But restaurants aren't known for diabetic-friendly menus. You might find the transition a lot easier at home, where you can do your grocery shopping and plan menus. That is my only concern. That is the point."

"Shannon, give me your phone." My niece glances at Ginny, shrugs her shoulders, and hands it to me. I go to the Google machine, get the results, and hand the phone back to her. "Read it and weep."

"Since when did you learn how to use the internet?" Shannon's mouth hangs open.

"Ha. I've learned all kinds of stuff," I say, sitting up a little straighter in my bed. "Chain restaurants do offer food I can eat. And even if they don't, Ginny and most certainly Adele will help me make choices. Have you met Adele?" I ask Shannon. "If anyone can keep me on the straight and narrow, it is her."

"Because here's the deal, girls. I'm going to Vegas. I still have things to learn."

CHAPTER THIRTY-FOUR

Audrey

I once dated a customer, a nurse who'd spent a tour of duty at a combat support hospital in Salerno, Afghanistan—a MASH-type unit on the Pakistani border. He was a great guy with a big heart, but he was tortured. Just the smell of grilled meats or the whop-whop of helicopter blades would set off vivid flashbacks of the soldiers and Afghan kids he cared for. Their blown-off faces, amputated limbs, and burned flesh haunted him.

He drank to forget and found the perfect drinking companion in me.

We did not stick, but our time together made me realize that you don't have to deploy to some war-torn country to suffer emotionally. Trauma comes in all flavors, and even seemingly unrelated events can elicit intense fear and self-loathing.

That's how I feel now: anxious, ashamed, and afraid—the same way I felt as a twelve-year-old kid, then searching for a father figure to love me like my daddy did. Something terrible happened back then, but no one knows about it. Who would have believed me anyway? Not my mother.

I pull into the driveway, my boxed breakfast on the passenger seat. My hands are quaking so severely that I can barely put the car in park. I sit there for a while, trying to control my rapid heart rate, when I notice my neighbor—a plain-looking woman, a busybody—who tries to engage in chit-chat whenever she sees me. She is opening her side gate, tethered to her little white yip-yap with a pink-colored retractable leash. A conversation is the last thing I need, and I slouch in my seat.

She is out of sight before I climb out of my Toyota sedan, a step up from the old Chevy that brought me here. The rental is a step up, too, compared with the dumpy, rundown trailer in South Carolina. The place is lovely. However, I can't help but notice that all the houses in Vegas look almost identical, with their red-tiled roofs, earth-tone exteriors, oversized windows, and tiny walled-in yards. Sometimes I wonder where the kids play, but that is not my problem.

Right now, thinking about kids, especially my own, is at the bottom of my list. I don't need reminders of my colossal mistakes, and I most certainly don't want to consider my future. The thought of pounding the pavement searching for a job sends my heart racing faster than ever. I have only thirty days, one month, to find a job and steer my sinking ship back to safety.

That leaves the alternative.

I go to the kitchen, fix myself a drink, and plop down on the sofa. As usual, the booze quiets the angst, giving me the courage to evaluate a strategy. I twirl the Rolodex in my mind, but can't think of a single person who might give *Peaches* a chance that doesn't come with conditions.

I've been on that carousel and don't want to ride it again.

Danny spoiled me.

My glass is empty, and that won't do. It's five o'clock somewhere. I pour another vodka, this time in a Slurpee-cup-sized glass, before checking the time. I should be standing behind the Cork & Barrel bar, dispensing nonsense to the barflies, telling stories, and playing the irrepressible Peaches with my exaggerated Southern accent. But I am not. I'm holed up in my house, fighting anxiety with my favorite depressant.

Oh, to turn back the clock to the fateful night at the Cork & Barrel where I did my faceplant. If I could do it over again, I would have never believed my married boyfriend when he claimed he was planning to divorce his wife, the woman who, according to him, would never understand him like I did. Seeing him at the tavern, all lovey-dovey, set me off. I had never felt so stupid and betrayed in my life.

My phone jingles as I take a sip.

Could that be Danny? I am delusional. He just fired me, for crying out loud. Even so, I rip through my purse looking for the phone. As usual, it's buried at the bottom, along with the business card Danny had given me earlier at the restaurant. My shoulders slump.

"Hey." I force my voice to sound bright, unworried, but Angel sees through my act.

"How far are you into your cups?"

"Second and counting. I guess you heard."

"I did. And the bar feels like a morgue. Your posse of admirers is threatening an insurrection unless you're reinstated."

"Well, that won't be happening anytime soon."

Her voice grows serious. "I may have an idea on how you might get your job back."

"You're nuts."

"No. Hear me out. The Duke University School of Law accepted me, and I'll be moving to North Carolina in a couple of weeks to settle before classes start this fall."

"Good on you, Angel. But how does your good news translate into my reinstatement?"

She tells me.

Why she goes the extra mile for me is hard to understand. I should be mothering her, not the other way around. We sign off after I promise several times to clean up my act. A sober Peaches is the linchpin in her plan.

The jumbo drink goes down the drain, followed by the contents of every liquor bottle stashed in my house. Glass clinks against glass as the weight of my habits collides inside the garbage bags. Am I making a rash decision? It's too late now to reconsider.

Angel has thrown me a lifeline, and for now, I will cling to it. But the drowning will come later.

CHAPTER THIRTY-FIVE

Audrey

Angel is as good as her word—promises made, promises kept. Within an hour or two of our initial conversation, Angel has discussed the situation with Danny, and the news is good.

Her laughter sounds musical, and it makes me smile.

"With me leaving, I argued that he'd be losing an experienced bartender, and that he should consider giving you another shot, especially since you have a loyal following," she says. "Of course, I assured him that you would curtail your drinking. He has agreed to think about it. Isn't that wonderful? You should expect a call. He does have a soft spot for you, and so do I."

She rings off. One of these days, Angel is going to make a great lawyer. She certainly proved her mettle when she pleaded my case to Danny.

I smoke a cigarette to keep my hands busy and swallow a Xanax to smooth out the rough edges as I wait for Danny's call. The pill works its magic, but music would complete my mellow mood. I douse the cigarette, tap my Pandora app on my phone, and choose a New Age channel. The instrumentals, the sounds of crashing waves, lift me and transport me to a nearly forgotten place and time: the Georgia coast and the last Smith family vacation before tragedy set us adrift.

I close my eyes and relive the moment—the sandcastles, the seagulls. I can smell the sun on Daddy's broad, capable shoulders as he carries me and Adele piggyback into the surf, while Mom watches and smiles from beneath the beach umbrella, a paperback resting in her lap.

The ringing phone brings me back to Vegas, where I came to forget.

"Hey. What's up?" I sit up straighter. The sky beyond the window is shifting, warm hues of gold and crimson melting into the deepening blue of twilight. It is the kind of sunset that deserves appreciation somewhere far from the neon glow of the Vegas sprawl. I draw in a deep breath.

"I said a lot of things this morning," Danny begins. "And I meant every word I said. But Angel is quitting, and, frankly, I am up to my eyebrows in alligators. If you want your job, show up tomorrow afternoon—sober, and then stay that way."

"Of course, I want my job back. But you seemed so adamant this morning. Why are you doing this for me, Danny?"

He doesn't speak for what seems like minutes. "I don't know. You remind me a little of my mom. Life was hard for her, but no one ever offered a hand up or a second chance. I am doing that for you. But it does come with a warning and a request."

"What's that?" I dread what I think might be coming next.

"Don't make me regret this, Audrey. You pull one of your stunts, and you are done." This isn't a warning. It's a statement of fact. "I don't want to see that happen." He lets that sink in before continuing in a gentler voice. "Did you look at that card I put in your purse?"

"I glanced at it."

"I can't force you to do anything, Audrey, but you should talk with her. If money is the problem, I will pay, with no strings attached. This is a gift."

Danny gets my thanks and a noncommittal acknowledgment. I am not a charity case, and I do not need my head examined by some chick specializing in substance abuse. Furthermore, AA, Celebrate Recovery, and any other "I'm an addict" group will never see me among their ranks, pouring out my sad little story.

I am going cold turkey.

With the phone wedged between my ear and shoulder, I make sure I have rid my house of every bottle of booze, including those stashed in hidden places. I am determined to prove to Danny, Angel, and myself that alcohol has no control over me; so obsessed, I nearly miss what he says next.

"By the way, I got an interesting call from some dude in Atlanta. Uh, I think his name is Jacob Hudson. Anyway, he claimed he is a very good friend of your daughter, but has lost track of her. He hopes you might know where she is." He pauses. "I didn't know you had a daughter."

I am poised at another crossroads. *Should I tell him the truth?*

"I do have a daughter. But I don't know this Jacob person."

He leaves it at that.

Even before we disconnected, a pit started forming inside my gut. It's growing exponentially, like an aggressive turbo cancer. I couldn't protect my sweet Laurel, who died trying to fend off Jimmy. The image is indelible and impossible to forget. Now, my latent maternal intuition tells me that Ginny needs my protection, too. *Who is this man? What should I do?* I have no answers.

The plastic garbage bags, lying in mounds on the kitchen floor, are filled to overflowing with cast-off liquor bottles. They mock me. What I would give for a glass of vodka now. I could always count on a nice drink to assuage my guilt. I'm almost ready to grab my keys and head in the direction of my favorite liquor store when the ringing phone jolts me to my senses, reminding me of the promise I had made to Angel. I see the caller's name, and this time I pick up.

CHAPTER THIRTY-SIX

Jacob

My conversation with the tavern manager, a guy named Danny Mason, went as well as I could have hoped. Since the barkeep had given him a heads-up, he was prepared for my call. Although he seemed hesitant to share personal information about Audrey, he accepted my reason for wanting to talk with her directly. He sounded a bit surprised when I mentioned Ginny. Regardless, in a roundabout way, he confirmed where Audrey worked, which gave me confidence about finding Ginny.

"Come on, Jacob. I want to go to Vegas, too." Red is lying in my bed, sulking as I pack my carry-on bag. The morning light catches in her hair, but there is no soft glow—just a tangled mess of red-hot strands against the sheets, a visual of the tumult she has introduced into my life.

"I deserve a trip." She drapes one arm over her stomach, a lazy, absent-minded gesture like she is protecting what is growing inside her. "We haven't celebrated yet."

"Celebrating? What's to celebrate? Furthermore, you're not going anywhere with me."

She gives me a pouty look. "Don't be silly, Jacob. We have lots to celebrate." She climbs out of bed and saunters toward me, hips swaying.

And, of course, I can't resist her seductive smile. She is a maestro. I sweep her into my arms and carry her back to bed, drawing her into a deep, passionate kiss. Her response confirms that I will get my way in more ways than one.

She will pay for putting me in an impossible situation.

Minutes later, Red's eyes are closed. As I caress her willowy, porcelain-colored arm with my fingertips, she sighs, a contented smile forming on her face. Little does she know what's coming.

"I asked you a question a few minutes ago." The caressing has stopped, and my voice sharpens. Her eyes flicker open, sensing the shift in tone. "Don't lie to me, Red. You purposely stopped taking your birth control pills, didn't you?"

I can see the hesitation in her eyes, a split second too late to cover it up. She bobs her head.

"Why would you do that?" I grab her chin and force her to look at me. I hold it just long enough to make her squirm. "You tried to play me. Manipulate me. And then you dare to suggest we have something to celebrate?"

Red's lips tremble. "How can you say that, Jacob? I love you. You love me. I want to be the mother of your children. Please don't be mad at me."

The desperation in her voice is the sweet kind of submission I am accustomed to. She is a puppet caught in her strings, uncertain over whether I will come to her rescue—let her dangle. I slide out of bed to dress, then glance over my shoulder. Lying in the bed alone, she looks small and pitiful.

I am unmoved.

"You know the situation. You're still the other woman. The homewrecker." I point an accusatory finger at her, my voice merciless. "A pregnancy brought to term would only sully your name. Is that what you want? It's already bad enough. Your reputation precedes you." I lift my eyebrows and throw out a lifeline. "You can make this right. Make the appointment today."

Her face is a canvas of sorrow; her flushed cheeks are stained with tears. She bows her head. "I'm sorry, Jacob," she mumbles. "I had no idea you would react this way."

"Make sure you make that appointment." I sling my bag across my shoulder and head for the door. I pause mid-stride. "Make sure you make the bed before you go."

The sounds of her sobbing follow me down the hallway. I don't care. No one gets away with trying to trap me.

I glance at my watch before opening the garage door. Good. I have plenty of time to mop up loose ends at the office before my flight leaves later this afternoon. Driving to downtown Atlanta is infuriating due to the city's infamous bumper-to-bumper traffic, but the commute does give me time to consider how I will manage Dad.

I find him at his usual post—his desk, wrapping up a call.

"Dad, thanks for setting me straight yesterday," I say, strolling into his office, wearing a somber expression. "I've given our conversation a lot of thought, and you are right. I haven't handled the situation with Ginny properly." He points to the chair, but I decline and start bouncing on my toes, my hands clasped behind my back. I stop. It's a gesture I do when I want to project superiority, but that's the wrong impression to make. I want him in my camp. "I haven't done right by her and want your advice."

"Take a seat," he insists, and I comply this time. He seems to be in a good mood and smiles at me.

"What would you do, Dad?" I tap my lips with my steepled hands. "I love Ginny. I want my family back."

"I thought I told you to give her time." He leans back in his chair, adopting the pose of a sage prophet.

"You did. But I found her. She is visiting her mother in Las Vegas."

A little white lie—no confirmation, just a hunch, but my gut tells me that her mother holds the key to finding Ginny.

"Do you think I should fly out to see her? Maybe get married there in Vegas?

Dad gives me a look that I can't interpret. "Why are you asking me? You've already made up your mind. Just go," he says, narrowing his eyes. "But don't embarrass yourself or dishonor the family. Remember, I have an election to win."

"Yes, sir." We shake hands, exactly the way he taught me in one of our few father-son interactions growing up. "I appreciate you."

In a few hours, I will be in Vegas, settling in at the Wynn, a forty-five-story glass tower of opulence. Nothing but the best for me. I deserve luxury after what both Ginny and Red have put me through. And then what? Who knows? I'll play that by ear. But two outcomes are assured.

Ginny won't resist me, and Rachel won't be carrying a baby when I get home.

CHAPTER THIRTY-SEVEN

Ginny

Oralyn has become resolute and will not be swayed. She has made it clear that she is staying with us. Although Shannon is not thrilled about leaving her diabetic aunt behind, she has accepted this reality. We say our goodbyes at the rundown garage where we parked the van a few days ago. With one final glance in our direction, Shannon climbs into the driver's seat for the long drive back home to Oklahoma.

No one speaks as we watch her slow progress along a rutted desert road, billowing clouds of dust marking the van's progress toward the highway. When she vanishes from view, we silently climb into the Escalade to begin the last leg of this trip to my mother. Perhaps, like me, Aunt Adele and Oralyn are wondering what the next few days will hold.

Oralyn is the first to break the silence.

"What are you in the mood for?" Oralyn's finger hovers over the buttons, ready to press one of her preprogrammed radio stations. This should be interesting. Oralyn's love for country and bluegrass music had my aunt's eyes rolling in their sockets the other day.

"Oh, I don't know. Your choice." Aunt Adele tucks a strand of hair behind her ear. "You get to play queen for the day."

"The tiara fits me better, anyway." Oralyn's laugh is infectious. She finds a classic rock station and begins her inimitable warbling. Soon, Aunt Adele joins in, and I marvel at these two. Only a few days ago, they needed a referee. Despite their differences, they seem to have found common ground.

Although Oralyn is a few years older than my aunt, they belong to the same generation and share familiar cultural touchstones. As I sit in the back with Laurel, they begin to recount these memories with excitement. Both learned to read with *Dick and Jane* primers, practiced addition and subtraction with flashcards, and by the third grade had begun to write in cursive. At night, they both gathered in their living rooms to watch shows like *Leave It to Beaver*, *My Three Sons*, and *Bewitched*. Their childhoods were shaped not only by the images of war that flooded the nightly news but also by personal connections to some of the young men who were drafted to fight and die in the jungles of Vietnam.

People can find common ground if they look for it—a valuable lesson for everyone. However, I can't help but wonder who or what contributed to the peace between them. And then, as Aunt Adele drives past the Continental Divide and billboards advertising Indian fry bread, something in their relationship seems to shift once more.

Their conversation deepens as they peel back layers of grief and regret. It feels as though I have vanished, becoming a silent and unseen witness to their confessions about what they would do differently if given the chance.

"I should have shown more empathy to my sister when Daddy died," Aunt Adele says. "She was especially close to him and took his death very hard. No one understood her struggles, especially not me."

"I know that feeling," Oralyn murmurs. "When my daughter died, I—" She swallows hard, her words trailing off, but the weight of her emotions lingers in the air.

I watch them, two women connected by past mistakes and a shared desire to turn back the clock. Their bond deepens with every mile we travel. Then, as my eyelids grow heavier, the truth settles over me—this trip isn't just a journey. It's a second chance for each of us. We are on a road to redemption, and none of us will ever be the same again.

In our own ways, we have already begun the transformation. Aunt Adele has become softer and more compassionate, while Oralyn has grown bolder and more confident about what she thinks is best for herself and others. The days of taking the back seat in her affairs have ended for her.

And me?

I will know the answer in the next day or two when I see my mother for the first time in twenty years.

Aunt Adele informed me of this certainty as we prepared to leave the Albuquerque hotel this morning. Before going to bed last night, she had decided to call Mom again to let her know that she would be in town and wanted to see her. Shockingly, my mother picked up.

"My mom knows we're coming?" I asked, loading our bags into the back of the Escalade. "How did she sound?"

"She sounded a little spaced out, but all in all, cogent. She asked about you. She wondered if you were okay."

"Well, she'll soon find out, right?"

"I didn't tell her you were coming." Adele dropped that nugget without fanfare. "I didn't tell her about Laurel, either."

"Why not?"

"Good question, and one I can't answer." Adele looked across the parking lot. Her eyes were fixed on the Sandia Mountains in the distance. "She sounded fragile… Like she might break into a million different pieces. I didn't want to be the person who threw the first stone." Aunt Adele shrugged and shut the hatch. "She thanked me for calling and told me she had to go to bed."

Since beginning this journey ten days ago, I assumed I would catch Mom off guard. It seems that's going to happen, and I'm uncertain it's the right move.

CHAPTER THIRTY-EIGHT

Adele

As Oralyn and I chat, driving past Gallup, New Mexico, and into Arizona, Ginny and Laurel sleep in the back. I almost forget they're back there until we arrive at our destination and I turn off the ignition.

"Where are we?" Ginny straightens as she rubs her eyes and tries to soothe Laurel, who starts to whimper.

"Standing on a corner in Winslow, Arizona..." Oralyn croons. She'd been looking forward to this pit stop and warned I would pay a king's ransom if I didn't stop. Few people our age had ever heard of Winslow until the Eagles put this little town on the map.

We pile out of the Escalade and spend more than an hour posing with the Glenn Frey statue, snapping selfies by the mural of the red flatbed Ford, and rummaging through the corner gift shop. Oralyn may have sworn off pastries, but when it comes to collecting souvenirs, some habits die hard.

"Isn't this precious?" Against her chest, she holds a T-shirt ideal for a tweener.

"I suppose. Who would you give it to?"

"Me." She gives me a what's-it-to-you look.

Not much of a souvenir shopper myself, I slip out of the store and sit on one of the benches. While sipping a Route 66 cream soda—my only purchase—I pull up Robert's number and calculate New York time in my head. Ten o'clock. *Good. Not too late.* I tap the number.

"Adele, my sweet. Where are you?"

I laugh. "Ogling Glenn Frey."

"Ah-ha. Having fun?"

"I am," I say. "I don't know how Ginny does it. No wonder old babes don't have babies. And Oralyn is keeping her chin up and adjusting to her new reality. Everything is good, but..." I see Oralyn pushing the stroller, and Ginny struggling with multiple bags. They're laughing as they walk out of the store. At this rate, someone will be riding on the roof because there will be no room inside the car. "Hang on, Robert." I get their attention and point to a restaurant across the street. "Girls, let's get dinner. I'll be in after I'm done with this call."

Oralyn gives me a thumbs-up, and I return to Robert.

"Hey, I need your advice on something," I say. I then tell him about my conversation with Audrey late last night. I had withheld a fair bit from Ginny, afraid of upsetting her.

"I think Jacob is still trying to find Ginny," I say, recalling Audrey's mention of a man who had called her boss inquiring about her. "Who else could it be?"

"You may be right, but that doesn't mean he's in Vegas. Are you worried?"

"Of course, I'm worried. He's been tracking her down like a psychopath. I don't trust him and put nothing past him. He should be in a straitjacket."

"How far away are you?" Robert asks. "I mean from Nevada."

"Waze says four and a half hours. If we left after dinner, we would arrive after midnight. What do you think? Should we push through or wait until morning?"

Robert doesn't rush. He is a plodder and makes decisions rationally, much like me—usually. His answer doesn't surprise me.

"Get some rest, Adele. You have a baby, a diabetic, and a niece who is likely nervous about seeing her mother for the first time in decades. Why add more stress?"

Robert's counsel is on target. We all need to regroup after the past few days.

"You're right. If he's there, he's there. We'll deal then."

"If you need anything, and I mean anything, call. I can fly to Vegas in a snap. Do you hear?"

I may have to take him up on his offer and feel myself shiver.

CHAPTER THIRTY-NINE

Audrey

It's been a whole day and counting—no cocktails and not even a Xanax. I feel a little shaky, but I arrive at Cork & Barrel thirty minutes before my shift starts at three o'clock. I help the kitchen staff, run a few food orders, and chat with customers—anything to distract myself from what I really want: a drink.

As soon as I move behind the bar, bouncing from customer to customer to take their orders, someone hits the jackpot. *Whoop-whoop.* Video time. Now all my Instagram followers know the machines are hot. I am busy. Thankfully so.

I am chatting with a handsome stranger with auburn-colored hair and snow-white teeth when my phone vibrates in my back pocket. "Excuse me." I read the text message. Adele is arriving around noon tomorrow and wonders where she should stay.

I type without hesitation.

Instead of offering a bed at my place, I suggest a well-appointed resort in one of the Summerlin communities close to my house. Entertaining a sister who has always looked down her nose at me could be tense, and Lord knows, I don't need more stress. For the life of me, I can't understand why she would reach out to me now. The last time we spoke, four months ago, the conversation ended on a sour note. She had called to tell me about Mom's passing and funeral arrangements. Her condescending tone rankled me, and I let her have it, telling her that I had no family in Georgia. My family was here.

A total lie.

My close friends can be counted on one hand. Or can they? Not one close confidante—aside from Angel, and even that seems unlikely—comes to mind. It is okay. Look at what happened when I shared confidences before. My high-school bestie, a cousin of Jimmy's, had set me up with her no-account relative. Ultimately, he would kick the life out of our daughter and then leave me for dead. I never heard from that so-called friend again. She didn't even show up at Laurel's funeral, a grim day for everyone.

I pocket the phone and focus on the stranger. "What's your name? New to town or on vacation?"

"I'm on a mission." The man's accent reminds me of the South, specifically the state of Georgia.

"Ooh. A mystery man." I wink at him and start a drink order placed by one of the waitresses.

The Cork & Barrel is rocking. I want to think my video contributed. Shouts erupt from the corner. Another lucky person has hit the jackpot, which means a good tip night for me. Danny arrives amid the ruckus for one of his unannounced pop-ins and signals for me to follow him to the other end of the bar, next to the soft-drink dispenser, where he takes a stool.

"How are you doing?" he asks, his face etched with concern.

"Great. Couldn't be better." All bravado, of course. A headache is coming on, a dull throbbing behind my carefully made-up eyes, and I can't keep my hands from shaking. I push them into my pockets, imagining the pleasure of a well-mixed vodka and tonic, garnished with a juicy orange wedge.

Don't go there. You can do this.

"Can I get something for you? Wings? A sandwich?"

Danny must not hear my question. He dips his head and asks under his breath, "Who is the dude over there? He's staring at you."

I glance over my shoulder and shrug. "No idea. I guess he's here on business."

Danny sits up straighter and crosses his arms. His mouth tightens as he looks hard at the mystery man. "Okay. Keep an eye on him." The barstool scrapes across the floor as he stands. "I'll be in the back office."

No one is wise to how I really feel. I glance at my watch—three more hours to go. One of my favorite patrons, an older man with kind eyes, smiles from ear to ear as he takes a seat next to the stranger, who is occupied with his phone. "Peaches. You're a sight for sore eyes. If only I were younger."

"Aww." I laugh and lean over to give the old guy a peck on his whiskered cheek. "We would've made quite the couple. Huh? What can I get you?"

From the corner of my eye, I notice that the stranger has put his phone down. He's now leaning back on the barstool, studying me with an intensity that would unnerve anyone. I decide to ask point-blank.

"Do we know each other, *mystery man*?" I cross my arms and peer into his face, noticing his vivid blue eyes.

"Should we?" He chuckles and drains the last of his sparkling water. "You remind me of someone I know. That's all."

"Is that good or bad?" I offer a flirty smile.

"That depends."

Bar-side flirtations are my stock-in-trade—a skill encoded in my DNA. But something is off with this man. The corners of his mouth have turned up as if he is withholding an essential piece of information.

"Okay, then…another drink?" This time, I don't wink.

"My check." He flashes a smile and pulls out his wallet, handing me a Benjamin. "Keep the change. See you soon… Audrey, or do you prefer Peaches?" And in a blink, he is gone, weaving through the Friday-night crowd. I grab the counter to keep myself from falling.

"Big tipper," the older patron says, shaking his balding head. "These guys act like the world revolves around them. Do you know him?"

"Nope. I've never seen him." A lump has formed in my throat.

"Huh. He sure acted like he knew you."

Looking past the crowds, I spot him talking with a group of men all wearing ball caps emblazoned with the Atlanta Braves logo. Their eyes are glued to one of the suspended televisions near the door. A pitch. A hit. The Brave rounds the bases and scores, eliciting raucous cheers from the stranger and his fellow travelers. They high-five before he leaves the building.

Who is he? The guy who called Danny? I talk myself off the cliff. No way. He's just another businessman, but how did he know my real name?

By eleven o'clock, I am done—sober as my mother.

I walk to the back office to say goodbye to Danny, who I sense stayed on-site to keep an eye on me.

"Danny, remember that stranger? The one who was staring at me?"

Danny lifts his head from a stack of papers piled on the desk. "Yeah, did he cause trouble?"

"No... I'm just wondering if he's the one who called you?"

"I don't know what he looks like. We talked on the phone." His brow furrows. "Do you want me to walk you to your car?" He doesn't wait for a response and walks around the desk toward me. "Time for me to go, anyway."

I blow a kiss to the old-timer as Danny escorts me to my Toyota parked close to the tavern's entrance. Standing sentry like a guard, his eyes sweeping the parking lot, he waits until I unlock the door and slide in. The seatbelt latched, I roll down the window, and he leans in closer, his hand gripping the door frame to create a protective barrier between me and the world. What would I do without him?

"Thanks, Danny. Thanks for everything." The ignition turns over, and the engine hums. My head pulsates. I give him a feeble smile and pull out. He is visible in the rearview mirror, still watching as I turn right onto the four-lane highway that takes me home.

He is like a father, like my daddy might have been.

CHAPTER FORTY

Jacob

Who needs a detective? I can do my own stakeout and do a better job at that. There is no question in my mind. After all, I found Ginny's elusive mama. My only surprise was her *extraordinary* likeness to the little mouse. They are duplicates down to the dimples.

To kill time while waiting for Audrey to leave the tavern, I search for her name on social media. Many results appear, but no one checks all the boxes. She probably posts under her Peaches alias. Given her temptress-like nature, especially with strangers, it would make sense. And then, for grins, I tap Ginny's name into Instagram. Nada. She must have removed her account. Did she post on other platforms? I scratch my head and decide not to check. It is getting late, and I'm getting bored. Did Audrey slip out while I had my head in the phone?

My eyes dart around the parking lot until I spot her with a man, who is being a gentleman by opening the tavern door for her. They walk side by side, his hand resting on her lower back as he guides her toward a Toyota parked near my BMW crossover. Her boyfriend? Husband? I have no idea, but his bearing reminds me of Melinda's husband, the meathead. I have no interest in tangling with him, so I slouch lower in my seat. Time drags on.

Good grief. Move on, bro. I'm getting uncomfortable. Finally, I hear an ignition and allow myself a look-see. The man's muscled arms rest at his sides as he watches Audrey pull out of her space. She pulls onto the highway, and only then does he walk to a truck, his back now toward me.

My cue to get moving.

She is no speed demon and uses her blinkers to warn drivers of her every turn. She reminds me of her daughter, the rule follower who would give me a boatload of rubbish because of the way I drove. One incident from about six months before the old bat finally kicked it comes to mind as I track the Toyota a few cars ahead of me.

Ginny's dumpster-fire-of-a-car had been in the shop, and she'd begged me to take her to her grandmother's place. She hadn't visited in weeks and needed her Granny fix. When we finally arrived, I put on my best grin and played the part of Ginny's doting fiancé, yammering on about an impending visit with the Justice of the Peace. Ginny gnawed on her lip, her face gray, as she touched the noticeable baby bump. Just as I was about to wrap her grandmother in a warm hug, good old Granny stiffened and pulled back, her nostrils twitching like she smelled something rotten. She might have said something, but all that registered was the sharp sting of rejection—a feeling my father would elicit. It flared in my chest, but I smothered it beneath a carefully measured sigh.

Fine. If she wanted cold, I would give her ice.

I flopped onto the sofa with an exaggerated groan, draping an arm over my eyes like some tragic figure, muttering about a headache just loud enough for her and Ginny to hear. The air in the room grew thick with unspoken words, but I had made my point. We barely lasted thirty minutes before I suggested we leave; my patience was thin, but my performance was flawless.

Anxious to get home, I blasted the horn, tailgated drivers hogging the passing lane, and then flipped them off as I sped past. Ginny—already unhappy about my truth-stretching and my insistence that we go home—started yelling and demanding that I pull over. She would drive, she announced. Dream on, sweetheart. Not a chance. I told her to sit back and enjoy the ride. *Driving Miss Daisy*, that's what I called it. The silent treatment, my go-to technique for keeping her in line, lasted for a day or two.

Now, the past fades as Audrey pulls into a planned community and bears right before turning into a driveway, the garage door already lifting. I drive past, slowing to capture as many details as possible in a neighborhood where every house looks the same. Unlike her neighbors—and even her own mother—Audrey does not seem to be into landscaping. Not even a cactus adorns her property: just sandy dirt and a few rocks.

The street past Audrey's winds through the rest of the community and takes me back to the entrance, from where it is a relatively easy drive back to the Strip. After the valet relieves me of my Beamer, I head for the craps tables. The gambling gods are with me.

In more ways than one, I go to bed richer. While I was cashing in my chips, Red left a voicemail. She has an appointment on Monday, and I will sleep like a baby.

CHAPTER FORTY-ONE

Oralyn

We are within a stone's throw of Flagstaff when I realize that we're on Pacific time. I learn this fun fact when I call Monty at seven o'clock and discover he is knee-deep in breakfast customers.

"Woman, you haven't been gone that long. You should know better than to ping me at nine on a Saturday." The diner sounds like a hive of industry, with clanking pots, clattering plates, and shouting voices.

"Then why did you pick up, you old fool?" I am teasing him—just our way around each other.

He ignores my question and goes on to tell me that Shannon has rid my refrigerator, freezer, and cupboards of my crackers and cookies, the microwavable dinners, and boxes of Kraft macaroni and cheese.

"Why did she do that? I'm perfectly capable of taking care of myself."

"Ahh, geez." I can see him running his hand across his shiny dome, disturbing his few remaining strands of combed hair. "Why are you getting all hot and bothered? Maybe she does these things because she loves you and wants to take care of you." I don't comment, and he goes on to tell me that he parked my van in my garage and dropped my bags of souvenirs on the kitchen table. "I noticed the baby seat Ginny and I bought at Walmart. Did y'all forget it?"

"Nah, there was no room in the Cadillac," I say. "Maybe you should return it or give it to Goodwill."

"Maybe I will. When are you getting home? Do you miss me?"

I chuckle. To quote that threadbare cliché, home is where the heart is, and I *am* missing Monty, Shannon, and my favorite customers. Even the old biddy has crossed my mind, but not enough to hightail it back to Oklahoma—at least not yet.

"I'll let you know," I say. "I don't know what to expect once we get to Las Vegas. Ginny's mother is expecting us by early afternoon."

"Taking your meds and eating right?" Monty asks. It's a non sequitur, a word Shannon likes to use when conversation bounces from topic to topic and doesn't follow a nice, straight line. The shattering of glass interrupts our conversation… "I'll get it. Just move those orders." He returns to me. "Where was I? Oh yeah, psychopaths."

"Psychopaths? We were talking about me."

"Whatever," Monty says. "I was thinking about Ginny's husband-to-be. I was just wondering if anyone has heard from him—maybe her aunt or that friend in Atlanta?"

"Not a peep," I say, in disbelief that he is still chattering with me, given the chaos I hear over the phone. "It's like he fell off the face of the earth… But here's a new twist. Ginny's friend said a detective had questioned her about Jacob. She gave him an earful. I wonder if it's the same detective who stopped by to talk with you?"

I doubt he caught a word. He is shouting again, and I suspect the pimply-faced grill jockey is the target of his wrath.

"Sorry, Oralyn, I gotta run. I'm too old for this nonsense. Hey, your job is still open if you want it back." He chortles and hangs up without saying goodbye.

The conversation took longer than I realized. While I yapped with Monty, the Escalade, with Adele at the wheel, flew past the exit for the Coconino National Forest. She didn't slow down for anything, driving with purpose, always in a rush. As we moved farther west, the landscape shifted. The towering pine trees around Flagstaff had given way to low, scrubby desert plants and jagged, weathered rock formations. The air grew hotter and drier, the kind of heat that dehydrates your skin. I glance at my crepey-looking forearms and am about to ask Ginny for some moisturizer when Adele shouts.

"Ladies, the next stop is the Roadkill Café and O.K. Saloon." She treats us to a hearty laugh. "The motto is…drum roll, please… *'You kill it. We grill it.'*"

Good Lord.

She is beginning to remind me of me. The uptight Adele has gone missing. I must admit to having a hankering for the new version.

"Americana at its best." Adele waxes lyrical as she pilots the Escalade to a small town called Seligman, an exit off Interstate

40, and we're back on historic Route 66, lined with motels, emporiums, burger joints, and souvenir shops, their parking lots filled with vintage cars and trucks. "Robert would love this place."

"Robert?" Ginny asks, sitting in the back, playing with Laurel.

"My significant other." Adele sounds exasperated. "I've told you about him."

"No, you haven't."

"Yes, I have."

It goes back and forth until I intervene. "Ginny, she's been dating Robert since the dawn of time, and you were napping yesterday when she dished."

"Do you have a picture?" Ginny pokes her head between the bucket seats, her eyes twinkling.

Adele hands me her phone and offers the passcode. "Pull up my photos. I took a selfie before I flew out."

The image shows a giant of a man with a thick mat of silver-colored hair. His arm hangs around Adele's shoulders, and her head is in his armpit. He is one of those ear-to-ear smilers. I find myself grinning back at him before showing the image to Ginny.

"Wow. He's a looker, Aunt Adele," Ginny says. "Why haven't you gotten married? You could honeymoon there." She points to a one-story motel. "That one has vacancies."

"I just might." Adele thumps the steering wheel and turns right into a gravel parking lot. "We're here."

We eat our breakfast—coffee and scrambled eggs for me and far more interesting fare for them—before I mosey over to the saloon side, bedecked with a snarling cheetah and a zoo of other taxidermy. So much to see and so little time.

"You ready? Ginny's already outside," Adele says, bouncing a jabbering Laurel in her arms. She had mentioned over breakfast that we were headed for a resort not far from her sister's place in northwest Las Vegas. "I'm thinking we should stop at Audrey's *before* we check into the resort. Maybe we could have dinner at the Cork & Barrel later." Adele then frowns. "But on second thought, a tavern might be inappropriate if we're toting a baby."

I caress the baby's cheek. "I'll look after her if you and Ginny want to go." I pause. "Have you talked with Ginny? It seems like you've changed the plan."

Adele chews on her lips. "Well, we don't really have a plan. Audrey suggested the resort, and that's about it." The look on Adele's face tells me she's worried about something else. I wait until she says, "Audrey doesn't know Ginny is coming."

My stomach tightens as we walk toward the Escalade. "Make that right, Adele." The words come out harsher than I intend. Not everyone enjoys a surprise, especially one as big as this, given their bad blood. Shoot, I wonder how I would feel coming face-to-face with a daughter I hadn't seen in twenty years because of something I did. Of course, that would have never happened, but even so. Popping in without warning could get ugly fast.

Adele nods and climbs into the driver's seat. The heft of the secret hangs between us as a silence falls over the Cadillac. I feel storm clouds coming, and notice Ginny hasn't said a word.

CHAPTER FORTY-TWO

Ginny

My stomach is in knots.

Maybe it's Aunt Adele's pedal-to-the-metal driving through the mountains past the Hoover Dam and Boulder City, then into Henderson. The air feels stifling, the heat pressing in, just like the tightness in my chest. More likely, a debilitating case of stage fright has prompted my white-knuckled grip on the grab handle. Mom has no idea that Laurel and I are along for the ride, and the closer we get to Mom's, the more nauseous I feel. The countdown has started as we close in on Las Vegas, its skyline barely visible through a thick haze, caused—at least according to a snippet heard on the news—by wildfires in Canada. My breathing intensifies.

How is she going to react?

I try to put myself in her shoes, but it's tough. Impossible. She's a stranger. My impressions, both good and bad, formed when I was just a kid, barely old enough to recall anything other than the source of my trauma on that hot and humid afternoon in South Carolina and then her desertion months later when I needed her the most.

What am I supposed to say now? "Hey, Mom, did you miss me?"

"Ginny, do me a favor." Adele glances at me through the rearview mirror. Her face has lost its color, and worry lines form channels across her forehead. I don't know whether she is reacting to my foreboding or hers. "Text your mom on my phone. Tell her we're stopping by her house first and to expect us shortly." She draws in a big breath of air. "It might be wise also to tell her that I'm not traveling alone."

"Don't you think Audrey might appreciate knowing specifically who's coming?" Oralyn snaps. "Why the mystery?"

Everyone is uptight, but it's not too late to turn back and stop the foolishness before we're standing toe-to-toe with Mom on her territory.

"We don't have to do this," I say, hoping my travel companions will see the light. "She didn't invite us; we invited ourselves. If she knows I'm coming, she'll probably refuse to answer the door. This is a terrible idea." I grip the handle harder and stare out the window, wishing I were anywhere but inside this car, hurtling toward more emotional turmoil.

"Stop it, Ginny. This isn't about Audrey or how she'll react." Oralyn's voice elevates in pitch, drowning out the drone of tires on asphalt. She turns her body to face me, sitting in the back, covered in a sheen of rank sweat. "This is about you." She points her finger at me. "This is about letting go and moving on—second chances. Have you ever considered that your mother might have her own forgiving to do? Courage can be infectious. All it takes is one brave soul to get the conversation started."

Oralyn has never raised her voice at me, and I am shocked that she did. My spineless dithering has set her off.

"When I get back to Oklahoma," she continues, "I'll be in the same boat as you are right now. People have hurt me, too. But I'm just as guilty as they are. I gossiped about them and enjoyed every minute of it. What does that say about me? Condemned people condemn. I'm a sinner, too. Now get over yourself."

No one speaks as we zip along the highway. The tension hangs heavy. But Oralyn's wisdom has struck a nerve.

"Where's your phone, Aunt Adele?" I ask.

"Here." Her hand shaking, she transfers the phone to me. "Sorry, Ginny. I'm on edge."

"We all are."

I then write the text.

And within seconds, a thumbs-up emoji appears.

CHAPTER FORTY-THREE

Audrey

After two or three days without a drink, having visitors is the last thing I want. Why is Adele stopping by today? Did she mention that Ginny is coming too? I can't quite remember the details of Adele's text. I have never felt so confused and out of sorts in my life. A dreamless sleep might help take the edge off, and so would a carefully crafted vodka cocktail.

I bring the phone closer to my eyes and squint, barely able to make out the time. Cripes, I've overslept. I need to get up and pull myself together. I stumble to the bathroom and splash cold water on my face. Yesterday's makeup is caked beneath my eyes, and my complexion has taken on an unhealthy hue. I look twenty years older. Perhaps a cold shower will give me the boost I need to get through the next few hours.

Moving in slow motion, I manage to turn on the shower, but my knees feel weak. I grip the grab bar, my fingers trembling, as a cold sweat breaks out across my face and down my chest. I try to steady myself by focusing on the sharp sting of cold water as it hits my skin. The dizziness passes, and with a mechanical slowness, I wash myself before toweling off—an activity performed while slumped on the bathroom stool.

Whew. I am drained and wonder what's wrong. The dryness of my mouth is worse than any hangover I've ever experienced. But even my fogged brain tells me a hangover isn't possible. I stay seated until I muster enough energy to get dressed in one of my cotton Cork & Barrel cotton shirts and a pair of baggy shorts.

The doorbell rings, shocking me out of the brain fog. Should I be expecting company? For the life of me, I can't remember. *Am I losing my mind?*

My body sways as I move slowly down the hallway toward the door, every muscle tight and uncooperative. I peek through the sidelights. His back is toward me, but I recognize the auburn-colored hair.

The mystery man.

What is he doing here? I'm sure I didn't tell him where I lived. I never tell anyone—a precaution to avoid unpleasant encounters like this.

That leaves only one possibility.

He followed me home last night.

And the hairs on the back of my neck stand up. The doorknob rattles. I hear him curse. He beats the door again and then rings the bell—repeatedly. I cup my ears and take several clumsy steps backward. Everything moves in slow motion as I fall to the floor, and pictures start flashing through my mind.

Jimmy.

The trailer.

Laurel.

I need to run. But I don't know where to go. Toward Laurel? But it's too late. Jimmy is standing over her unmoving body, but Ginny has a chance. Go, sweet pea, go. Hide in my bedroom and dial nine-one-one.

And that fast, the flashback ends.

I am slumped against the wall, kitty-corner to the door, my head resting between my pulled-up knees. I try to catch my breath, fill my lungs with air, but the room spins. Are the voices I hear beyond the deadbolted door real or imagined?

"Can I help you?" A woman's voice and the yapping bark of a dog waft through the door. My neighbor. The talkative Bella? Barb? Bonnie? Did I ever know her name?

"Yes, ma'am." The man's voice sounds polite, accommodating, even friendly, but I know from first-hand experience at the Cork & Barrel last night that he's anything but kind. He gives off a sneaky, manipulative vibe that makes me think of Jimmy. "I stopped by to see Audrey Smith," the man continues. "She is expecting me, but she isn't answering the door. This isn't like her. I forgot my phone. Could you call her to make sure she's okay? Better yet, do you have a key to her house?"

No. No. No.

"I've seen her, and she's fine," my neighbor says. Her dog's yip-yap has turned into a full-throated growl. "Even if I had a key, why on God's green earth would I open the door for you? I don't know you. But if you're concerned, I'd be happy to call the police for a wellness check."

"Uh, that's okay," he says, laughing, and bangs the door again. "Maybe I got the time wrong. Have a great day."

Then silence.

I should thank her, but I don't dare open the door. Instead, I hoist myself up and stumble to the back of my house, to a corner that I think is invisible to people who might peer through the windows or the sliding-glass door. But in my anguished mind, my pursuers find me, anyway. Their mouths contort as they jeer and mock me, screeching that I am beyond saving because I hadn't saved a child who needed my protection.

In a moment of clarity, I realize that my mind has gone rogue and that the tormentors are not real. I need help, so I dial a number I know by heart.

"Please, God, let him pick up. Please. Please. Make him answer."

Danny picks up on the third ring.

"I'm scared." My voice sounds distant, as if I'm trapped inside a tomb far, far away. "I need your help. Come quickly." I hear glass shatter, and then everything goes black.

CHAPTER FORTY-FOUR

Ginny

Something is wrong.

We pull into my mother's driveway and park next to a truck. A man is at her front door, banging and yelling, "Audrey, open the door."

"Now what?" Aunt Adele turns off the ignition, already rattled because she had gotten lost before finding my mother's house in a tidy neighborhood enclosed by stucco walls.

The man must hear our car doors slam. He turns to face us. "Are you Audrey's daughter?"

If my uneasiness could grow worse, it has. My heart pounds in my chest, pulsating inside my head and down my arms. Another worry has replaced the dread and fear I felt earlier. *Where is my mother, and who is this man?* My voice sounds clipped as the hair on the back of my neck stands up. "Yes, I'm Ginny. This is her sister, Adele. And who are you?"

"Danny Mason." He comes off as levelheaded, unaffected by the unfriendly tone of my voice. His hand is extended, and he answers the unspoken question banging inside my head. "I'm Audrey's boss."

"What's going on?" Aunt Adele steps forward, matching calm for calm, but her eyes give her away. They look wild as they dart between me and Danny. "My sister is expecting us."

"I'm not sure," he says. The rocks lining the foundation get his full attention, like he's looking for something. "Thank God, I was only minutes away when I got her call."

What? I have no idea what he is talking about.

"Your mom called just a few minutes ago. She sounded confused," he says, apparently reacting to the uncertainty on my face. "She was terrified and told me to come." The foundation gets another look. "Do you have a key?"

"No." Aunt Adele runs her hands through her hair before pushing past Danny. She starts pounding the door, shouting, "Audrey, open the door. Let us in."

I glance over my shoulder and see Oralyn. Her eyes are wide and round, resembling the shape of a saucer as she leans against the Escalade, bouncing the baby on her hip. Up and down. Up and down—like a jackhammer. Clearly, she doesn't know what else to do. No one seems to know what to do.

Except for a woman who is now hurrying across her postage-stamp-sized yard.

"I called nine-one-one." She is out of breath. "That guy made me nervous. I thought he'd left, but maybe he got into her house somehow. Oh my gosh. That's his car over there…" She points to a car, the only one parked at the curb of my mother's quiet street.

It's funny what your mind registers when adrenaline pumps through your veins. Before bounding up the short sidewalk, I had noticed the BMW—the only brand Jacob would consider driving—but I let the thought pass. *It couldn't be Jacob. No way.* He's hundreds and hundreds of miles away, probably entertaining, more likely tormenting, his redhead. I have a smidgeon of sympathy for her. She has no idea what she's in for.

"Which man?" Danny asks.

"He was just here." The neighbor's voice rises in tempo, and her hands flutter about her face. "He claimed Audrey was expecting him, but he was aggressive. I got a bad vibe and told him to get off her property. I then called the cops."

Events are moving faster than my fear-soaked brain can process. In the distance, I hear the wail of a siren; the sound gets louder and louder until a police cruiser arrives and screeches to a halt in front of Mom's house, a commotion that has drawn the neighbors from their air-conditioned cocoons. They congregate on the sidewalk, murmuring among themselves.

"Is the door locked?" one of the two cops asks, moving in lightning speed.

"Yeah. I just tried it, but we need to get in quick," Danny's head pivots between the two officers. "I just spoke with the woman who lives here. She said she was scared and needed help."

The neighbor nods and then adds her account of what has happened. "I called nine-one-one because a strange man showed up just a few minutes ago and insisted that Audrey was expecting him." She takes a breath. "He gave me the creeps."

"Get the battering ram," one of the two cops shouts as another cruiser arrives.

"We need to get out of the way," Aunt Adele says, placing her arm around my shoulder and guiding me to the yard as still more law enforcement personnel show up.

Bang.

Bang.

Bang.

The door swings wildly on its hinges, eliciting a blood-curdling scream from the neighbor. "That's him. That's him." Her shaking finger points at someone inside the house, but I can only see a cavalry of men wearing sand-colored uniforms charging through the door.

Amid the clamor inside, an officer bellows, "Drop it. Now." A thump sounds, and then the shuffling of feet. "He's down… Victim in the back… Potential load and go."

I feel nothing but blind terror. *Did I hear 'load and go'?* The situation must be life-threatening. The howl of another siren adds to my panic, and without thinking, I leave Aunt Adele, who is watching the EMTs unload their stretcher. They race toward the door, with me now at their side.

As I step through the entryway, a beast of a man, a gun holstered at his hip, blocks my path. "Ma'am, you can't go in."

"But the woman who lives here is my mother." I twist to see past this human boulder, but his fingers dig deep into both of my arms. "This is a potential crime scene. You must wait outside." He is talking, but I am not listening. I break free of his grasp, but I don't get far before my hand flies to my mouth, and I gasp.

The perp who prompted the neighbor's emergency call and ear-splitting shriek is not a stranger.

The perp is Jacob.

He is lying on the floor, just inches away from shards of glass and a large rock. His hands are cuffed behind his back. Did he break the door and then bash my mother's head with that rock? My mind goes blank, overloaded with conflicting emotions. Disgust. Regret. My poor choices have now put my mother in peril. An inexplicable protectiveness lies over me, and I want to punish the man responsible.

Jacob lifts his head, his face glistening in a layer of sweat.

"Ginny, honey, I didn't do anything." The mask has slipped. That smug countenance I had seen so many times before is no longer present. He has lost control and is seeking an escape. "I'm innocent. I found your mother unconscious on the floor. I would never do anything to hurt her or you. I love you."

It takes a few moments for me to collect my thoughts about the man I once loved. He is evil, only happy when others are in pain. He tormented me, and now he has hurt my mother. Looking down on his prone body, I shake my head and in a strong and steady voice that doesn't sound like my own, I say, "I see what you are doing, and your feelings aren't my problem, Jacob. I'm not interested in your opinion or anything else you have to say. This conversation is over."

"Do you know him?" The cop has once again taken hold of my arm.

"Unfortunately, yes." My voice sounds flat. "His name is Jacob Hudson."

"Okay, we'll need to take your statement."

I shrug.

My only interest is the stretcher now rolling past me.

I sidestep the policeman, my legs pumping to keep pace with emergency personnel who are sprinting toward the door. "Mom, it's me. Ginny." Her complexion looks waxy, and her breathing is shallow. She is bleeding from her forehead. I touch her face, clammy to the touch, as we step over the threshold. The bright sunshine nearly blinds me. "Hang on, Mom. You'll be okay."

A sense of déjà vu washes over me. Hadn't Granny done the same thing? She, too, wouldn't leave Mom's side, gently stroking her swollen, battered face as medics rushed her from the broken-down trailer in South Carolina. I watched from the back of a police cruiser, feeling alone and scared.

Jimmy had wrecked my mother's body and perhaps even her spirit. Was Jacob, my misguided choice for a life partner, responsible for what's happening now?

So many questions, but answers can wait.

My immediate concern is for Mom.

The crowd has grown larger. My eyes dart around, trying to find Aunt Adele. She is exactly where I left her, wringing her hands and standing next to Danny.

I know what I must do.

"I'd like to ride with my mother if that's okay with you," I tell the medic, who has already started IVs and taking vitals. "I'm a nurse—not that it matters, but I feel like I need to be with her."

He glances at my face and then Mom's.

"Okay, get in the front."

And so begins one of the longest trips of my life.

CHAPTER FORTY-FIVE

Adele

The ambulance, with Ginny and my sister onboard, streaks out of the neighborhood. I recall reading that first responders are judicious about when to use sirens, reserving them for truly life-threatening situations—a piece of information better left unknown. The siren starts blaring before the ambulance pulls away from my sister's house.

Tears begin to trickle down my cheeks, and I can't suppress my emotions any longer. What if Audrey dies? What if I never get the chance to apologize to her? Why, why, why? I am filled with so many regrets. Danny wraps his arm around my shoulders, reminding me of Robert, who is unflappable in a crisis—the kind of person you can rely on during difficult times like this.

But the truth is, Danny's calm does not soothe my tangled nerves or allay my escalating sense of helplessness. I can't control this situation even though I try. I sent Ginny a text and left a voicemail just moments after the ambulance whisked her and Audrey away—too early, I know, but I couldn't stop myself. The police aren't providing any reassurance either, with their vague requests for me to stay put for questioning.

Despite my blurred vision, I can see Audrey's neighbor sitting on her stoop, gesturing as a uniformed female officer writes notes on a pocket-sized notebook. Then, I notice that Oralyn—the baby secured in her arms—has moved closer to us, standing on the other side of Danny.

"I can't believe this is happening," I say to no one in particular. I reach into my purse for a tissue and blow my nose before turning to face Danny. "I'm sorry, did you say that you're Audrey's boss?"

"I am." He stares at Audrey's front door, his taut jawline twitching. "She's worked for me for...geez, I can't remember." He massages his temples. "A long time." Moments pass before he continues. "She's a good woman, but she's had some problems... I don't know what's going on because she doesn't talk much about herself. Shoot, I didn't know she had a daughter until the other day."

Unaware of my sister's latest struggles, I am about to ask him for details when we're interrupted by a commotion at the door. Whoever had entered Audrey's house—most likely through a back window or door—appears at the front entryway, surrounded by Metro police. They guide him, his head bowed and his hands cuffed, down a step, and then across the yard, moving slowly toward a parked cruiser behind the Escalade.

My breath catches, and my hand goes to my chest.

Oralyn swings her head in my direction. "Do you know him?" she asks in a hushed tone, her graying eyebrows lifting as she ignores the baby's fascination with the readers dangling from her rhinestone lanyard.

"Jacob. Jacob Hudson." I feel like my mind has disconnected from my body.

"That's him?" Oralyn's mouth forms a perfect circle as she wraps her arms tighter around Laurel, as if she's afraid that he'll break loose and steal the baby. "How did he find us? I thought we had thrown him off the track. Oh my gosh. I need to sit down." She hands Laurel to me and drops to the curb.

Danny gives both of us a quizzical look. "Did you say Jacob Hudson?"

"Yes, Ginny's fiancé, the baby's father. Ginny left him—no, she ran from him—more than a week ago," I say.

"That's the man who called me a few days ago, claiming he had lost track of Ginny and thought Audrey would know where she was. He called her by name. I thought nothing of it. He made me think he was on the up-and-up." Danny squints harder at the procession, moving at a glacial speed just feet in front of us, deep crow's feet forming at the corners of his eyes. "He showed up at the tavern last night."

The pieces are falling into place. *What in God's name was he planning to do?* My body trembles as I watch the police shove Jacob into the back of the cruiser, nonplussed when his head bangs hard against the cruiser's doorframe. They slam the door. Jacob turns his head and looks out the window. Our eyes connect. The stare-down lasts for a moment before he casts his gaze in another direction. His arrogance takes my breath away as another shiver runs down my spine.

What would he have done to Ginny?

I feel like I could get sick. I cover my mouth with my hand as all thoughts of Audrey's struggles—the problems Danny had alluded to earlier—evaporate in the scorching heat. In retrospect, this was a mistake. Answers to my questions could have made all the difference.

I reach for my phone and call the only person who can comfort me at this moment.

"Robert, please come. I need you. Something has happened..."

CHAPTER FORTY-SIX

Ginny

The waiting room is packed with people of every flavor. Most appear lost in thought or distracted by their phones, including me. I try calling Aunt Adele, but the call goes to voicemail. I don't bother with Oralyn. Running alongside the stretcher, I had noticed her chalk-white complexion and the tight grip she had on Laurel. Her predictable life in Oklahoma must seem like a distant memory to her right now.

"Ginny Carmichael?" an ER nurse calls.

I follow her labyrinth like path to where my mother lies, connected to medical equipment. She looks small and vulnerable lying on the bed.

"Your mother, correct?" an ER doctor asks, holding a clipboard.

I nod.

"Your mother has had a grand mal seizure," he says, turning his detached gaze on Mom, whose twitching has stopped. She appears lost in a haze, unable to communicate.

The goose egg on her forehead has grown larger, but the bleeding has stopped. In a few days, the small blood vessels under the skin will likely break, leaving purplish-colored bruises around her eyes. Not a first for her, having lived with Jimmy.

"The seizure may have come on because of a concussion or a blow to her head," he continues, "but until she tells us, we won't know whether the suspect struck her, or she fell. However, we need to consider other possible causes. Is she epileptic? Anxious? Does she have PTSD, a history of migraines, or substance abuse?"

His questions make me feel inadequate, much like how Jacob would make me feel. It didn't matter what I did or said; somehow, I never quite lived up to his expectations, and now I'm not living up to this doctor's. I don't even have the basics about my mother's medical history. We have no history at all. All I can do is shake my head.

"Okay." He exhales and orders an EEG, a comprehensive metabolic panel, a toxicology screen, and other tests. "We'll have a much better idea of what's happening once we get test results."

He glances at the door and sees a plainclothes police officer waiting beyond the threshold next to the nurse's station. "We've already told him that your mother is in no condition for questioning, but he may want your statement." The doctor brushes past me without saying another word.

I take in a big breath and stroke my mother's face before leaving her—reluctantly—to talk with the officer, who is chatting up a nurse as her colleagues rush from one curtained examination area to the next. The scene is one I have seen many times before, yet it feels different today.

ERs have a life and rhythm of their own, a constant ebb and flow that's almost predictable. The beeping machines, the hurried footsteps—a pattern that brings a twisted sense of comfort to me. I know this world. Here, second chances can happen, moments to right wrongs or save lives. But sometimes, no matter how well you know the rhythm, the door closes, and nothing you do can change the outcome.

Is that the case here?

The nurse directs us to a small room tucked away in the corner. We both take our chairs directly across from each other at the table. He pulls out his notepad and taps his lips with a pen.

"I have a few questions."

The interview takes longer than I expected. As events unfolded, I hadn't realized how valuable my testimony might be—a far cry from the information I had offered just minutes earlier while speaking with the doctor. Shouts and curses from an anguished patient interrupt my narrative about Jacob's use of tracking technology and a private investigator to pursue me across the country. I do all the talking, while he avoids the questions I want addressed.

"What are you charging him with?" I ask, standing as he closes his notebook.

"Several charges are possible, but we must finish our investigation."

"You will be charging him with something, right?" My voice sounds more aggressive than I intended. Although I no longer believe Jacob can affect me emotionally, I want more. Legal trouble might discourage him from ever coming near me again.

"I don't want to live the rest of my life looking over my shoulder because of him." I feel my eyes narrowing.

"Ma'am, I understand. You might consider getting a restraining order."

I roll my eyes. "What good would that do me?"

"Added protection." He stands and takes one step toward the door when his phone rings. "I gotta take this." He turns his back on me.

From the one-sided dialogue, I gather that the call concerns us. "I still haven't spoken with the victim. She's in no condition to talk. Have you interrogated him?" he asks, then pauses, nodding at whatever the caller is divulging. "Alright, I'm finished here and on my way. We can question him together." He ends the call and looks at me. "I need to go downtown. I'll be back to talk with your mother."

An hour later, I still haven't heard from the detectives, but Mom's condition is becoming clearer.

CHAPTER FORTY-SEVEN

Ginny

I walk the short distance to my mother's bed following the detective's interview, numbed by the scene.

My near-catatonic mother has mutated into a raging lunatic. The small, curtained space is crowded with muscled security staff and a new contingent of nurses—all male—who are trying to subdue her. Her strength seems supernatural as she claws and kicks. Before the beefier reinforcements arrived, she had delivered a well-aimed kick at a young nurse whose nose now runs a bloody river, spotting her scrubs and the floor. Someone hands her a towel.

"I've never seen anything like it," the freckle-faced RN says, her voice tinged with hysteria, proving at least to me that she is a newbie to emergency-room medicine. How many times had I dodged a fist or kick to the groin? No one seems to be listening to the woman as she dabs her nose with a bloodied towel. She is of no use in this rapidly devolving situation.

Whether alerted by my mother's shouting or by a nurse's report, the doctor elbows his way in and positions himself next to Mom's bed. As she bucks and curses, infuriated by the mittens now shrouding her hands and the tethers binding her wrists and ankles, he looks at her as if she were a curiosity.

"You're all devils," my mother snarls, tugging on the restraints. "Take them off. I'm not a criminal, but you're treating me like one." She collapses against her pillow, her blue eyes darting back and forth as if she is searching for a liberator.

Her eyes find mine. "Who are you?"

I step forward and touch her arm, hoping a gentle touch and a soothing voice might calm her hysteria. "Mom, it's me, Ginny."

"Take these off," she yells, showing not even a flicker of recognition. I am a stranger to her, another tormentor among everyone else.

"Mom, please—"

"Ma'am, who is the president?" The grim-faced doctor speaks over me, asking just one of the handful of time-and-place questions medical staff ask when patients show a cognitive break.

"Ronald Reagan." She doesn't miss a beat. Her eyes become wide as her body arches like a scene from *The Exorcist*. "Remove these straps now. How am I supposed to save the children? They need me."

"Ms. Smith, the restraints stay on." The doctor's face is inches from hers. "You attacked a nurse, and for your safety and ours, we can't take them off. If you want to blame someone, blame me." She quiets—for a second—before arguing her case for freedom at decibels likely heard in the waiting room.

He is about to say something when a nurse interrupts.

"Doc, her blood pressure is spiking… Her heart rate is all over the map."

He glances at the medical-monitoring equipment, as if not trusting the pronouncement, and shakes his head slightly, frowning. "It would be enormously helpful if *someone* knew her history." He says this under his breath.

It's so true, but I don't have answers. I reach into my cloth bag, searching for the burner among the jumble of items. I dial a memorized number, but the phone rings. "Come on, Aunt Adele, pick up." She doesn't answer, so I'm forced to leave a message.

As I run alongside the medical professionals rushing my mother to the ICU, I learn that test results show a different diagnosis. A heavy sense of dread washes over me, extinguishing any hope that this was a one-time occurrence. My mother's grand mal seizure probably had nothing to do with epilepsy or a head injury. Most likely, Jacob hadn't caused my mom's medical emergency, either. Her issues could have started days, maybe even years, ago.

This could be bad—very bad.

CHAPTER FORTY-EIGHT

Jacob

My bedroom closet looks like the Taj Mahal compared to the drab, gray interrogation room where I sit, my arms folded, at a cheap Formica-topped table. Other than providing my name, I will keep my mouth sealed until my lawyer arrives.

I am suspected of first-degree burglary, a Category B felony in Nevada, and possibly other charges, including assault and battery. The circumstantial evidence against me is quite damaging, according to the Keystone Cops, who brought me to this room, but they are full of it.

So is my father.

His head is exploding. Before arranging legal counsel with a hotshot criminal practice here in Vegas, he told me—through what sounded like gritted teeth—not to return to Atlanta until the dust settles. My mausoleum of a house, which he owns, will no longer be a home to me. Whenever authorities see the light and release me, I will be moving to the coast to assume operations there. Dad thinks he is punishing me, but he couldn't be more mistaken. I am tired of Atlanta and his political campaign. I am tired of everything.

I'm the victim—not Ginny, her mother, my dad, or anyone else.

Once I spotted Ginny's mother lying on the kitchen floor, I grabbed the first rock I could find, chucked it at the sliding-glass door, and then called nine-one-one. I still can't figure out how Metro police got there so fast. Within seconds of my reporting an emergency, they were busting down the front door, catching me in the kitchen, standing amid the broken glass. They should be thanking me for my rapid-fire, selfless thinking, not accusing me of a crime. Had the consequences of my good deed been known then, I would have left the way I came in, leaving Ginny's look-alike mom prostrate on the floor.

A knock on the door disturbs my thoughts.

A man of average height, with slicked-back dark brown hair, peeks around the door, escorted by one of my interrogators, a woman of about my age. He is dressed in a tailored suit that practically shouts success—a promising sign. "Thanks," he says, flashing a warm smile at the female cop. "Give us a minute." She nods curtly, shoots me a glare, and shuts the door behind her with a definitive click of the latch, locking me inside.

"My name is Rodriguez." He strides into the matchbox-sized room and shakes my hand with a firm, practiced grip. He pulls out a legal pad from his shoulder bag and takes a seat in the plastic chair across from me. "Your father was wise to contact us first." His gaze stays fixed on mine. "As you may be aware, you are suspected of burglary. The investigation is ongoing, but they believe they have enough evidence to charge you. If convicted, you could be facing a significant amount of time in jail. Can you tell me what happened?"

My story comes out in measured tones. The longer we talk, the better I feel. No good deed goes unpunished, I say.

"Did Ms. Smith invite you into her home?"

"She was expecting me, and when she didn't answer the door, I grew alarmed and started pounding on the door." I lean back into my chair. "Her neighbor promised to call in a wellness check, and I initially decided to leave, but then I thought better of it. I opened the side gate to the backyard and then looked through the windows and sliding-glass door. That's when I saw Audrey Smith lying on the kitchen floor."

The lawyer nods and screws up his eyes as if trying to imagine the scene I just described. He taps his pen on the table.

"Someone did call in an emergency but left no name. Was that you?"

"Of course, that was me. I've already explained the situation. My girlfriend's mother had collapsed on the floor, and since I have some medical training, I thought it was best to get to her as quickly as possible. I found the rock and broke the glass. Good grief, is that a crime?"

"That depends. Ms. Smith's neighbor also called nine-one-one. She reported she became concerned about a man's aggressive behavior. Was she referring to you?"

That witch. While I debated whether to sneak through Audrey's side gate, the busybody neighbor apparently was on the phone reporting me as a suspicious person. No wonder the police arrived guns blazing—the injustice of it all. She will also be hearing from my attorney.

"This is a big misunderstanding," I say, drumming the tabletop with the tips of my fingers. "When can I get out of here?"

Rodriguez takes his time answering. He reads his notes. "Much depends on Ms. Smith's statement," he says, preoccupied with his scribblings. "And, of course, your account of what happened." He lays his pen on the notepad, his eyes drilling into mine. "You are to answer their questions truthfully. Do not volunteer information. If they overstep in their questioning, I will recommend that you refrain from answering. Cops are not your friends. I am. Do you understand?"

His attitude strikes me as pompous. Of course, I understand. *Does he think I'm stupid?* I've seen enough cop shows to know how they work—good cop, bad cop. They will lie, imply, and accuse me of all sorts of crimes, hoping I'll break under pressure and admit to doing something that I did not do.

Rodriguez stands and knocks on the door. "We're ready."

Ahh, a co-ed team. The woman will be like putty in my skillful hands.

"What is your relationship to Audrey Smith and her daughter, Ginny Carmichael?" the woman asks as if we are best friends.

"Ginny's my fiancée." Rodriguez gives me a look, and then I remember that I had described her as my girlfriend just moments earlier, and it's too late to correct the statement. *At least I didn't call her my wife.* I lean back in my chair and cross my legs. With Rodriguez's okay, I then recount my side of the story about how I'd been worried about Ginny and flew to Vegas to find her. Blah. Blah. Blah.

"You are a nasty piece of work," her cohort snarls, his eyes squinty and mean. "You stalked Ms. Carmichael, and then you stalked her mother. You wanted to harm Ms. Smith, possibly her daughter. And guess what, dude, you succeeded. You'd better pray Ms. Smith recovers from her injuries because we'll throw the book at you."

The interview goes downhill from there. My cool has evaporated like the morning dew. Sweat forms at my neck and drips down my back, especially when they read my Miranda Rights. Crimes I did not commit could tarnish my good name.

"You'll be cooling your heels in a holding cell until the judge sets bail," the woman says before she and the co-inquisitor stand, scraping their chairs across the floor.

"This can't be happening," I tell Rodriguez as soon as they slam the door. I rub my five o'clock shadow. I need a shower and a shave. "Have you any idea how bad this is for me? I have standing in Atlanta."

"Don't worry yet. Their case is weak." Rodriguez gathers his legal pad and swings his bag over his shoulder. "However, much depends on Ms. Smith's testimony." He pauses. "Is Ginny Carmichael your girlfriend or fiancée? You seem to have trouble remembering."

At that moment, a cop opens the door. He's taking me to a holding cell, and all I can see are the veins bulging from my father's neck and the smirk on Rodriguez's chiseled, good-looking face.

CHAPTER FORTY-NINE

Oralyn

After the police interview and a quick stop at the grocery store, we finally arrived at the rented three-bedroom penthouse apartment. In all the commotion, Adele had forgotten to check her phone. When she finally did, she gasped and rushed out the door. That was hours ago, and I still haven't heard from her or Ginny. I'm exhausted and feeling much too old for this endless turmoil.

I lift myself off the large sectional sofa, my joints creaking as I make my way over to check on Laurel, who is sleeping soundly in her portable crib next to the fireplace, sucking her thumb. Thank God for small blessings. Baby girl had turned into a little demon at her grandmother's house, and nothing seemed to calm her. I still can't find that blasted binkie, but at least she has discovered her thumb.

If I weren't an old lady, I'd suck mine, too. Yep. A good pull on the thumb might calm my nerves.

This apartment doesn't relieve anything. It echoes. Five of my houses would fit inside this palace, with its cathedral ceilings, fancy-pants kitchen, pool-sized soaking tubs, private elevator, and Lord knows what else.

I walk into the kitchen and put away the rest of our groceries in the fridge and cabinets. As I do so, I catch my reflection in the sliding-glass door that leads out to a spacious balcony. It offers a view of man's relentless march to tame a once inhospitable desert. My goodness, just look at my hair! The humidity hasn't caused this helmet of frizz, which looks more like a well-used steel-wool pad. Neglect has, and it's no wonder, considering my recent hospitalization, constant traveling, and now Jacob's latest surprise. I could use a nap, but the mountain vista, bathed in a kaleidoscope of color, seems so much more inviting. I unlatch the door and step outside.

It's hot and dry—like an oven. But I ignore the heat and plop down on one of the balcony chairs, trying to make sense of my impressions. I've always wondered how the other half lives and made that one of my goals when I agreed to take part in Ginny's journey—her path to redemption, and perhaps even my own. Thanks to Adele's deep pockets and her over-the-top generosity, I've gotten a taste of how bougie people live. Shoot, not even a fever dream would have landed me in a place like this.

I'm not ungrateful, but this lifestyle doesn't feel like me.

I want to go home.

This trip has taught me the value of simplicity and the importance of appreciating what I already have. It's not about grand gestures or extravagant locations—it's about finding peace in the small, quiet moments. I miss my home, my routine, and the things that bring me comfort. Nothing seems permanent here. When a casino loses its allure, demolition experts wire it with explosives, and before you know it, it's gone. Living in the past doesn't help anyone, but ignoring your history seems foolish, too. You need a starting point, a reminder of where you've been.

The good Lord has blessed me with a fulfilling, if predictable, life in Oklahoma, surrounded by people I've known since I was knee-high to a grasshopper. Much to my surprise, I even miss Wilma, whom I've maligned for years as the "old biddy."

I hear Laurel fussing through the partially opened door, reminding me that I'm still needed here. Who knows how long we'll stay, but I'll make the best of it. Whatever happens, happens, but in the meantime, I can take comfort in knowing I've scratched an item off my life list. I will return home a changed and, I hope, a better person.

CHAPTER FIFTY

Ginny

Mom's condition hasn't changed, but at least Aunt Adele and I now understand what we are dealing with, and my heart breaks seeing her like this.

She is suffering from delirium tremens, a severe and life-threatening form of alcohol withdrawal that occurs when chronic drinkers stop drinking abruptly. She has all the classic symptoms, including seeing things that are not there. In her fractured reality, she imagines desperate children who plead for her help. It could take another two or three days before she completely detoxes, aided by benzodiazepines to calm her overdriven nervous system.

This day feels like it will never end.

Aunt Adele slips out of Mom's darkened room, filled with beeping machines and clinical smells, to call Oralyn and let her know that we will not be home for several more hours, adding another layer of stress for me. Oralyn isn't entirely well herself.

And then there's Jacob.

The detective—the man I had spoken with earlier in the ER—said Jacob is expected to post bail soon and will likely fly back to Georgia to await trial. "More charges are possible," he assured me when we spoke on the phone. "But this case hinges on what your mother remembers, and she may not remember anything, which isn't unusual in cases like this."

I want Jacob to pay a price, any price, for his sociopathic stalking of me and my mother. At this point, I can only hope the seizure and withdrawal haven't affected her cognitive function.

I study her plundered face. Blood is already collecting beneath her eyes. Within a day, she will look like a battered wife—a far cry from the perky, confident Peaches persona she projected in the video—the video that proved my mom was alive and well.

"Who are you?" The words tumble from my mouth before I can snatch them back. I want to know and love her.

She mumbles, and my phone vibrates—an unfamiliar number flashes on the screen.

I lower my voice. "Hello?"

"I spoke with your aunt. She gave me your number. What's going on?"

"Hold on." I notice a chair tucked away behind the machines, next to a plate glass window affording an uninspiring view of the rooftop. "Thanks for calling, Danny. Given the test results, the doctors believe she probably fell because of a withdrawal-related seizure, not a blow to the head." My voice comes across as measured and calm, as if I were discussing a random patient, not my own flesh and blood. However, I would be of no use to anyone if I let my emotions take over. "She has a drinking problem, a big one," I continue. "Did you know?"

He takes in a deep breath. "Oh boy...I had no idea—"

"Yes, and DTs have complicated the detoxing." I stand to peer past the monitors to get a better view of her. Her arms and legs are flailing again. I hear her murmuring, reacting to whatever her embattled mind has conjured. At least she stopped screaming.

"Which medications are they administering?"

Danny's voice is steady as he asks the question. It's not the kind of thing most people would think to ask, but his tone suggests personal familiarity with the issue, as if he's been down this road before and knows the drill.

"I'm a nurse, Danny. I've seen this before, but watching someone you know... It's scary. I can't do anything but make sure she gets the best medical care."

"I know how you feel," he says without offering more. "If it's okay with you, I would prefer to have this conversation in person. Would it be okay if I stopped by your rental tomorrow morning? Afternoon? Maybe we could meet for coffee? I think it would be easier on you and your aunt if I shared my observations face-to-face."

At that moment, my mind crosses time and space. TC would have made the same suggestion.

Of course, that would be okay, I tell him. I end the call, noticing only then that Aunt Adele had slipped in while I talked with Danny. She has positioned herself next to my mother's bed, leaning over, her hand resting on Mom's exposed shoulder. The thin hospital gown has slipped down, exposing

Mom's bony shoulder. "Sister, do you know who I am?" my aunt whispers, her mouth close to Mom's ear. She motions to me to stand next to her. "Ginny and I have come a long way to visit you."

Mom opens her glassy, unfocused eyes. She lifts her right hand as far as the strap allows, bends over, and starts biting the mitten. Somehow, she manages to free her hand of its covering, and the nurse appears as if beckoned by a silent alarm.

"Aren't you the magician?" the nurse says, gently working Mom's hand back inside the mitten. The nurse looks in our direction and gives us a sad smile. "Ladies, I think it might be best if you go home for the night. She's highly agitated… Not your fault, of course—just the nature of the beast."

"Are you sure?" Aunt Adele asks.

The nurse nods. "Withdrawal is ugly and hard to watch, especially for family members." She goes on to tell us about a pastor, a closet drinker, who had landed in the ICU because of a heart attack. He was less than truthful about his alcohol habits, and, of course, his wife had no clue about his addiction. Within two or three days without a drink, his secret was out. "I pitied his wife…my goodness, the language he used."

Aunt Adele has offered to drive, mainly because she is already familiar with the route. However, I also suspect she needs to feel in control, and getting behind the wheel is her way of taking charge. I lean my head against the window, the air conditioning blasting, watching as we pass one community after another, stitched together into a large patchwork quilt.

"Robert is flying out soon. I figure we'll be here for a few more days." Aunt Adele glances at me. "I hope that's okay."

"Sure. I want to meet him. Maybe you two can visit one of those little chapels," I joke because it's better than worrying… or crying.

She shrugs and gives me a lopsided grin. "You never know."

So true. We never know. We don't even know the people we should know.

We ride the private elevator to our apartment, and the smells of a home-cooked meal greet us. Laurel is lying in her crib, gurgling the way happy babies do, pulling her feet toward her mouth. A scene of domestic happiness. All is well with the world, even though it isn't.

"Ah, baby girl." I lift her and hold her tight, nuzzling her neck and breathing in her sweet, milky scent. "Did Miss Oralyn give you a bath?" Laurel coos and waves her fat, dimpled arms. I raise my eyes and catch Oralyn's attention.

"Thank you," I mouth.

She winks and removes a sizzling casserole from the oven.

Thank you, Lord, for Oralyn. But please give my mom another shot. We still need to make things right.

CHAPTER FIFTY-ONE

Jacob

I swing my carry-on bag over my shoulder and glance at my Rolex. It is early—very early. I could have called an Uber, but I thought, why not give Red a buzz? She doesn't have anything else to do on a Sunday morning except pick me up from the airport, take me home, and help me load my convertible.

Pack only the essentials, dear old Dad had advised last night, after posting the hefty bond to ensure my court appearance back in Vegas if it comes to that. But according to Rodriguez, I have nothing to worry about. His well-placed sources told him that the case has nearly fallen apart. Ginny's mom is a drunk—big surprise—and is still incommunicado. No one is expecting much from her.

I am done with Ginny and her mess.

Especially now that I am on home turf.

Red sees me standing in the passenger pick-up area before I see her behind the wheel of her late-model Lexus crossover. She lowers the passenger-side window as I approach. “Hey, babe,” she says, her voice filled with uncertainty.

I flash her my signature megawatt smile. “Darlin’, thanks for doing me the solid. Whew, what a trip.” I toss my bag onto the back seat before leaning through the open window, bringing her lips to mine. All the air seems to leave her body as she cups my face with her manicured hands and pulls me in for a deeper kiss.

“I’m so glad you are home,” she whispers in her kitten-like voice, her Georgia accent thick and heavy.

“Me too.” Those words are spoken with sincerity.

She must take that as a good omen because she starts chattering about all sorts of trivial things as I slide into the passenger seat. I’m careful to avoid mentioning the topic that had brought her to tears the day I left for Vegas. As she talks, I barely pay attention. I have more important matters on my mind.

“Hey, Jacob,” she says, driving past one mansion after another in my exclusive neighborhood. “Did you know that your dad is leading in the polls?”

That gets my attention.

“Oh yeah?” I glance at her. “I didn’t think you followed politics.”

She gives me a pouty look. “Of course, I follow politics. It’s your dad. Our families go way back.”

Ah, yes, our family connections. I almost forgot about Dad’s heavy-handed demands—delivered with all the subtlety of a bulldozer—when he insisted that I cut ties with Red. Hadn't he called her a tart? I stored that accusation for later recall and even questioned Red in a roundabout way before leaving for Vegas.

It turns out that Dad had pulled her onto his lap at a family gathering several years ago. At the time, I was away at boarding school and knew her as a flirty teenager who wore suggestive clothing. When I asked her about it, she laughed it off and attributed his inappropriate behavior to having drunk too much. She never gave it another thought, she said, because it never happened again. However, her account might come in handy when I update Dad on my plans.

What a moralistic fraud.

As she pulls into the driveway, I give my house a long look before unlatching the seat belt and striding toward the front door, the keys jangling in my hand. Red slides next to my side and nestles her hand into mine. I don't care who sees us, most especially the nitwit neighbors who loved Ginny and the kid as if they were family and made sure I knew it. I pull Red close to my chest and nuzzle her swan-like neck. She wants more and nearly drags me up the foyer stairs.

"Later, Red. I have packing to do."

"You're going somewhere?" Her mouth turns downward.

"Yes—a surprise."

We are walking past the nursery, and I stop, my hand frozen on the doorframe as I survey the room. It is a little girl's dream—a pastel-pink nightmare. I paid for every inch of it, every single detail. A delicate, hand-painted mural of a large, leafy tree dominates one wall above the custom-made white crib. The ruffled curtains, the children's books neatly arranged on a shelf beneath the window seat—their price stickers still attached—and the perfectly positioned rocking chair make a statement: Look at what I can provide.

None of it ever mattered to Ginny. She never appreciated how hard I tried to make everything perfect for her, for us, because she was always too busy searching for something better. That child, the one who probably isn't even mine, will act the same. They are spitting images of each other.

I take two heavy steps into the room, feeling the load of frustration land hard against my chest. The room is pristine, still untouched by any real life. It is a lie, a reminder of everything I have done for people who never deserved it.

"Dad has asked that I take over coastal operations. We have big plans. Anyway, I'm headed there today." I pause for dramatic purposes. "I think this furniture would look great in my new house." I let my arms swing open, as though I am offering a gift for her to consider—one of my specialties. No one can ever accuse me of not knowing how to manipulate a moment. "What do you think, pretty lady?"

The corners of Red's eyes crinkle. She then catches my drift and rushes to the upholstered window seat before sitting, her hand clamped over her mouth. Her eyes sweep the room, taking in the nursery's pricey accoutrements.

Even though I had done something similar with Ginny at one of my parents' dinner parties, I take a knee and ask for Red's hand. This time, however, I don't slip a pop-top ring on her finger like I did with Ginny. I have something better to present. I twist off a silver signet ring embossed with my initials, noticing the grayish coloring around my ring finger. "This is temporary,"

I say, looking at my ring, another gift from my mother. "Will you marry me?"

"Oh, Jacob. Of course, I'll marry you." Her eyes leak tears as I fit my too-big jewelry onto her slender digit. She then envelops me in a tight hug, rocking me back and forth. Bored with the histrionics, I stand up. Deep furrows fill the space between her eyebrows. "But what about my appointment tomorrow?"

"Cancel it. You're gonna be a mama, Red. A beautiful one."

"What about Ginny?" She sucks in her lips.

"Done, my love. She won't be showing up around here again." I laugh, lifting her into my arms. This is too easy. She literally soaks my shirt with her tears. She is gung-ho, raring to go. Our life together is her dream come true.

I call Dad from my downstairs den and shut the door, not wanting Red to overhear my conversation.

"I'm headed out. When is the house going on the market?" I resent the way he has taken control of my home, but knowing Dad, I suspect he will invest the proceeds into the company. His dedication to ensuring Peach State Holdings' success, despite the economic downturn, is admirable and assuages my resentment—until he drops this nugget.

"What kind of question is that, Jacob? Of course, we're not listing it yet," he says. "You should know better. If you haven't noticed, the market is soft, and until it improves, a friend of mine will house-sit. But we need to clear out your belongings."

I know better than to ask who this friend might be and suspect this person is of the female persuasion. Is he moving me out to make room for his honeypot? If that's the case, a mystery is solved. An illicit love interest would explain his distracted behavior lately.

Talk about indiscretions; talk about putting yourself first—my dad in a nutshell.

"Look, son, I appreciate your cooperation," he continues, apparently oblivious to his hypocrisy or determined to keep the focus on my supposed gaffes. "But your relocation is for the best. What happens in Vegas, stays in Vegas, right?"

Please leave it to him to haul out that overused cliché. *Nothing happened in Vegas, but something most definitely is happening in Atlanta.* I wonder if Mom is aware of his shenanigans, or would she even care? No doubt, she has already begun planning her first star-studded dinner party as the wife of a state senator and would likely look past his improprieties.

Already annoyed and eager to end the conversation, I nearly lose my temper when he brings up Ginny. "If she demands child support, don't contest it," he advises. "We don't need more trouble."

"First of all, those charges will be dropped because I was falsely accused," I say through clenched teeth. "Furthermore, that baby may not be mine—something I learned while I was in Las Vegas. You should be grateful that things turned out the way they did. I did you a favor in more ways than one. I'm moving on, and you'd be wise to do likewise." *Yes, Dad, your secret arrangement is safe with me.*

He coughs and changes the subject. "Okay, great. Look, I must attend another fundraiser. Call me as soon as you arrive at the beach." The line goes dead.

Maybe I will; maybe I won't. *Won't he be surprised when Red moves in with me?* I chuckle to myself.

As I pull out of the garage, Red blows me a kiss. "See you next weekend," she shouts before climbing into her Lexus, which is packed with my clothes and mementos that she'll deliver later. She has a few loose ends to tie up before she moves to the coast, giving me plenty of time to check out the scene.

Like father, like son. I have other opportunities to pursue.

I peel out of the driveway and onto my tree-lined street, not looking back.

Jacob Hudson is on the move.

CHAPTER FIFTY-TWO

Ginny

I tiptoe from our bedroom. Waking Laurel is the last thing I want to do. I need alone time to think, meditate, and prepare for whatever the day brings. The sun has already begun its ascent over the mountains, painting an abstract in cayenne, coral, burnt orange, and powder blue. It's beautiful—a reminder of Granny. She saw God in everything, especially in the dawn of a new day when the colors arrest your senses and God's dominion humbles you.

"Sunrises are as unique as your fingerprints, sweet pea," she'd say, sitting on her front porch, sipping coffee, much like what I'm doing now on the balcony. "Not one is like the other—just like you and me. Everyone is beautifully and powerfully made, and don't ever forget it, not even on your worst day."

The memory makes me smile and gives me courage, something that had been in short supply a day ago. I call the hospital to check in on Mom. The update is neither good nor bad. It's neutral. She is going through the process and sleeps most of the time, the nurse says, recommending that we wait until later to visit.

I hear the sliding-glass door open. Aunt Adele is cradling my baby, who is making noisy gulping sounds as she guzzles her bottle; the spit rag is draped over her shoulder.

"This kid is a chowhound," my aunt says, taking the chair next to me. She laughs. "I'm no expert, but I think she needs *real* food."

Her observation is spot-on. Laurel is always hungry, but I would feel more comfortable discussing this with her pediatrician before introducing cereals. I run my fingers through my hair and make a mental note to call the doctor tomorrow morning. This is becoming ridiculous. It's probably time for a checkup, and, of course, I have no intention of ever going back to Atlanta. I must settle down and grow roots, find a home and a job. I need to create a new life for myself and Laurel, but the question is, where would we go?

"Have you seen Oralyn?" I ask, suppressing the internal self-talk. "She's normally up at the crack of dawn. I think she wanted to catch a livestream of her church services." I smile to myself. Lately, she has taken to technology like a duck to water.

"She's propped up on her pillows and already watching on her phone. I heard a few seconds of his sermon—whew. There is nothing shy or retiring about that pastor."

"You should see him in person," I say as Aunt Adele thumps Laurel's back.

"Big burp, sweet baby," she murmurs before glancing at me. "Have you called the hospital?"

"Yes. No change. The nurse said Mom is arousable but gets agitated. She wants to keep the number of visitors to a minimum.

We could probably wait until later today or tomorrow to visit."

I shake my head and ask a nagging question. "Did you see this happening?"

"Not this necessarily, but I'm not surprised." Aunt Adele places the empty bottle on the table separating us and adjusts Laurel into a sitting position on her lap. "You didn't grow up with her. I did. She's a broken person, Ginny, and I'm starting to think she has endured more than Daddy's death… I'm beginning to see her in a different light."

"Why?" I ask.

Aunt Adele raises her pointer finger toward the sky. "The Almighty has shown me the error of my ways."

I'm dumbstruck—not just by my aunt's acknowledgment of God, which surprises me, but also by her observation about my mother. It reminds me of something TC had told me during our miraculous encounter—an insight I had almost forgotten. "*Your mother didn't have the benefit of counseling,*" he said. "*Is it possible she experienced another shock?*" I consider sharing TC's observations, but Aunt Adele, after a brief pause, has picked up where she left off.

"Your mother looked like an angel—much like the little one here." She caresses the baby's crown, her eyes distant as she gazes toward the horizon. "She sang like one, too. Mom was over the moon when Audrey began serving on the altar guild, helping with communion, and singing her solos. Everything seemed fine until one Sunday. After that, she threw a fit and refused to go to church. Of course, Mom won those arguments."

I suck in my bottom lip. "What do you think happened?"

Aunt Adele shrugs.

Neither one of us speaks until Oralyn breaks the silence, stepping out onto the balcony. She looks thinner, and her face has a healthy glow—a vast improvement over yesterday, when worry carved deep creases across her face. She lowers herself onto the chaise lounge and stretches out.

"What time are we meeting Danny?" Oralyn chirps. "If I were younger, I'd be after that one." She gives me a grin. The woman knows how to lighten the mood.

* * *

Danny is waiting outside when we arrive for brunch. He greets us with a broad smile, offering his right arm to Aunt Adele and his left to Oralyn. I follow in their wake, noticing the approving glances from the women we pass. He exudes a rugged, laid-back charm, which is so different from the overly coiffed Jacob. I find myself wondering how many women wish they could be holding onto Danny's arm. My two middle-aged companions certainly sparkle at Danny's chivalrous attention.

After the server takes our orders, Danny directs the conversation to Mom.

"I feel somewhat responsible," he says, taking a sip of water. "I fired her for getting blind drunk and then rehired her the next day. She was short on money—she's always short on money—and I felt sorry for her. I wanted to give her a second chance." He takes a deep breath and drums the table with his fingers. "I told her to stay off the sauce. Obviously, she took my warnings to heart. Maybe I should have insisted she get professional help first, before giving her the job back. It may have prevented all this."

We all shake our heads. Aside from Oralyn, who has yet to meet my mother, we could all find reasons to blame ourselves. A long silence stretches until he lifts his head, and our eyes meet.

"I see a lot of similarities between your mom and mine."

"What happened to your mother?" I ask.

"She was a nurse, like you. She was very good at her job, and people loved her, like how they react to Audrey." A sadness crosses his face. "Like many people, my mother carried a lot of emotional baggage. When she injured her back moving a patient, her doctor prescribed painkillers. It didn't take long before they had her by the throat. It was painful to watch." Danny looks past my shoulder, staring at nothing. "Look, I'll do whatever I can to help. I think the world of Audrey."

I nod. "Where is your mother now?"

One look at his face and I wish I hadn't asked.

"My sister and I spent nearly a fortune on rehab and recovery centers—the best that money could buy in Kansas, where I grew up on a farm. She relapsed and died of an overdose. I was overseas, deployed with the Reserves. My sister and I thought she had turned the corner. Her death was the saddest day of my life because I hadn't been there for her."

He stands. "If it's okay, I'd like to visit Audrey once her symptoms start to subside."

He is as good as his word, and I don't think I could have managed without his strong presence two days later.

CHAPTER FIFTY-THREE

Adele

It is Monday. Robert took the red-eye flight from New York last night and has already made our secret arrangements. He is now fast asleep in his hotel room several stories above the high-end hair salon where we are currently sitting. While his arrival may not be a surprise to my travel companions, the plans we had made are.

This day of pampering is on me, a woman with an ulterior motive.

Ginny's messy updo appears effortless, which, of course, is the point. In contrast, mine is meticulously styled and tinted—just as I had requested for a day that I thought would never arrive. My only regret, of course, is that my sister cannot be here. However, I didn't want to wait. If this trip has taught me anything, it is that life is too short.

"Oralyn, you look stunning," I exclaim, rising from the salon's rich leather sofa to admire her reflection in the floor-to-ceiling mirror. "You are a genius," I add, addressing the stylist—an effusive, diminutive man who evokes the image of *Edward Scissorhands.* With remarkable speed and precision, he has transformed Oralyn's once-frizzy crown of gray coils. He continues to perfect her look, rearranging the soft, wavy curls to beautifully frame her professionally made-up face. Satisfied with his work, he finally brings his fingertips together and raises them to his lips.

"Magnifique." The word flicks into the yonder. He beams.

Oralyn, who had kept her eyes closed as the hairstylist snipped and layered, blinks her eyes open, and then blinks again. "Dang, I look good," she says, tilting her head from side to side. She purses her lips to distribute her coral-colored lipstick, something I thought I would never see. "Girly-girl" is not a term that usually describes Oralyn. "What do you think, Ginny?" she asks.

"Perfect. You look beautiful." Ginny's eyes have taken on a lighter shade of blue. Is it her eye shadow or a reflection deep from within her soul? She wraps her arms around Oralyn's shoulders and says, "No one will recognize you back home in Oklahoma."

Oralyn sighs, a frown forming. "I suppose it'll take some time getting used to. I kinda grew attached to the old mug." She narrows her eyes as if trying to puzzle out a problem. "I have no skills in the hair department and don't own any of the lotions and potions to make my hair look like this."

"Ah, madame, the cut will make it easy, but use a little of this." The hair maestro rubs a glob of hair gel into his hands and reveals his styling technique on his own head. "You see—it's easy. A child could do it. I will sell you a bottle." He taps his lips and gives Oralyn an appraising look. "But you must buy some of this, and this, and this. Do you have a hair dryer?"

"Do I look like I would own a hair dryer?"

He laughs before bending down to peck her cheek. "What is the word? Ah, *oui*… I believe the word is card. You, madame, are a card."

He seems to think Oralyn is kidding.

"Let's get it," I interject, pulling out my credit card. The anti-frizz hair treatment, shampoo, conditioner, and styling gel go into the salon's lavish shopping bag. A round styling brush is thrown in for good measure. Oralyn protests, but I tell her to hush. "This is my gift, my treat, and you're spoiling my fun." I glance at my watch. "Ladies, we must go."

We fill the back of the Escalade with our new purchases—a sleek, cream-colored sheath for me, a similar style in blue for Ginny, and an emerald-colored pair of palazzo pants and a fitted blouse for Oralyn. Even Laurel will wear a lacy, white dress with matching pantaloons and a headband.

"All this fuss for nothing," Oralyn says as we take the elevator to our apartment for a quick wardrobe change. She thinks we're getting "doodied-up" to see a show and then dinner on the Strip. As we head back out, dressed to the nines, she gives herself a long look in the mirror, as if unsure the image is real. A small smile forms as she smooths the front of her blouse. "A new me," she mumbles before taking my hand. "Thanks, Adele. This is another first for me. I can't wait to see what happens next."

I bet she can't.

I am as giddy as a twentysomething bride-to-be and laugh. What would my former colleagues think? Like Oralyn, I, too, am about to experience a first, and no one, especially me, saw it coming.

CHAPTER FIFTY-FOUR

Ginny

Aunt Adele and Robert have something in common with Billy Bob Thornton and Angelina Jolie; both couples tied the knot at the historic Little Church of the West. However, unlike the movie stars, I would bet Aunt Adele and Robert make their union last.

Talk about surprises. Somehow, Aunt Adele managed to keep her wedding plans a secret. It wasn't until she drove onto South Las Vegas Boulevard and the chapel's sign came into view that the true purpose of our "day of beauty" became clear.

"Are you lost?" Oralyn had asked, sitting in the back with Laurel. "All I see is a cedar chapel, not something you'd expect to see in these parts."

"Not lost—just crazy," my aunt said, pulling into the parking spot and telling us to hurry.

I still can't believe it. What happened to my uptight aunt? She was as silly as a teenager on a first date and couldn't keep her hands off Robert at the post-wedding celebration. Likewise, for the charming and easy-going Robert, whose eyes shone every time she spoke. Their easy affection made me happy, and I wondered if I would ever be so lucky in love.

If the shock of a surprise wedding hadn't been enough, Robert then dropped another bombshell as we lifted our glasses of bubbly in honor of them in a private restaurant dining room.

"We're moving," Robert said. "Isn't that right, Adele?" He pulled her close to his side and leaned over to kiss the top of her head before tussling her carefully crafted hairstyle. She slapped his hand and laughed before planting a tiny kiss on his lips.

My jaw dropped at the news. My aunt—the quintessential career woman who seemed content living a go-go urban lifestyle—had made an about-face. Her eyes shimmered as Robert revealed their plans to move, possibly to Wyoming, where Robert wanted to buy a ranch and return to his agricultural roots.

As a white-gloved waiter started cutting the cake, Aunt Adele stole a glance at me. "I love you," she mouthed, bringing tears to my eyes. She had never revealed what I had meant to her, and I hadn't told her, either. Holding Laurel, I rushed to her side. "We can't let distance separate us ever again," I whispered. We then clung to each other, rocking, until Laurel, smashed between us, started to yelp.

While her future is set, mine is as elusive as ever—an unsettling thought. I have so much to think about.

"If I ever get married again, I'm doing it Adele's way." Oralyn interrupts my thoughts.

We have made ourselves comfortable sitting on the apartment's large sectional sofa. *Jeopardy* is playing on the billboard-sized TV as Laurel pinwheels her arms and legs while lying on a blanket spread out on the floor. She is babbling, still wearing the white ruffled dress bought for Aunt Adele's special occasion.

"Adele eloped, doggone it, and is now spending the night in that glitzy hotel wedding suite," Oralyn says. "What's not to like about that? No fuss. No muss—right up my alley."

"You're getting married?" I ask, moving to the floor to play peek-a-boo with Laurel, trying to keep my voice light. My emotions are all over the place—elation, doubt, and fear, and then back again.

"You never know. Stranger things have happened." Oralyn has propped her feet on pillows and runs her fingers through her wavy hair. "I still can't believe this. This whole trip feels like a dream."

My head bobs. It does feel like a dream—yet another. However, when I wake up this time, I won't have a mission or a destination in mind. I will be a refugee, with no home to call my own. I bite my lip.

"What's up with the worried look?" Oralyn asks, drilling her eyes into mine. "I've noticed the look all day… Let me have the baby." She pats the sofa cushion. "Come and sit; talk to me."

As usual, Oralyn is spot-on in her observations. I have been stewing in uneasiness, and it feels like every time I take one step forward in trying to keep an even keel, I end up taking two steps back. I transfer Laurel into Oralyn's outstretched arms and then settle in next to her. She gives me a small smile before raising her eyebrows.

"I'm just worried, that's all," I say with a shrug.

"Why worry?" Oralyn fluffs one of the pillows to make herself more comfortable, weighed down by Laurel, whose eyes have begun to droop. "What does Matthew say?" She rubs her chin, dramatic-like, because she knows what the scripture says, and so do I. "Let's see, doesn't it say something about not worrying about tomorrow because tomorrow will worry about itself? Today was a happy day. You should hold onto that." She tilts her head to the side, her eyebrows arched. "What is really bugging you?"

I exhale loudly and lift myself off the sofa, walking toward the sliding-glass doors. "Two weeks ago, I took a risk. I hopped into my car and drove off without a thought, other than to see my mother—not my usual style." I raise my hand to stop Oralyn from interjecting. "Yes, the risk was worth taking."

"Okay, what's the problem then?" Oralyn gently rubs Laurel's back, an act that fills me with tenderness. This dear, sweet woman, whom I met by happenstance—much like how TC and I had become acquainted—is a mother to me, the only mother I have ever experienced other than Granny. And then, another miracle happened. I never dreamed I would have a relationship with Aunt Adele, but I have one, and I don't know what I'll do without her.

I'm afraid my cobbled-together family will break apart. The puzzle pieces will go missing, never to complete the picture we've assembled since our journey began. Oralyn will go home to Oklahoma, and Aunt Adele and Robert will start a new life in Wyoming. And I will be set adrift—again—without even a guarantee that I can start over with my mother, who has big problems of her own.

Each day does indeed have its own troubles.

"Girl, I'm not going to your pity party. Do you hear? I may not be the brightest bulb on the circuit, but it seems God has given you everything you need." Oralyn rises slowly from the sofa to prevent Laurel from waking. "Regardless of what happens with your mother, which I suspect is at the root of all this, you will always have me and Adele. You will always have the good Lord, too. Where is your Bible? I think you may need a refresher."

I hold Oralyn's words close to my heart.

CHAPTER FIFTY-FIVE

Audrey

It's clear that I'm in a hospital, but I don't understand how or why I ended up here. Everything feels blank, as if someone has wiped my memory clean. Perhaps the amnesia is a blessing, considering that I am shackled to this uncomfortable bed like a common criminal.

What did I do?

"How are you feeling?" a nurse chirps as she bounces into my room.

It's an insipid question. I feel awful. A film of grime coats my teeth, and I can smell the sour odor emanating from my body. She ignores my uncharitable response as she moves around my bed, checking IV lines and medical monitors. Her cheerfulness and efficiency drive me crazy.

"Take these off...please." I pull at the ties, noticing the bracelet of bruises around my wrists.

Deep lines form between her carefully plucked eyebrows as she leans over to examine my hands. "Gee, I'm sorry. I can't make that call, but your doctor is making rounds—" She glances at the wall clock. "In an hour or so. How about I mention it? Does that sound good?" She nods with enthusiasm and then glances at the fishbowl window. My eyes follow hers.

Standing beyond the glass is another stranger. He is dressed casually, but his body language gives no hint of an easygoing temperament. He drums the counter with his fingers, his eyes on the move, twitchy-like, until they land on me. My nurse frowns and mumbles under her breath. "He is dogged. I'll give him that." She smiles at me and squeezes my shoulder. "He wants to talk with you and get your testimony. Are you up for it?"

"Who is he? I don't know him." Panic rises. I am trapped and give my bound wrists and feet a good tug.

"He's a Metro cop."

"What did I do?"

"You know what?" She squeezes my shoulder again. "I'll tell him to come back later. The goal is to keep you calm." She sails through the door and returns within minutes. "I bought you some time, but he wants to take your statement. He says he'll wait."

"Why?"

"Do you remember our conversation yesterday? Do you know why you're here?"

Her non-answer—her questions to my question—only infuriates me more. Of course, I don't remember. I don't remember anything at all.

"Why won't you answer my questions?" I struggle to keep my voice steady.

"Ah, here she is."

Another scrub-wearing woman, presumably my doctor, strides into the room. "You're back among the living, Audrey." She smiles at me, showing me her straight, white teeth. I detect an Indian accent and watch as she scans her clipboard. She lifts her head to study me before she talks with my nurse.

"The restraints aren't necessary. Let's get her up and moving around." The nurse nods. "I'm sure you would like that."

"What I would like," I say in response, "is a cigarette, a shower, and a toothbrush—in that order."

The doctor laughs. "No cigarettes, but we can manage the shower and toothbrush."

With the doctor's approval, the nurse frees my arms and legs and mentions that she'll grab a nicotine patch and return later to remove the catheter and help me into the shower. I can't imagine why she seems so cheerful. She gives me a tiny wink before walking out of the room, leaving me alone with the doctor, who has taken a seat next to my bed, her clipboard balancing on her lap.

"How are you feeling?" she asks, her mocha-colored eyes fixed on mine. "You seem a bit agitated, which is to be expected. You might experience lingering memory issues, depression, and a host of side effects, but look on the bright side. You've made it through the worst of it. Detoxification is difficult—"

"Detoxification? What are you talking about? No has explained anything to me, including why I woke up this morning to find myself tied down in this bed."

"Fair enough. You seem to be straightforward, and I appreciate that." She crosses her legs and leans back into the chair. "You are withdrawing from alcohol. Along with increased irritability, nausea, and a racing pulse, your situation was further complicated by seizures, delirium tremens, and hallucinations. You could have died from this." She pauses, perhaps to let the gravity of the situation sink in before continuing. "As for the restraints, we had no other choice. You had become aggressive and posed a risk to our staff and to possibly yourself."

"Come on, doc. You're making this up to make me feel worse than I already do." I start laughing, but it sounds forced. "I'll admit to enjoying a cocktail or two, but I am not an alcoholic, which is what you seem to be implying."

She frowns. "First and foremost, no one is condemning you. You're not the only person with an alcohol abuse disorder. My only concern is your well-being," she says, raising her hand to keep me from interrupting. "I plan to release you tomorrow, but I strongly recommend admission to a treatment and recovery center. Outpatient services are available, too, though most people profit from more intensive care."

"Nope. I'm not doing it," I say, rubbing my wrists and examining the bruises around an IV puncture wound. "Even if I had a drinking problem, I'm not sure how pouring out my sad little story would help. Furthermore, these centers are expensive, and I can barely make my rent."

She sighs. "Outside a court order, no one can make you do anything. This is a decision only you can make on your own, but let me give you the facts." Her voice is calm and measured. "Intensive counseling in a safe setting could provide the tools and strategies to maintain sobriety. The next time, you might not be so lucky."

Glancing at her wristwatch, she stands up. "Think about it, okay? Our Outpatient Services Department can help with the details. We'll talk later today."

With that, she leaves the room, and I'm left alone with my jumbled thoughts and fragmented memories. I had sworn off alcohol and poured my bottles down the drain. Now, to my dismay, I find myself without the means to satisfy my cravings. All I want is a drink.

CHAPTER FIFTY-SIX

Ginny

We sit at a table in the hospital cafeteria once Danny and a woman named Angel arrive. At least they had the sense to grab a cup of coffee on the way. The brew I'm drinking tastes like sludge and is only making my upset stomach worse. I take a few sips and set the Styrofoam cup down.

I am terrified.

Rejection is a hard pill to swallow, and I have no reason to expect a perfect, Norman Rockwell-style reunion when I speak with my mother for the first time in decades. Regardless of how she responds to me, I must accept her wishes and count my blessings. Even so, my emotions are all over the map as I fiddle with the turquoise-colored memory band that TC gave me.

Interestingly, meeting Angel and listening to her stories begins to soothe my jangled nerves. Of everyone at the table, Angel is the closest to Mom. She fills in the details that help me form a clearer picture of my mother's life and relationships with others. What stands out to me is the unique bond they shared. Even though Angel is about my age, my mom often turns to her for guidance.

"She could be so frustrating," Angel says. "She would ask for my advice and then do the complete opposite. When I confronted her about it, she'd shrug and say, 'Doing what I do best…screwing up my life.' When I asked why she would purposely make things harder for herself, she would bite her lip, stare off into space, and change the subject." Angel shakes her head back and forth. "My goodness, I had no idea you or Adele existed."

Angel's words sting, but hadn't Aunt Adele and I done the same thing, writing her off as if she hadn't lived?

Oralyn, who had been listening quietly, finally speaks up, and our heads turn in her direction. "Why did you try to help her?" Oralyn asks, sounding as if she already knows the answer. "Why didn't you throw up your hands and give up?"

"Because beneath all the chaos is a wonderful person with a big heart," Angel replies. "She's in pain, and I've always believed that, especially now that I've met her family. Something must have caused her to struggle like this, and that's why I kept reaching out, trying to draw her out. I hope that if I were in her shoes, someone would show me the same kindness. I want her to find peace."

Oralyn pats Angel's hand and shares a knowing expression with Aunt Adele and me.

We ride the elevator to the ICU in silence. When the doors open, Oralyn, who is pushing the stroller, heads for the adjacent waiting room, while we move in the opposite direction. I press the buzzer, and the double doors of the ICU swing open with a soft whooshing sound. As we round the corner, a nurse greets us as if she is expecting our arrival and taking charge of the situation.

"What's going on?" I ask.

"The detective investigating your mother's case is taking her statement," she says, guiding us to a small conference room at the end of the hallway, where she believes we will be more comfortable as we wait for the interview to conclude.

"Maybe I should sit in on that conversation, or at least wait outside the door," Danny says, striding past her. I admire his confidence and assertiveness, and I wish I could see the detective try to turn him away. It's no wonder my mother respected him and aimed to do right by him—a detail Angel had shared as we sat at the cafeteria table.

"How is she?" I ask the nurse.

"Medically, she's out of the woods and is scheduled for release tomorrow, but I have concerns. She's not the first patient to battle addiction, and she's not the first to think that rehab is an expensive waste of time. She is resisting treatment. I hope you can influence her otherwise."

A soft rap on the doorframe interrupts our conversation. The same detective who interviewed me a few days ago stands in the doorway. "Is this a good time to talk?" He doesn't wait for an answer, brushing past me to take a seat at the conference table. I can't read his expression, and it makes my stomach flip.

"Where's Danny?" I ask him, noticing that Aunt Adele has abruptly stopped her conversation with Angel.

"Ah, talking with the victim…your mother." He places his notebook on the table and frowns. "Look, I haven't spoken with the prosecutor yet, but I want you to know that I will recommend dropping the burglary charges against Jacob Hudson. We must prove beyond a reasonable doubt that he entered your mother's home with the intent to commit larceny, assault, or some other felony. Right now, we can't do that." He leans forward in his chair. "Unfortunately, your mother doesn't remember what happened, and without her testimony—"

My arms fly above my head in a gesture of defeat. In my preferred scenario, Jacob would be locked behind bars, and I would never have to worry about him ever again. Now what? I don't know what to think or do.

"Let it go." Aunt Adele's voice is crisp. She raps the Formica-covered table with her knuckles, adding emphasis to her words. "I have no doubt he meant to harm someone, whether it was your mom or you. The sooner that man is out of your life, the better."

Since leaving Jacob, my emotions have swung between fear and doubt, only to shift back to confidence and certainty, as if I'm stuck in a continuous loop. Yet, amidst all this, I haven't felt an abiding joy; in fact, I am more disquieted than ever. Aunt Adele plans to join Robert in Wyoming once we help Mom settle in. And Oralyn has informed me that Monty will be driving my Honda to Las Vegas and then flying home with her. Their futures are all set, while mine is still unsettled.

I want peace—more than anything.

"Aunt Adele, you're right," I say, grateful for her unwavering guidance. "By letting this go, I can move on. I can begin to live."

"I'm sorry you've had to go through this." The detective stands and accepts my handshake. "I'll be in touch if anything changes."

I follow him out the door, only to collide with Danny.

"Whoa, sister." Danny grabs me around the waist. I see a spark in his eye as he leans in closer, smelling like soap, to whisper in my ear. "Your mother knows you're here, Ginny. She also knows about the baby. She wants to see you. Go."

"Really?"

"Really." He squeezes my shoulder and nods in the direction of Mom's room.

"What about Aunt Adele and Angel?"

"No, honey, you go." I do a double-take. Aunt Adele's voice has taken on a Southern cadence not heard in years. "Angel and I can wait."

The walk down the hallway feels like a death march. The destination, the reason for this journey, lies just beyond the threshold. I came to set things right, and here I am—ready to mend fences. But is she? I pause outside her room and take a deep breath. Gathering my resolve, I place one foot in front of the other, taking cautious steps toward my mother.

She lifts her head and stretches out her arms, tears welling up and streaming down her cheeks as she speaks words I never thought I'd hear.

"I don't deserve it, sweet pea, but could you find it in your heart to forgive me?"

FOUR MONTHS LATER

CHAPTER FIFTY-SEVEN

Audrey

Adele was more demanding than ever, but for the first time, I chose to ignore it. I didn't have the energy to argue, especially since Danny supported her, insisting that a ninety-day "vacation" from my everyday life could help me avoid relapsing as I adjusted to a new lifestyle free from alcohol and nicotine. So, off I went to the rehab and recovery center recommended by my doctor.

Was it easy?

Not at all.

Facing my past and acknowledging my destructive tendencies was a monumental challenge. I cried a lot, especially when the questions turned to my childhood. I spoke openly about my father and began to understand how his death had affected me. My emotional growth had stalled, and a six- or seven-year-old version of myself took control. Only now do I recognize why Jimmy—a man older than me, reminiscent of the married men and high rollers I had consorted with in Vegas—was so appealing. I yearned for a daddy figure, someone who would take care of me.

In the end, only the bottle would do.

Four months after my release, I am still feeling unsteady, grasping for anything to keep me from falling. As Ginny brews a pot of coffee in the kitchen, I sit on my sofa, playing patty-cake with our chortling mini-me, little Laurel—one of two bright spots in my otherwise depressing life.

The possibility of failure—both financially and otherwise—is very real, despite the encouragement I receive from Danny, Ginny, Adele, and even Robert, who have all become my most enthusiastic supporters. Deep down, I know I have much to be grateful for, and I keep telling myself to buck up and stay strong.

My goodness, Adele has taken care of my rent and recovery bills, refusing to let me pay her back when I get my feet under me. "Don't worry about it, sis," she said when we spoke on the phone last night. "It's the least I can do." She also offered me a job and a place to live on her sprawling cattle ranch nestled in a mountain valley, fifty miles east of Jackson Hole. I told her I'd keep the offer in mind for the future.

As it stands, I do have a job. In a couple of days, I'm set to start my new position in the finance department of Cork & Barrel's corporate headquarters—imagine that. I'll be learning a valuable skill. Even though my salary will be far less than what I could earn tending bar and collecting tips, Danny believes it's smarter to avoid a job that revolves around slinging drinks. Given how I feel right now, he's probably right.

I'm on edge and feel worthless—a charity case who's buried

beneath a pile of mistakes. It all weighs on me like an anchor, threatening to drag me under.

"Mom, I'm proud of you," Ginny says as she carries two cups of steaming coffee into the living room. The ever-present Danny, who always lifts her spirits, has just left. She's more exuberant than ever, especially about my chances of overcoming my worst impulses, which have always involved wasting money on shiny baubles, booze, and any mind-altering substance I could lay my hands on.

Can I stay clean?

She sits down next to me and Laurel, placing my hot cup of coffee on the coffee table. As she blows on her steaming brew, she begins to talk about her faith and the existence of miracles—a topic that even my sister seems to enjoy. A change has indeed come over Adele. Like me, she used to attend church mainly to appease our mother, but now she speaks of God and His power to transform even the most hardened hearts.

"I wavered and second-guessed myself, but God never left my side," Ginny says, reaching over to tickle Laurel's belly, as she shows off her four new teeth. "He introduced me to special people, like TC, then Oralyn and her boss, Monty. They made sure nothing, including Jacob, could stop me from being with you."

I don't know what to think of all this.

She leans back to rest her head on the cushion. "Mom, I hope you realize how much progress you've made in your recovery. You're working the steps: You've taken a moral inventory and you've reached out to people you think you've hurt," she continues, counting my so-called achievements on her fingers.

She then pauses, lifting her head and trying to make eye contact with me, but I look away. "But I sense you've breezed past the most critical steps. Have you asked God for help, and do you believe that He can restore you?"

The questions hang like a heavy, wet blanket.

"You can do this, Mom," Ginny then says. "People love you. I love you. More importantly, God loves you, and He has wonderful plans for you."

She reminds me of my mother.

I bury my nose in the baby's soft, roly-poly neck, breathing in her pure, comforting scent. Ginny's words drift past me, empty and insubstantial. Nothing anyone says can change my mind. I long for the effervescent Peaches—the woman who let me escape myself, if only for a moment. The real me fills me with revulsion, and I wear self-hatred like an old, worn-in sweatshirt. Deep down, I know the source of my pain, but I'm not ready to face it; instead, I push it down and find myself asking: If God truly loved me, as Ginny and Adele so passionately believe, why did He let these things happen to me?

"I'm working on it, Ginny," I say, giving her a small smile and wiping the tears welling up in my eyes. "How about we talk about something else…take a walk or something? The walls are closing in."

"Absolutely, Mom," she says, rushing off to get Laurel's baby stroller.

As we step outside, I notice her staring at me, gnawing on the inside of her cheek. Her expression makes it clear that she wants to tell me something, but she isn't sure how to bring it up. I have my suspicions about what it could be: either the moonstruck

Danny—the side of him I'd never seen before—or that job offer in Wyoming. Either way, I can tell she's worried about how I might react—another worry for me. My issues shouldn't hold her back.

"It feels like an oven out here," Ginny says instead, biting back what might have been on the tip of her tongue. She wipes her brow and fans her face as I push my granddaughter in the stroller.

"This is nothing," I say. "Wait a few months; it gets hotter than blue blazes."

Ginny laughs. "I haven't heard that phrase in a long time. You sound just like Granny."

I could cry. My mother is gone, and I never got a chance to apologize for the misery I put her through or to thank her for raising my beautiful, loving daughter, whom I don't feel I deserve.

It's as if she can read my mind. "Oh, Mom, don't you think Granny already knows? She's in high cotton, looking down on all of us. Her family is now whole."

I nod, wishing I could believe it.

ONE YEAR LATER

CHAPTER FIFTY-EIGHT

Oralyn

I was home maybe two weeks before boredom set in. How often can you vacuum your rugs, water your plants, or weed your garden? Monty was more than happy to offer me a part-time job.

Word traveled fast on my first day back. You would've thought I was the homecoming queen; every booth and barstool was occupied. While Monty and his business partner counted their loot in the back, I basked in the attention. Even Wilma—aka the old biddy—stopped by for a cup of coffee, her eyes squinting as she tried to figure out my new look.

"My goodness, Oralyn, you're almost pretty," she said, patting the gray, frumpy head covering she calls a hairdo and sucking in her gut. "I'm thinking I'm due for an update. What do you think?"

Here we go again, I thought, before remembering my lecture to Ginny when she had wanted to quit our trip to Vegas, just miles from the finish line of her odyssey. The words came back to me in a flash, along with my promises. This is about letting go and moving on—second chances, I told her. Let the anger go.

So, instead of getting torn up by Wilma's backhanded compliment, which I would've done, and then marinating in the noxious brew for the rest of my life, which I also would've done, I extended an olive branch. I thanked her for noticing the new and improved Oralyn, then offered to drive her to my la-di-da salon, which I would never have found on my own.

Thank the Lord for Shannon. How would I ever manage without her? She always encourages me, and that quality shone through when she picked Monty and me up at the airport on our return.

"Aunt Oralyn, you look awesome," she had said, oohing and aahing as Monty grinned, announcing in his baritone voice that the body snatchers had whisked me off and left an imposter. Shannon gave him a withering look before touching my gentle curls and stepping back to appraise my new outfit—something Adele had chosen for me. "I know just the stylist for you, as well as a boutique," Shannon had said, wagging her finger. "No backsliding—men will drool over you."

I'm not sure about the drooling part, but compliments are nice to hear, and I made sure to compliment Wilma after my hairdresser snipped and styled, making her look years younger. However, she completed the transformation on her own. She smiled, erasing the ever-present downward pull of her jowls, grasped my hand, and thanked me for taking time to spend the afternoon with her.

This confirms what I have always understood: New hairdos and clothes—the outward appearances—don't bring lasting happiness. In fact, they are fleeting, short-term fixes to whatever ails you. What matters is the condition of your heart, and mine and Wilma's needed tune-ups.

For me, it took a madcap trek across the Southwest to diagnose and repair my broken parts. For Wilma, I'm not sure, but we understand each other a whole lot better and have more in common than either of us had ever imagined. I'm not suggesting that we're best friends, but she doesn't look down her nose at me, and I don't run for cover when I see her at church. We're downright friendly. All it takes is a willingness to walk around in someone else's shoes for a while.

As I sit on my front porch, already dressed, my bags packed, I allow myself to reflect on the lessons I learned. For so long, I had let the hurtful words from my father, my ex-husband, and, yes, even Wilma, influence my opinion of myself. I saw myself as inconsequential, perhaps even unlovable, before sweet Charlie came into my life. When he took his promotion and moved his operations to heaven, however, I resorted to old habits, the deeply grooved ruts. I felt sorry for myself, refusing to recognize just how important I was to people who mattered. Not even the Spirit could convince me otherwise.

We're all great in our own unique ways.

Although it's early, I'm already hot. I dab the perspiration gathering between my breasts and then glance at my Timex, which no longer leaves a trench on my wrist. Shannon, Monty, or whoever agrees to chauffeur me to the airport will arrive shortly. I am headed for Georgia—another part of the country I've never seen. This reunion with Ginny and Adele isn't a happy occasion, but my presence is necessary.

My phone buzzes. Shannon is on her way.

Before I pocket the phone, I notice an image that has appeared on the screen—a photo of me, holding baby Laurel, surrounded by Adele, Audrey, Ginny, and Danny. Despite subzero temperatures, we posed on a mountaintop overlooking Adele and Robert's expansive ranch far below, and nothing could bushwhack our celebration.

The day is still vivid in my mind, as if it happened yesterday, not six months ago.

* * *

Ginny and I were hiding in one of Adele's spacious bedrooms, acting silly as we modeled our cowgirl boots, Stetsons, and flouncy embroidered dresses. Without my even noticing, Ginny's teasing and laughter stopped. I could tell something had gotten stuck in her craw. She plopped down on the edge of the bed, gnawing her lip, a tic I had come to know well during our own *Thelma & Louise* moment stuffed inside my old van, both running from our pasts and into our futures.

"Do you think I'm being too hasty?" she asked.

"Maybe. You haven't been dating Danny long, so I can understand why the short courtship might seem a bit rash to an old worrywart like you," I said. "But I have a good feeling about it. Remember what I told you in the diner shortly after you landed at our doorstep?"

"Not really."

"Well, let me remind you. I said that when the Spirit speaks, I listen. I've made too many mistakes by ignoring His counsel in the past."

A tiny smile appeared on her face. "Didn't you also say you sometimes ignore His counsel?"

"That's true, but right now, He's yelling in my ear." I gave her hand a reassuring pat. "Trust the Lord, Ginny. He put Danny Mason in your path because that handsome honey is meant for you."

"Okay. Okay." She took a deep breath and then let it out, her eyes scanning the room until they landed on a log house in the distance, with smoke billowing from the stone chimney—a vintage Currier and Ives print. "Did I tell you we're moving into that little cabin over there?"

She had mentioned it—maybe fifty times or more. But who was counting? The girl was a bundle of nerves, unable to calm herself, voicing every thought that came to mind. I decided to help distract her by asking about my favorite little person.

"What's going on with baby girl?"

"She's great, growing like a weed." Ginny glanced at me and shook her head. "Jacob keeps insisting he's not her father and has no interest in being a part of her life, but Danny demanded, through our attorney, that he take a DNA test. He wants to make everything legal and airtight."

"Did you get the results?"

She frowned. "Oh, for heaven's sake, Oralyn. Of course, he's the father. He's agreed to give up his parental rights. At least that's what his lawyer told our lawyer."

As far as I could see, it was good news all around, but Ginny seemed troubled—beyond the usual jitters about what was supposed to take place in Adele's cathedral-like great room downstairs in an hour or so. My eyebrows raised.

"What if Jacob decides to back out? What if he causes more trouble?" She buried her head in her hands and then looked up at me. "You know he's more than capable."

"Girl, he'd be the last person I'd worry about," I replied, leaning in to look her square in the eyes. "Nobody is going to mess with you—not with Danny around."

"I guess you're right. Of course, you're right. I have nothing to fear. Right?"

While on the road, Ginny and I had shared hotel rooms, mothering duties, and our stories. I got to know her better than most people and could read her emotions like a book. To my ear, her words sounded like false bravado. After seeing what Jacob had put her through, I understood her trepidation. But it was time to move on. He occupied way too much of her headspace, and it wouldn't change until she let go and left him in the past.

When I told her as much, the corners of her eyes narrowed. "I promised to move on before, but I can't stop thinking about him, even though I know I should. I'll work on it, Oralyn. I promise."

She then took my hand, and together, we headed downstairs. Within an hour, Ginny Carmichael had a new husband and a new last name. One that baby girl would share if the good Lord was willing and the creek didn't rise.

* * *

A horn sounds and breaks my reverie.

"Do you need help with your bags?" Shannon is already bounding up the steps, taking hold of my suitcase, yammering about traffic and Lord knows what else. Some things never change, and that's okay, too.

Because sometimes life throws fastballs, catching you unawares, making you wish you could stop the clock and live as you always had. This unplanned trip to Georgia is a testament to that.

CHAPTER FIFTY-NINE

Jacob

I am the son of an ambitious state senator, and I use that to my advantage. Just mentioning my father's name opens doors for me. However, his position and financial acumen, which guided Peach Street Holdings through the economic downturn that troubled less capable companies, are not the only reasons for our stratospheric success. While the economy has rebounded, I have also proven my worth. I not only excel at the real estate game, but I have also mastered the art of skullduggery. Exploiting incriminating information has become second nature to me.

Information is power, and I wield it like a pro—ask my father. As I always say, what happens in Atlanta stays in Atlanta.

"Honey, your parents just arrived." Red steps through the French doors onto our screened-in porch overlooking the Atlantic Ocean. The ever-present baby is at her chest. We've lived in this sprawling beach house since we got married a few months after law enforcement dropped those ridiculous charges in Las Vegas. Despite my dad's initial dislike of her, Red has become the Queen Bee in his eyes.

She gave birth to a boy—an heir to the *Hudson Family Kingdom*—and my dad's accusations were all but forgotten, along with Ginny and the kid. Not that they cared before, but my mom and dad never mentioned them again. Any inquiries from friends, political supporters, and business associates—people who had been acquainted with my former "wife"—were brushed off, and Dad deftly steered the conversation to more neutral topics, often with a well-timed joke or compliment.

To this day, Dad wants to avoid negative attention, including discussions about my unwarranted arrest and the reasons for my move to the coast—the best thing that ever happened to me.

"Let bygones be bygones, Jacob," he told me when I showed him the correspondence from a law firm in Wyoming. A quick Google search proved the attorney's legitimacy. "Why contest a paternity test? Why contest an adoption if it comes to that?" Dad's eyes bored into mine. "You're off the hook financially and otherwise, and stirring up trouble only exposes you and me to more questions better left unasked." He paused to let it sink in before continuing his lecture. "It's best for the family."

What a hoot—his concern for the family—but Dad had a point. A legal battle with Ginny or a confrontation with her new man wasn't worth the trouble. Pops had his heir, after all, and I had his trust, which I've secured with the secret about who's living in my old house in Atlanta. Still, I sometimes find myself wondering about Ginny. What bothers me most is that she beat me at my own game. I ended up getting the boot, and I won't let that happen to me again.

No siree.

I give Red an appraising look as she steps closer to the chaise lounge where I spend weekends, especially on warm, breezy days like this. I swallow the last of my iced tea. "What did you make for dinner, honey?"

I roll my eyes when she tells me. "I thought you'd make something less fattening. What's it been? Five months?"

I pinch her love handles playfully. Her lips quiver—always her reaction when someone offers constructive criticism. But then I notice a tiny squint at the corner of her eyes, an expression that Ginny would make before threatening insurrection. To win in situations like this, I change tactics, which is precisely what I do.

"Oh, baby, I'm sorry. That came out the wrong way," I say, gently cradling Red's chin in my hands. "You're beautiful—perfect. You know that, right?"

Her mouth turns up as she bobs her head, the reaction I was hoping for. She caresses the baby's fluff of scarlet-colored hair while I lean down to kiss both her and Jacob Jr. on top of their heads.

It's a game, of course, and I make the rules. Everything is exactly as I want it. I call the shots around here.

CHAPTER SIXTY

Ginny

Granny's old house, located an hour south of Atlanta, is cramped beyond belief. Aunt Adele and Robert have taken over Granny's old bedroom, while Danny and I sleep on the roll-out couch in the well-worn living room. Oralyn, meanwhile, has settled into my old bedroom, sharing the space with Laurel. It's a relief that Aunt Adele decided to wait before putting Granny's bungalow on the market. Being here one last time is comforting.

"What time is it?" Danny asks, rolling over to squint at the mantel clock next to the framed photo of my mother and older sister, taken a few weeks before I was born. I can't believe I once debated photoshopping Mom out of that decades-old photograph when I created a digital copy for myself. When we go home in a few days, that framed photo will join my other special keepsake now displayed like a priceless Fabergé egg inside the glass curio cabinet.

"Why are you keeping that?" Danny asked when I removed the bubble wrap and placed the empty wine bottle on one of the shelves shortly after we moved into the cabin. "There is nothing special about that vineyard or label."

The look on my face had told him otherwise. TC *had* come. He had left that bottle to remind me of our time together and convey the message he wanted me to hear. If he hadn't come when he did, who knows where I'd be today?

Certainly not with Danny—likely dead, just like my mother.

A lot can happen in a year.

"Seven-thirty," I murmur, sitting up and groaning. "Ugh. I don't want this day to happen." I flop back onto the lumpy pullout mattress, curling myself into a fetal position as I watch Danny roll out of bed, dressed only in boxers and a T-shirt.

"Where did I put my jeans?" His eyes scan the room, which hasn't changed since Granny's death, searching for his pants. I point to Granny's chair by the fireplace. Danny begins pulling on his pants, one leg at a time, his muscled arms rippling as he glances over his shoulder. "You look tired. Why don't you get more sleep?" He zips his fly and sits next to me on the bed, caressing my cheek with his calloused thumb, a testament to the physical labor needed to raise livestock on Robert and Adele's ranch. "I'll make the coffee and take care of Laurel as soon as she wakes up. This won't be an easy day for you."

It's just like Danny to think of me before himself, a trait that stands in sharp contrast to how Jacob might have behaved. My husband of six months is also grieving—heartbroken by the loss of a friend. He never stopped believing in my mother.

"Angel is coming. Driving down from North Carolina. She's wrecked, too." He tucks the sheets around me. "Get some rest. You're going to need it."

The squeak of an old door hinge and the soft padding of little feet interrupt our conversation. Peeking around the doorframe is Laurel, who toddles toward us with a smile around her thumb, dimples forming in her chubby cheeks. She clings to the last gift my mother gave her: a fluffy, stuffed white bunny with pink eyes and ears that goes everywhere with her.

"There she is. Good morning, sunshine." Danny's morning greeting is always the same. He sweeps his soon-to-be officially adopted daughter into his arms and brushes strands of her wild, platinum-colored hair from her eyes. Those eyes, like my own, remind me of my mother. "Help me with coffee, baby girl. Your mommy needs her sleep."

But I don't sleep.

I remember.

Everything.

* * *

The memories bring tears, not from bitterness, but from a place of profound gratitude. In the twelve months I spent with my mother, we had our do-over. We became friends and confidantes, forming a female bond neither of us had truly experienced growing up. At last, we found a kindred spirit in each other. She amazed me. Nothing about my life escaped her attention. She was the one who pointed out Danny's growing affection, which I also felt, but ignored, perhaps because I didn't trust myself.

"I hope you don't think Danny stops by to check on me," she remarked a few weeks after her release and Aunt Adele's move to Wyoming. We were kneeling at the tub, bathing Laurel. "Trust me, girl, he likes you." She didn't smile; her tone was serious. Smiles, in fact, were rare in those early weeks. "I may not know much, but I can read men. You can't go wrong with him."

"Oh, Mom, cut me a break. Look at my track record."

"Look at mine. But one of these days, I will find my Prince Charming, someone who looks at me the way Danny looks at you."

She then grew quiet—a familiar pattern as she navigated her struggles and embraced sobriety—but this silence felt different. I sensed a deeper unrest within her. When I asked what was on her mind, she waved it away. "I'm good…terrific. I have you."

In so many ways, she was right. The weeks that followed were restorative. A few days before I moved to Wyoming to start my new nursing job—plans for marriage and Danny's relocation already underway—Mom announced at my going-away dinner that she had accepted Aunt Adele's offer to help her and Robert manage the business side of *R&A Ranch.* She would be moving, too.

Aunt Adele wasn't the only Smith girl with a knack for numbers. Mom had a savant-like skill for business—a talent that she had buried beneath the weight of self-doubt and then addiction. While working at Cork & Barrel's corporate offices, she began to realize her true potential—a gift that probably surprised her the most.

"You've been hiding your light, Audrey," Danny said, shaking his head in wonder after we finished dinner at her kitchen table.

"Never, never underestimate yourself. The tavern will be losing a genius, and Robert and Adele will be gaining a pro."

"Yeah, yeah, yeah," she replied in her signature drawl. "And you, sweet boy, are gaining me as a mother-in-law and a neighbor to boot." She tousled his hair. "It's like winning the jackpot, huh? We'll be one big happy family as soon as I take care of loose ends here." I'll never forget the joy in her voice and the laugh lines around her eyes. In that moment, she seemed like she'd truly let go of her worries; the change was unmistakable on her face.

Later that night, after Danny had gone home, however, she couldn't sit still. She paced back and forth, jumping up to wipe down the already spotless granite kitchen counters and to remove imaginary smudges from the sliding-glass door.

"Mom, what's bothering you? Please sit down; you're making me nervous."

She stopped mid-scrub and, in a voice that I'd never heard before, she said, "I'm going to be straight with you, and I hope you'll always be honest with me. I haven't told you the whole story. In fact, I haven't told anyone. But I refuse to drag my secret to Wyoming because it's weighing me down." She took a big breath before taking a seat across from me. "As we both know, nothing good happens in darkness."

She then went on to describe how the choir director had groomed her, she a pre-pubescent at the time. He had gained her trust through compliments, attention, and little gifts—the things she craved after her dad died—and then robbed her of her innocence behind a locked closet door. The abuse persisted for years until he moved away, no one the wiser, including the pastor, Granny, and the congregants who admired his dedicated service. Throughout it all, she never spoke a word, living in fear of his threats. It was a heavy burden to bear, yet she carried it like a vital accessory for most of her adult life.

"I blamed myself for that man's abuse. I blamed God," Mom said. "But today a feeling came over me, and the more I thought about it, the more I began to understand. First, I realized I hadn't done anything wrong; I was just a sad and vulnerable kid." She glanced at her hands before meeting my gaze. "However, living my life as a victim is just as harmful. I should know—I've done it for years, stuck in self-pity. No more." Mom took another breath. "And second, something more profound occurred to me: I came to understand my choices. I could either continue believing the lies or begin to see myself as God sees me—a beautifully created woman with purpose and worth. Your grandmother tried telling me that, but, of course, I didn't listen."

The rawness of her testimony pierced my heart because I could relate.

A smile spread across her face. "I could die tomorrow, but I would die a contented woman. You now know the truth, and I have a thankful heart. Never forget that we have a choice in how we deal with the good and bad in life." After that, she went to bed, leaving me alone at the kitchen table with my thoughts. We never spoke of past hurts or mistakes again. What would be the point? The past was the past, and we tacitly agreed to leave it there.

Getting ready for bed that night, still reflecting on her long-held secret and its ugly repercussions, I remembered the promises I had made to TC the day we first met at the festival, which seemed like a lifetime ago. After listening to my story, he agreed—no, he insisted—that I dedicate my life to helping people just like me—and my mother. Think about all the good you could do, he said.

With all that had happened, I had nearly forgotten those ambitions. Climbing into bed hours later, still wired by my mother's confession, I vowed to resume my studies, perhaps not in medical school, but certainly in a master's program. I would become a counselor. I would help young victims navigate trauma. Too much was at stake. Look at what had happened to us, my mom and me.

* * *

Lying on Granny's sofa bed, my pillow is damp from tears. I flip it to the drier, cooler side and pull the sheet over my head, listening to Danny's easy chatter with Laurel in the kitchen. As I am about to nod off, a loud rap on the front door jars me to wakefulness. I hear heavy footsteps across the hardwood floor. I don't move. I feign sleep, not ready to greet visitors. That will happen later.

"Can I help you?"

"Uh huh… Yeah. I hope…" I don't recognize the woman's voice, but she sounds like a local. "You're Adele, right?"

"I am. Do I know you?"

"Yeah… maybe." The woman pauses. "Look, just give this to Audrey's daughter. It's important."

I hear the door latch, and curiosity gets the better of me.

"Who was that?" I sit up, disentangling myself from the covers.

"No clue." Aunt Adele shrugs and then hands me a tattered envelope, my name scrawled across the front. "She said it's for you."

I stare at the unfamiliar handwriting, praying the letter doesn't bring more unexpected and earth-shattering news, like when a local cop came to the ranch two weeks ago to inform me of my mother's death.

The irony of it all was striking.

She had been steadfast in her sobriety but died instantly when a drunk driver T-boned her as she drove home from a Celebrate Recovery meeting—her last in Vegas. She was supposed to join us in Wyoming the very next day.

In a daze, I half-walked, half-ran, stumbling along the rutted dirt road leading to Aunt Adele's, little Laurel clutched to my chest. Through my sobs, I delivered the heartbreaking news. *How could this happen? Why would God take her from me?* Aunt Adele and I stood there, clinging to each other, overwhelmed by grief, when we both noticed it. Off in the horizon, rays of sunlight began to peek through a bank of fast-moving clouds. The light was brilliant, drawing our attention to the human-like formations far above our heads. Granny, my mother, and TC had come together in the rearranging clouds.

It felt like a miracle. The Lord gives and the Lord takes away. While I may not understand why these special people passed on, I must trust in His better plan.

On this day—the final chapter in my mother's story—I choose to find comfort in that understanding. The people I love most have gone home. As my mother said, I have a choice in how I react to the good and bad in life.

CHAPTER SIXTY-ONE

Ginny

The letter remained unopened for several hours after we laid my mother's cremated remains in a burial plot next to Granny, my grandpa, and my big sister Laurel. The turnout surprised me. In addition to my friend Melinda and her husband, Hank, who had driven down from the Atlanta suburbs, all manner of people came to pay their last respects—Granny's friends, Mom's childhood friends, and some of my own, and Adele's.

Most touching, at least to me, were those who traveled long distances, such as Angel and other former colleagues, as well as Mom's favorite customers—mainly older men who would visit the tavern daily to spend time with her. Her over-the-top flirty persona lifted their spirits, serving as a balm for their lonely hearts.

"We had nothing going on," one man told me after the service, hunched over and leaning on his cane. "But she made me laugh. Around her, I didn't feel like a worthless old man."

He scratched his forehead. "It's funny; I had no idea her real name was Audrey. To me, she was always Peaches. I'm really going to miss her."

So will I.

The service is over, and the mourners have gone home. Danny and I sit at Granny's kitchen table while Oralyn, Aunt Adele, and Robert take Laurel for a walk. We are alone.

"Ginny, there's no time like the present," Danny says, offering the envelope that I had tucked into my cloth satchel. "You should open it."

"Do I have to?" It feels like an unwanted gift.

"Yeah, I think you do. It could be important. You never know." He massages my neck for a moment and then strides toward the front door. The screen door slams, and through the front window, I see him making himself comfortable in one of Granny's porch chairs.

Danny is right. I fill my lungs and run my finger along the envelope flap, extracting a dog-eared letter written in a messy, childlike cursive. My hand flies to my mouth as soon as I see the sender's signature and the name of the city where he has lived for the past twenty years in a correctional institution.

What could he possibly want?

Dear Ginny,

I know I'm the last person you expected to hear from, and I wouldn't blame you if you decided to throw this letter away.

My cousin informed me about your mom's passing and promised to deliver this letter to you. I want to offer my heartfelt condolences. Your mom was a wonderful girl, and so were you and your big sister. I could come up with countless excuses for my past actions, but I won't. I take full responsibility for everything that happened, and I am genuinely sorry.

May the Lord bless you and heal you, Ginny. One day, I hope you can find it in your heart to forgive me, but I understand if you can't. Some things are just beyond redemption.

Sincerely,
Jimmy Carmichael
Enoree, South Carolina

I remember Jimmy as a drunk, a cokehead, and an ignorant brute. I remember his diabolical anger, the overturned furniture, and the threats when Mom's suppers didn't suit. I remember my sister and me running from the trailer when he came home from work—always eager for a fight—and her drilling nine-one-one into my six-year-old mind just in case of an emergency. Above all else, I remember my sister's innocent blood seeping into the stained, dirty rug.

Anger surges through me. Jaw clenched, I crumple the letter and hurl it at the trash can, but it ricochets off the rim and lands on the floor. Frustration mounting, I seize the plastic napkin holder and fling it. It explodes into fragments, but even that isn't enough. My fury feels justified. Let him rot in hell for what he did to Laurel, Mom, and me.

Minutes pass, and then more time goes by. I try to calm my heaving chest, confused by my outburst. Where did that come from? I hadn't thought about Jimmy in years, and when I did, I found myself behaving in ways that felt unrecognizable to me.

Oh boy, Ginny, this isn't hard. You know what the problem is here.

An undetected malignancy has taken root. If I don't cut it out, it will spread, poisoning every aspect of my life—Danny's, little Laurel's, everyone else I hold dear. Choosing to forgive Jimmy doesn't mean I forget the pain; it simply means that I dethrone its power, just as I did with Mom and later with Jacob. Breaking free from these emotional shackles was exhilarating, and I want that feeling again.

A decision is made.

I toss the broken pieces of plastic into the trash before trying to straighten Jimmy's note. Stepping out into the Georgia heat, I dangle the creased letter from my fingers. "Danny, I won't be flying back with you."

"What's up?" he asks, his eyes opening as he taps his lap. "Sit." I snuggle in close, breathing in his scent—a mix of soap and line-dried laundry, so fresh and pure.

"I must take care of some unfinished business in South Carolina."

"Jimmy?"

I nod and hand him the letter.

He gives me a curious look and then scans the letter before smoothing out the crinkles himself. "It might be time." That's the thing about Danny—he can read my mind. "Ginny, do what you know in your heart is best."

"I'm getting good at this, huh?"

"A good muscle to exercise," he replies. His eyes close, and I hear his sigh; it's been a long, emotional day. We rest in a comfortable silence, listening to the birds, the tree frogs, and the sounds of distant traffic.

"You know, Ginny, I've been thinking," he then says. "You know very little about your father. I can't imagine what could lead a man to attack a woman, let alone a child." He rearranges himself and me on the chair, his strong arms wrapped around my waist. I feel his warmth. "That note is tragic. His life is tragic. Take his words at face value. Grace is a gift you can give him. But more importantly, it's a gift you can give yourself. Live free."

As always, he is my lighthouse. Danny guides me to safe harbor with as few words as possible.

I close my eyes, resting my head on his broad shoulder, feeling comfortable and serene, confident in what I must do. As I told myself after TC came, the dysfunction must end here.

Voices coming from the cracked, uneven sidewalk in front of Granny's house break my peaceful mood. I open my eyes and see Aunt Adele and Robert, both pushing the stroller, and then the one person who might join me on this final leg of my journey.

Oralyn steps onto the porch, her gaze sweeping across our faces before settling on the letter clutched in my hand.

"Are you up for a road trip to South Carolina?" I ask her. "I'm looking for a trustworthy co-pilot, and I understand you have experience."

"My bag is packed. Just let me know when it's time to go."

EPILOGUE

TC

I didn't drive the second chance highway in its entirety—just a couple of off-ramps that brought me back to the same route. Not that I didn't want another go. After hurtling over the low head dam to my accidental death, I begged the Big Man for a second shot at the wheel, still enraptured by the world and its offerings, still convinced I'd wasted my life, succeeding at nothing.

"Surely, you have something more for me," I argued.

Chuckling, the Big Man showed me His hand, explaining over my vociferous protests that I had nothing to prove. My big, boisterous personality, which I'd taken advantage of and honed mainly to mask my self-doubts, had been custom-made for me. It had a purpose, the Big Man said, and I'd achieved what I was supposed to do.

"Furthermore, I can't risk your eternal soul," He added, clapping my back, His mouth curling into a wide grin. "You need to stay with me so you can't get in trouble. I need to keep an eye on you."

Of course, He was right. He's always right, but it took my death for me to understand this.

He explained all this after I'd sped through the light toward Him. Through videos—a fitting medium for someone like me—I learned the real story about myself. Though I had gotten waylaid, I had lived a noble life. But I—like Adele, Oralyn, Audrey, and Ginny—needed someone to help remove the blinders. Like them, I had to stop believing the lies.

Although my gift of conversation didn't seem extraordinary to me at the time, while I ricocheted against the walls, trying to find my purpose, the videos showed me just how profound it had been.

I did have a knack for connecting with people. Friends, family, and even perfect strangers liked me. No, they loved me. They wanted to be in my presence—drawn by something they couldn't quite put their finger on. They just knew they felt better about themselves after spending time with me, seeing themselves as interesting, engaging, and yes, lovable—the most powerful of human desires.

I was their friend when they needed one.

No, the second-chance highway wasn't on the itinerary. The Big Man wanted me with Him. But He did have one more mission for me—another chance, a pitstop—to convince me of my specialness.

He sent me to Ginny.

My job? To shine a light on her misguided thinking and lead her back to her true path, the one He had engineered eons before she'd made her debut on the world's stage. It was a big assignment—one that unnerved me. Clinging to my old thinking, the fear of failure nearly sidetracked me, but I should have known better.

How could I fail? The Big Man was always there, giving me the words that might pierce Ginny's heart and soul, opening her eyes to the truth. I was simply the messenger. After completing my mission, I returned home to the Big Man. I settled into my new reality, which is far sweeter than anything I ever experienced on earth—and that includes meeting Ginny, perhaps the most beautiful girl I'd ever met.

And here's my message to you: We all have a mission, a purpose—a job that only we can do. Through the power of dreams and my God-given talents, I did mine. I stopped Ginny from doing the unthinkable. Who knew I would become one of those special people Granny Smith had talked about?

The Big Man assures me that I can rest easy. Ginny will be fine from now on. She has learned that nothing good happens in darkness and to ignore the superficial validations of the world—a lesson I never learned. More importantly, she has discovered the dangers of having an unforgiving heart and understands that God places people in our lives to help keep us on track. Nothing is a coincidence.

Life won't be easy. It never is. She and Danny will experience trouble, setbacks, and great sorrow, but they will overcome. Through faith, she will walk in understanding: God does not cause the bad and ugly in the world; the thief does. Her job, therefore, is to transform negative experiences into something positive.

My spirit soars.

She will stay in the light and fulfill the purpose that God intended for her. With family and friends by her side, she will change lives for the better, achieving these wonderful things with the knowledge that I am not far away, and neither are Granny and her mother. As she gazes into the night sky, admiring the star-speckled canvas, she will intuitively understand that we are rooting for her just beyond the veil.

And what more can anyone ask?

The End

ACKNOWLEDGMENTS

Writing this novel wasn't part of the plan. I'd published the prequel to this story, a book called *Always Think of Me*, figuring it would be one and done. I'd fulfilled my dream of writing a novel and never looked beyond that one ambition.

One month after releasing the debut, however, I made an about-face and began laying the foundation for *Second Chance Highway*. What changed? What got me off my rumpus?

Encouragement.

Encouragement from friends and acquaintances, such as Janet King, Cherilynn Bisbano, and Sandy Redmon, who urged me to write a sequel that would chart Ginny Carmichael's course in her quest for freedom through forgiveness. By the fourth or fifth chapter, I can't remember which, I knew I had gotten myself in a fix. How could I write a plausible story about a young woman on the run if I'd never driven the cross-country route that Ginny had chosen?

I couldn't.

But I had no reason not to give it a try, and plans began to take form. I would head south from my home in Tennessee to Georgia, where Ginny's story starts as she flees an abusive fiancé, determined to make amends with her long-estranged mother in Las Vegas. My husband, Kevin Berry, threw in, agreeing good-naturedly to drive the entire trip through Alabama, Mississippi, Oklahoma, Texas, New Mexico, Arizona, and Nevada. As we traveled the miles, we had no idea where we would sleep at night or which tourist attraction we'd visit. We pretended to be on a Ginny-like journey.

Thank you, Kevin, for taking the wheel as I scribbled notes and snapped photos of what we saw along the way. Thanks to my cousin, Guyan Long, who let us crash at his home in Las Vegas and then introduced us to a tavern manager who provided insights into what makes that city tick.

Thanks, too, to Bobby and Mary Charles, who hosted us at their charming log home in Wyoming on our return trip home. If not for Mary and Bob's hospitality and desire to show us the wonder and beauty of western Wyoming, I may not have included this state in the novel.

A shout-out goes to my editor, Rebecca Andersen, and members of my Knoxville Writers Guild critique group: Marilyn Muscaro, Jeannette Brown, Melanie Sakalla, and Kelly Ferguson. This novel came together because of them. And I'd be remiss not to mention Theresa Shreffler Kidwell, a childhood friend and nurse who ensured the accuracy of all medical scenes.

Above all else, thank you, Kevin, my husband of forty-plus years, for putting up with me over the decades. A girl couldn't ask for a better partner in life.

ABOUT THE AUTHOR

Lori Keesey discovered her passion for writing at the young age of six when she wrote and illustrated a *very* short story about three puppies lost in a hatbox. Her first-grade teacher loved the story and encouraged her to continue writing, highlighting the vital role teachers can play.

Many years later, the study of Harper Lee's *To Kill a Mockingbird* in high school rekindled her interest in writing fiction. Captivated by Harper's young protagonist, Scout, Lori aspired to create characters as engaging as Scout herself. Years passed—during which she read hundreds, if not thousands, of novels before Lori achieved her goal. Her award-winning debut novel, *Always Think of Me*, was published in 2024.

Throughout her career, Lori has written for daily newspapers and trade publications. Her freelance work has appeared in regional and trade magazines, especially those specializing in space exploration and related fields. A space exploration enthusiast, Lori worked for NASA in public outreach for nearly 20 years.

She graduated from the University of Maryland, College Park, with a B.S. in journalism. Born in Washington, D.C., Lori now lives in Walland, Tennessee.

You can connect with her on Facebook, Instagram, LinkedIn, or X, or by visiting her website at https://lorikeesey.com.

DISCUSSION QUESTIONS

1. What did you like best about this novel?
2. How did the book make you feel? Did it evoke any strong emotions?
3. What themes stood out to you?
4. How did the characters evolve throughout the story?
5. Which character did you relate to the most? Why?
6. If you could ask one character a question, what would it be?
7. What was the most surprising twist in the plot?
8. How did the author build tension throughout the story?
9. Did any plot points feel unrealistic or forced?
10. How did the ending affect your overall impression of the book?

www.ingramcontent.com/pod-product-compliance
Lightning Source LLC
LaVergne TN
LVHW010558100826
845148LV00014B/2755

* 9 7 8 1 6 8 4 8 8 1 6 0 4 *